Praise for *Once Again a Bride*

"A near-perfect example of everything that makes this genre an escapist joy to read: unsought love triumphs despite difficult circumstances, unpleasantness is resolved and mysteries cleared, and good people get the happy lives they deserve."

—*Publishers Weekly*

"A bit of gothic suspense, a double love story, and the right touches of humor and sensuality add up to this delightfully fast-paced read about second chances and love's redeeming power."

—*RT Book Reviews*, 4 Stars

"Ms. Ashford has written a superbly crafted story with elements of political unrest, some gothic suspense, and an interesting romance."

—*Fresh Fiction*

"Well-rendered characters, superb writing, and gentle wit make this a romance that shouldn't be missed... Ashford returns with a Regency winner that will please her longtime fans and garner new ones."

—*Library Journal*

"Mystery entwines with the romance, as Ms. Ashford leads us astray... *Once Again a Bride* is great fun."

—*Historical Hilarity*

Also by Jane Ashford

The Marchington Scandal

JANE ASHFORD

sourcebooks
casablanca

Published by Sourcebooks Casablanca, an imprint of Sourcebooks,
Inc.
P.O. Box 4410, Naperville, Illinois 60567-4410
(630) 961-3900
Fax: (630) 961-2168
www.sourcebooks.com

Originally published in 1982 by Signet, a division of The New
American Library, Inc., New York.

Printed and bound in Canada
WC 10 9 8 7 6 5 4 3 2 1

Praise for *The Bride Insists*

"Perfectly delightful Regency romance... Remarkably executed."

"Ashford captures the reader's interest with her keen knowledge of the era and her deft writing. An engaging cast of characters...a charming plot, and just the right amount of sensuality will keep Ashford fans satisfied."

"A marvelously engaging marriage-of-convenience tale, and Ashford's richly nuanced, realistically complex characters, and impeccably crafted historical setting are bound to resonate with fans of Mary Balogh."

"Ashford establishes a union made for all the wrong reasons until trust and love can set things to rights... For all historical romance fans."

"A solid historical...the heat is palpable."

"A sweet historical romance that one can enjoy over a hot cup of happy and a warm blanket! Most assuredly a warm and fuzzy read!"

Praise for *The Marriage Wager*

"Exceptional characters and beautifully crafted historical details ensure a delightful read for Judith McNaught and Mary Balogh fans."

—Publishers Weekly

"Lively, well-written Regency romance sparkles with wonderful dialogue, witty scenes, and just the right touch of humor, adventure, and repartee."

—RT Book Reviews, Nominated for
Best Regency Historical Romance

"A riveting, emotional romance that will garner a place of prominence on anyone's keeper shelf."

—Rendezvous

"You're really going to enjoy *The Marriage Wager*. It is one of the finest marriage-of-convenience stories I've read."

—All About Romance

"Entertaining, colorful characters, romantic... An engaging and entertaining read."

—Caffeinated Book Reviewer

"An enjoyable Regency romance with complex characters."

—Book Lover and Procrastinator

One

"BUT, MY DEAR, YOU MUST COME TO MY BALL," SAID Lady Eliza Burnham emphatically. "All London will be there. And you cannot stay shut up brooding here forever, after all."

Katharine Daltry smiled. "Eliza! You know I never brood."

"Well, whatever you are doing, then. It can't go on."

"Can it not?"

"No," said the older woman, exasperated. "You must go out. Why, you are nothing but a girl still. And Robert has been dead these four years." Seeing a shadow pass over her friend's face, she added, "I don't mean to sound heartless, Katharine, but it is the truth. I know you loved him dearly; indeed, you made that only too plain when you went off to India in that amazing way, in spite of everyone's warnings. I have never understood why your father agreed to take you along."

Miss Daltry's lips curved upward again. "I told him I was in love. And his and Robert's regiment was posted to India for three years. We should never have been married if I stayed behind."

"Well, you weren't married in any case," replied her ladyship practically. "And why the general did not send you home directly Robert was so unfortunately killed, I don't know. But he always indulged you shockingly."

This time, the sadness in Katharine's face was sharper. "I suppose he did. I told him I couldn't bear to be away from him just then, and he understood. And then, time simply...passed. It did not seem at all like four years. And now Father is gone, too."

"And I am the greatest beast in nature to have mentioned him in that callous way. How can you bear me, Katharine? I'm sure I didn't mean to remind you of your bereavement."

The younger woman smiled again. Eliza Burnham did indeed chatter heedlessly at times, leading strangers to conclude that she was as empty-headed as she was fashionable. But she had been a close friend of the mother Katharine had lost when she was barely nine years old, and she had to some extent taken Mrs. Daltry's place during Katharine's adolescence, when General Daltry had been much occupied with the war in Spain. Thus, Katharine knew rather more about her, including her extensive charitable works, and had long since judged her kindhearted and well-meaning. "It is all right, Eliza. I'm not still mourning Father. I got over that on the voyage home. And it has been eight months. I shall always miss him terribly, of course, but I am...well, reconciled to it, I suppose."

"Poor darling. But if that is true, there is no reason at all why you should not begin to go out. Of course, you may not wish to dance or anything of that sort for a while, but…"

Miss Daltry shrugged. "My scruples are not so delicate, Eliza. If I wished to go to parties, I should. But I don't wish it. Father left me well provided for, and for the first time in my life I need consider no one but myself. It may be monstrously selfish of me, but that is precisely what I mean to do." She dimpled. "Think of me as a disagreeable old cat, disappointed in love and left on the shelf."

Lady Eliza looked at her despairingly. No one, she thought to herself, could possibly look less like an old cat than Katharine. She barely looked her twenty-seven years, and in any case, she was one of those women who merely become more beautiful with maturity. Her once-too-slender figure had filled out to perfection during her stay in India, and her piquant triangular face had softened. Her dark brown hair was as silken as ever, her skin had warmed to honey brown, and her sparkling amber eyes now held compassionate wisdom as well as spirit. Meeting those curious, almost golden eyes now, Lady Eliza saw a very characteristic glint of mischief. "Oh, I have no patience with you," she exclaimed. "I give it up."

"Good," laughed the other. "Then we may leave this tedious subject and have a comfortable coze. Tell me all your news. How does Andrew like Cambridge?"

"But, Katharine," wailed her friend, "what will you do? How will you live? You can't stay hemmed up here all alone."

"Alone? Have you forgotten Cousin Mary?"

"That poor little woman is completely under your thumb."

Katharine laughed aloud. "She isn't, you know."

"Nonsense. Of course she is. She is so sweet and quiet that she could never stand against you. I know you!"

Katharine let this pass. "Well, if you do, you should know that I am perfectly content. I have my house. I see my good friends whenever I like. I can go to the theater or the library if I require amusement. I ask for no more, certainly not the ridiculous 'gaieties' of the season."

"But what about a husband, a family of your own?"

The corners of Miss Daltry's mouth turned down. "Those are not to be thought of. Now, I insist you tell me about Andrew."

With a sigh, Lady Eliza gave in and began to talk of her eldest son, just gone up to Cambridge. And in retailing his doings, she soon forgot her firm resolve of the morning, to *make* Katharine promise to attend the ball she was giving in three weeks' time. Indeed, she left the house without raising this issue again, and it was not until she was removing her hat in her own bedchamber that she remembered it, and gave vent to a most unladylike expression.

At the same moment, Katharine Daltry was also expressing annoyance, though the cause was quite different. She had just finished reading a letter that had arrived with the afternoon post. "How unfortunate," she said aloud.

"What is unfortunate, my dear?" asked her companion, a small thin woman with pale hair and clear gray eyes.

"Cousin Elinor," replied the other curtly.

"Has something happened to her? She was perfectly

all right when I last heard from her mother. Indeed, she was about to be married."

"Nothing has happened to her. Or, that is, she was married, in January. And now she means to come to town for the season."

"Oh." Mary Daltry, for this was indeed Katharine's cousin and chaperone, looked doubtfully at her charge. "Is that unfortunate?"

"Well, I think it is. I haven't any wish to be saddled with a green girl."

"But isn't her husband coming, too? What is his name again? Marchington, that's it. Thomas Marchington. He's Sir Lionel Marchington's son."

"Yes, he's coming. But I understand that Tom Marchington is barely twenty years old, and Elinor isn't even that. They can no more look after themselves than...than babies."

"Oh, no. I'm sure you're wrong. Gentlemen are taught all about that sort of thing."

Katharine looked at her middle-aged cousin with amused exasperation. She did not know what she meant by "that sort of thing," and she was tolerably certain that Mary didn't either. She was fond of her cousin, but she often found her own opinions at odds with those of a forty-year-old woman who had been reared very strictly by a clergyman father. "Well, we can only hope so," she answered, refolding the letter. "But I think it is much more likely that they will expect me to squire them about and rescue them from all sorts of scrapes. I shall have to make it very clear from the beginning that I never go out."

"Of course, dear," murmured Mary soothingly.

"*And* that I do so by my own choice, not because I am not invited. Otherwise, I daresay they would be trying to help *me*."

Mary Daltry chuckled at this idea. "Surely not."

"No? I have not seen Cousin Elinor since she was a grubby schoolgirl, but I have a very vivid memory of her. Don't you remember how she positively persecuted that poor curate? Mr. Ambley, I think his name was. He was not being invited in the neighborhood, and she insisted he was being horridly snubbed. It turned out he was trying desperately to find time to work on his book."

Her companion appeared to be suppressing a laugh. "Well, but, my dear, her motive was very noble."

"God save me from noble motives. Elinor suffers from an excess of sensibility. Or did, at any rate."

Mary shook her head and looked down.

"Come, you must admit that Elinor's feelings are rather overenthusiastic. What about the spaniel she dosed with 'tonic' until it actually bit her?"

The older woman made a stifled noise. "Katharine."

"Well, she did. I could not invent such a story."

"Yes, but…"

Katharine burst out laughing. "You needn't try to humbug me, Mary. You think she is absurd, too."

Allowing her smile to emerge, the other agreed. "But I insist that she acts from the best of motives."

Katharine shrugged contemptuously.

"Yes, dear. And you know, I can't help thinking that you might perhaps enjoy getting out a bit with Elinor. I know you say you saw enough of the *haut ton* during your own come-out to last you all your life, but Elinor is very young and would give you a new perspective on things you have seen before. And she would no doubt welcome a little guidance. I do think—"

"Cousin Mary, are you feeling quite well?" interrupted Miss Daltry. "I had a notion that lobster might disagree with you. I said so last night, you recall. But I did not expect it would addle your wits."

"You may mock, Katharine, but I still think I am right. You should go out and meet some lively young people. From what you tell me, you spent far too much of the last four years alone, and you need some company other than mine."

Several emotions seemed to struggle with one another in her cousin's face. "I have all the company I require. And if I did not, I should certainly not choose Elinor to remedy the situation. I thought we had finished with this subject once and for all, Mary. I intend to do exactly as I please, and that means not going out."

"Yes, dear," replied her cousin serenely. "But I expect you'll change your mind. We have only been in London together for three months, after all."

"Are you trying to goad me into letting you go back to Hampshire, Cousin Mary?" said Katharine in a rallying tone. "I see it now. You are weary of my airs and want to escape, but you are too nice to tell me so. Instead, you drive me to distraction in the hope that I will send you away. Well, I shan't do it. You will have to speak your wishes plainly, and then you may do as you like."

Mary Daltry smiled. She had been closely acquainted

with her much younger cousin only for the three months mentioned, but in that time she had learned to distinguish her teasing from what she called her "true" voice. Katharine Daltry had an active wit and loved to take a topic to outrageous lengths in its service. At first, this had greatly disconcerted her less-spirited cousin, but she had soon become, if not resigned, at least accustomed to these flights. She was in no danger now of taking Katharine's talk of Hampshire seriously. Indeed, Katharine would not have made such a remark even three weeks previously. She had rescued Mary from genteel poverty in the country and knew her cousin was sensitive on the subject. But they had gone a great way toward establishing a comfortable, close relationship since then, and Katharine was certain that her bantering would do no harm. On the other hand, she hoped it might do some good in diverting Mary from the subject at hand. Katharine had found joking very useful in this line before now; it was one of her most practiced weapons.

"Well, dear, you know best, I suppose. It is early days yet," was Mary's only reply.

Katharine eyed her with a rueful smile. She had recently begun to realize just how deceptive her cousin's meek exterior really was. There were strong principles and clear common sense beneath her quiet, self-effacing manner, and Katharine was learning to respect her opinions more and more. Now she knew that her cousin had merely put off the issue of going out, not abandoned it.

Two

A SUNNY APRIL MORNING TWO WEEKS LATER FOUND
Katharine Daltry engaged in a very characteristic occupation. She was alone in one of the attics of her small
house in Green Street, and she was painting in oils.
This was an unusual pastime for a lady, who would
commonly have preferred watercolors, and Katharine
had rendered it even more eccentric, and quite scandalized her London servants, by the determined way
she went about it. The attic room had been cleared
out as soon as she purchased the house and its broad
skylight washed until it shone. The whitewash on
the walls was the only other improvement she made
before filling the corners with paints, canvases, and
various other artistic paraphernalia. She had begun this
sort of work in India, partly to occupy the long lonely
hours, after a very proper girlhood training in sketching and watercolor, and in the process of educating
herself in the new medium had become rather good
and extremely devoted to it.

To the rest of the household, however, excepting
Cousin Mary, her daily sojourn in her "studio" was

the subject of persistent gossip. The butler was impassively bland; the cook shook her head and wondered what would come of such goings-on; and the maids alternately giggled and marveled. Much of this talk had to do with the costume Katharine donned for these sessions. As now, she always wore a faded old muslin gown covered by an immense, and paint-bespattered, kitchen apron. Her dark hair was pulled ruthlessly back from her forehead and confined in an unbecoming knot on top of her head, and her slender hands were stained with varying shades of vermilion.

Yet in spite of her odd appearance, a visitor to the room, had such ever been allowed, might have been arrested by the sight of Katharine bent over her easel. For something, perhaps the rapt look in her amber eyes, offset all this dowdiness and lent her an aura of beauty despite it.

Today she was working on a still life. She had set up a vase of scarlet poppies, procured at some expense at this season, on a blue-draped table directly under the skylight, and she was just now trying to capture the exquisite blue-black center of one of the flowers on her canvas. It was a delicate operation, done with a tiny brush, and when a knock came at the door, Katharine's hand jerked very slightly and smeared the design a little.

"Damn!" she said, very improperly. She threw down the brush and strode over to fling open the door. "Mary! What is it? You know I am *not* to be interrupted in here. Indeed, you have never done so before."

"And I would not now," replied the other, "if I could have avoided it. I am sorry, Katharine; I know you value your mornings alone. But Elinor and her husband are here, and she positively insists upon seeing you. One of the footmen, the new one, unfortunately let out that you were at home, and it was only by promising to fetch you that I prevented Elinor from coming up herself."

Katharine sighed angrily. "Drat the girl. I knew she would be a nuisance. I suppose I must come down." She turned back into the room. "Tell them I will be there in a quarter of an hour."

It was rather longer than that before Katharine Daltry reached her drawing room. She had had to cover the painting, wash the pigment from her hands, and change her dress. And it must be admitted that she did not hurry overmuch. She did not at all look forward to seeing her Cousin Elinor, and she was still quite annoyed at the interruption of her work.

Finally, however, she walked down the stairs and across the hall to the drawing room, whence voices could be heard. When she entered, the three people seated near the fireplace turned and stood to greet her, Mary with a slight grimace at Katharine's truculent expression.

Katharine eyed her younger cousin and her husband with critical interest. Elinor, who was the daughter of Katharine's mother's younger sister, as Mary was of her father's elder brother, showed some resemblance to her hostess. Her hair was the same dark brown, and her figure had some of the extreme slenderness Katharine had exhibited at her age. But Elinor's eyes were of an undistinguished brown, and her face was constructed quite differently, being more round than triangular. Her husband, Tom Marchington, was a well-set-up young man with light brown hair, a high color, and slightly prominent blue eyes. Katharine knew from her aunt's letters that his family owned the estate next to Elinor's parents' and was very wealthy. The match had been made up years before by the older couples, but Elinor and Tom appeared happy enough with the result.

"Do sit down," said Katharine, doing so herself.

They all sat.

"I am so happy to see you, Cousin Katharine," exclaimed Elinor. "It has been so long. Indeed, I don't believe we have met these six years. You must remember me as a silly schoolgirl."

This clearly called for a demur, but since it was precisely what Katharine did remember, she replied, "It has been a long time. And now you are quite grown up. I must offer you my felicitations on your marriage." She included them both in her glance. "I am so sorry I did not return to England in time to attend the ceremony."

"Yes, we so wanted you to come," said Elinor. "But we couldn't put it off because Tom and I were determined to do the season, and we wanted all that out of the way."

Raising an eyebrow very slightly, Katharine looked at Tom Marchington. "This is your first visit to London also?"

"Yes. M'father never cared for town life, so he put me off whenever I asked to come. But now that I'm a married man, I suppose I can do as I please."

Katharine's eyebrow moved again.

"Tom is just like me," added Elinor. "He has always *longed* to see the *ton* and the season. You cannot imagine how disappointed I was last year when all the children came down with the measles just as Mama was about to bring me up to town for my come-out. I cried for days. And I still think she might have found someone else to... But that is all over now. We are actually *in* London! We mean to have a perfectly splendid time and go to every party there is!"

"Hah!" put in Tom. "I shan't spend every moment doing the pretty in some drawing room, Elinor. I have told you I mean to see some other sights as well."

The girl grimaced. "Oh, all those horrid gaming hells and boxing saloons. I cannot imagine why you want to waste your time there. But you must do as you like, of course."

"I shall start with a good tailor," replied the man unheedingly.

"Oh, yes! Cousin Katharine, we both mean to buy completely new wardrobes before the season really gets started. Can you tell me where I should go?" She looked over her cousin's elegant gray morning dress. "I want to be the *height* of fashion!"

Katharine smiled a little. "If that is your aim, you must go to Madame Gervase in Bond Street; she is all the crack, I have heard." She turned to Tom. "I fear I know nothing about Savile Row."

Mr. Marchington reddened slightly. "That's all right. Have the name of m' father's snyder."

"Isn't it thrilling?" Elinor clasped her hands before her bosom. "I can hardly bear the excitement. And, oh, Cousin Katharine, we want to ask you to present us to *everyone*. Mama says that you were a tremendous hit when you came out six years ago, and I mean to be the same. You must know all the *haut ton*."

This was the remark Katharine had been warily waiting for, and now she could not restrain a slight grimace.

"Your mother exaggerates, Elinor. I had a very modest success, I assure you, and most of that was due to curiosity, I daresay. I was the oldest deb in living memory because we waited for Father to return from France."

The younger girl shook a playful finger at her. "Now you are being modest, Katharine. Mother told me you took the town by storm, and refused scores of brilliant offers for the sake of Robert Adams." She sighed audibly. "I have always thought it the most romantic story."

Acutely embarrassed, Katharine clenched her fists in her lap. But she made a great effort to pass this appalling remark off lightly. "Hardly scores, Elinor. Not even several. And you know I have been out of the country for years. I really know almost no one in London now. However, a friend of mine, Lady Eliza Burnham, is familiar with all the people you wish to meet. I will ask her to present you to some of them. Indeed, she is giving a ball next week, as it happens, I will have her send you a card."

"Oh, that will be splendid. And perhaps you will permit us to go with you? I mean, uh, perhaps you will dine with us before and go on to the ball."

"Thank you, but I'm not attending."

"Not…? Oh, of course. Katharine, your father. I meant to say how sorry we are right away, but I…I forgot. Your blacks…that is…"

"I've left off full mourning. It has been nine

months, and Papa always loathed black. But I must tell you straight out, Elinor, that I am not going out. The activities of the *ton* bore me unspeakably, and I greatly prefer remaining at home, seeing a few friends occasionally. I fear I will be of little help to you during the season. But I will ask Lady Burnham to do what she can."

"You don't *want* to go out?" Elinor appeared to puzzle over this astonishing fact for a while; then her face cleared. "Oh, *of course*, dear Katharine. How could I be so stupid? You cannot forget Robert. You do not wish to relive moments that you shared with him." She sighed again.

Katharine made an exasperated sound. Her cousin was really impossible. If she had in fact been wearing the willow for a man more than four years dead, this reminder would certainly have depressed her spirits. As it happened, she had recovered from the death of her first love some time ago, but this did not excuse Elinor's thoughtlessness. She was about to deliver a blistering set-down when it occurred to her that here was an excuse to avoid Elinor's further importunities. She knew that the younger girl would never accept the simple fact that she preferred being alone to "society." But if she thought a broken heart was behind her solitude, surely she would leave Katharine alone with her "sorrow." Katharine raised soulful eyes to Elinor's, sighed, and dropped them again. Mary looked at her with astonishment.

"Poor Katharine," exclaimed Elinor. "Naturally, I understand. I will do nothing to intrude upon your grief."

"Thank you," answered the other brokenly.

"I say, Elinor," put in Tom Marchington. "We

must go. I promised we'd look in on my great-aunt this afternoon."

"Oh, dear. I am positively terrified of Lady Steadly." But Elinor rose and held out a hand. "I shall call again, Cousin Katharine, when we can truly *talk*."

Katharine's heart sank, but she shook hands and said, "And I shall speak to Eliza Burnham. You may expect a card for her ball."

"Thank you!"

The Marchingtons took their leave, and Katharine and Mary sank back down on the sofa. "What an abominable girl she is!" said the former.

"Perhaps it is a family failing," retorted Mary tartly.

Katharine looked up, met her cousin's censorious gaze, and, reprehensibly, giggled. "Don't scold me, Mary. Indeed, it was the only excuse I could think of that she would accept."

"But, my dear, you can't have thought. You know Elinor has a…well, a weakness for gossip. She will spread this ridiculous tale throughout the *ton* as soon as she is given the chance. She will *revel* in it!"

"Let her. I don't care a straw what the *ton* thinks of me. My own friends will know better, and the rest may prattle of my broken heart all they like. They have little enough to amuse them."

Mary shook her head. "I'm afraid you will be sorry, Katharine."

"Nonsense. I am never sorry for myself." She dimpled. "But at least I have got you to admit that Elinor is an abominable girl. For that, I will forgive her her untimely visit and her apparently doltish husband."

"Katharine!"

"Did you conceive a *tendre* for him? No, I cannot believe it. He is pure country squire come to town to see the sights."

"You really mustn't speak so of your own family, Katharine. He seems a very pleasant young man. And I do *not* admit that Elinor is abominable, only a bit unwise and inexperienced, perhaps."

Katharine laughed. "Doing it too brown, Cousin. You cannot say at one moment that she is a terrible gossip and at the next that she is an innocent child. It won't do. And as for me, if I cannot malign my own family, whom can I blacken? It is everyone's privilege to bemoan the family eccentrics."

"You do so enjoy your jokes, Katharine. It is one of the things I find so puzzling."

"My joking? Pooh, Mary, you are one of the few people I know who *does* understand them."

"I don't mean that. I simply cannot understand why someone who loves witty conversation as much as you refuses to go out. I know that *I* am no wit. I cannot keep pace with you for three minutes together. Yet you will not search out more amusing talkers. It is unaccountable."

"I amuse myself more than anyone else possibly could," laughed Katharine.

But her cousin shook her head. "You are so animated when you have a proper partner. I remember thinking so when your father's friend Sir Giles Overshaw visited us on his way from Vienna to take up the ambassadorship in South America. I had never before seen you so gay. Why not make a push to meet other such people, Katharine? I know you would enjoy it."

Seeing that Mary was not going to be put off with

a light answer, the younger girl sighed and said, "And where do you suggest I begin?"

"Why, among the people you are acquainted with in London. We are in the midst of England's most fashionable society. There must be many fascinating people who would be delighted to talk with you."

"Do you think so?" Katharine gazed into her cousin's kind, narrow face. She remembered, as she often forgot, that Mary had been reared very strictly in a country parsonage and had never been to a town larger than Grantham before she herself summoned her. "I fear I must disagree with you," she told her gently. "You know, Mary, I had two seasons before I went to India with Father. I met no one I liked enough to marry during the first, so they insisted I should have another, even though I didn't want it at all. I have seen a good deal of fashionable society."

"Yes, dear, I know." Mary eyed her anxiously. "And I know you didn't care overmuch for it. I understand completely. I am sure a great many fashionable people are quite shallow and silly. But there must have been *some* you liked."

"Of course there were. I still see them now. You have met them all."

"But, Katharine…"

"No, Mary. I am sorry, but I must insist that I understand this subject better than you can. Let me tell you something. I was quite as eager as you could wish when I first came out. I thought, as you do, that I should meet all sorts of wonderful people and have splendid conversations every night. But it simply wasn't so. Why, the man whom the *ton* calls the greatest wit alive is the most arrogant, unfeeling creature on earth! I have not the least desire to see any of them ever again."

The older woman gazed at her, still looking anxious. "Well, my dear, I must suppose that you are right. I have no experience upon which to base any argument. But, Katharine…" She hesitated.

"What is it? You look so worried. There is no need to be, I promise you."

"I'm not so sure of that."

"Why?"

Mary Daltry hesitated again, then said, "I don't wish to seem prying, or…or impertinent, my dear, but I can't help wondering what you mean to do with your life?"

"What I mean to do with my life?" repeated Katharine in an astonished tone.

"Yes. Twenty-seven is still very young. Do you mean to stay here in this house and grow old, chatting with me and painting and perhaps traveling to Bath in the summer? Is this to be your life?" She stopped, started to add something, then fell silent.

Katharine seemed genuinely struck. She did not reply for a long time, and her cousin was very satisfied with the expressions that followed one another across her face. Clearly she had never really considered this question before, and her companion astutely left her to visualize the future it implied.

At last Katharine looked up. Mary met her amber gaze. For a moment their eyes held; then, abruptly, Katharine laughed, throwing back her head. "You have planted me a facer, Cousin. I admit it. You are right. I shall not be content to do what I have been doing the past four months for the rest of my life."

Mary nodded.

"But," continued Katharine before she could speak, "that does not mean that I shall break down and embrace the *haut ton*. It only means that I must do some thinking."

"That is all I ask, my dear."

Katharine laughed again. "And a jolly good thing, too, for I shan't promise any more." Her smile faded. "But I must do that, clearly. I see suddenly that independence might be a very daunting thing. When one can do whatever one likes…" Her voice faded; then she murmured, "What do I like, I wonder? Besides painting."

Silence fell again, but it lasted only a moment before Katharine stood up. "That is all very well, but it cannot be decided in a moment. *Now*, I must write the promised note to Eliza Burnham, and then I am going back to my studio until luncheon." And she strode over to the writing desk and sat down.

Her cousin watched her scribble the note, smiling slightly as she finished and sealed it with her customary haste. But Mary's eyes showed concern, not amusement, and they did not change even when Katharine had hurried from the room and left her alone.

Three

THE SEASON OPENED WITH ITS CUSTOMARY BRILLIANCE, and Katharine Daltry resolutely ignored it. She passed her days in the quiet routine she and her cousin had established since their arrival in London—reading, walking, painting, and occasionally seeing friends at small private gatherings. Mary did not bring up the question of the future again, knowing that Katharine would puzzle over it in her own time. Elinor Marchington called on several occasions, but she was not encouraged to stay long, and she was never permitted what she called a "real talk" with Katharine, who was far more socially adept than her younger cousin and well able to deflect her rather obvious curiosity. Elinor was so excited by the new experience of going into society that these mild rebuffs hardly touched her. Lady Burnham's invitation had been only the first of many, and Elinor was thrilled beyond measure by the *ton* and the nightly parties and concerts she attended.

Thus, it was with some surprise that Katharine received her on an afternoon early in May, for as soon as Elinor entered the drawing room, it was clear that she had been crying. The younger girl looked around the room, then heaved a deep sigh. "Oh, good, you are alone. I *must* talk to you, Cousin Katharine. I don't know what I am to do."

"What has happened? Come and sit down."

Elinor sank onto the sofa next to her cousin and groped in her reticule for a handkerchief. Katharine saw with concern that tears had started in her eyes once again. "Oh, Katharine," she sniffed. "I wanted so much to come to London. I never imagined it would be like *this*."

"What is it? Has someone snubbed you? You know, Elinor, there are all sorts of odious snobs in the *ton*. It doesn't mean anything."

Elinor shook her head, her voice momentarily submerged in tears. Katharine waited as she struggled for control. "It is Tom," she blurted finally. "He has gone mad, I think. I don't know what to do."

For one vivid instant, Katharine pictured this statement as the literal truth. She saw the stolid Tom Marchington run mad, and her lips twitched. But she sternly controlled this lamentable reaction and said, "What do you mean, Elinor? Has Tom done something silly?" Various explanations occurring to her, she added, "You know, gentlemen are interested in the oddest things. If Tom has been to a cockfight or lost money in a gambling hell, it is no more than dozens of young men do every day. Quite unaccountable, of course, but I believe they get over it."

"Oh, if it were only that." Elinor took a shaky breath. "I know about gaming, and boxing, and all those horrid things. Indeed, Tom told me he meant to go to Jackson's and Cribb's Parlor and...and those sorts of places. It is not that." She looked at Katharine with wide tragic eyes. "It is a...a woman."

Katharine stared at her.

"He has become utterly infatuated with Countess Standen. He positively hangs over her at parties, and I know he goes to her house. Everyone is talking. Katharine, what am I to do? You must help me!"

"But...but, Elinor, you must be mistaken. You are not used to town manners. Perhaps you misunderstood some remark, or..." Katharine trailed off, unconvinced by her own feeble excuses. She had heard of the countess. The woman was notorious for her indiscretions, and for her complete indifference to both the world's opinion of her and the feelings of others. She had been pointed out to Katharine during her own first season, and though they had never met, she had seen the countess at more than one *ton* party behaving in a way to make any observer blush. Thus, even considering Elinor's inexperience, it was possible that she was right. Katharine could imagine that it might amuse the Countess Standen to entangle a twenty-year-old boy fresh from the country, and though she certainly would not remain amused for long by dazzled innocence, it might well be long enough to ruin Tom Marchington's marriage.

"I am not mistaken," said Elinor, hanging her head. "Other people have noticed it, too. Your friend Lady Burnham came to speak to me at Almack's last night, expressly to warn me. I nearly sank with embarrassment. I didn't know what to say to her. Katharine, you must help me before it is too late."

Katharine's eyebrows drew together. If Eliza Burnham had noticed this indiscretion, it must be real. She met her cousin's tearful brown eyes. But whatever could she do about it? She had never spoken to Countess Standen in her life, and she hadn't the least idea how to wean a young man who was nearly a stranger to her away from a dangerous older woman. Katharine had an uneasy suspicion that the countess would be up to any stratagem she could think of, not that she could come up with *any* at this moment.

"You *will* help me?" repeated Elinor. "There is no one else I can turn to. Mother is so busy with the children, and besides, she would never understand. She would only tell Tom's father, and then there would be a great scandal."

Katharine brightened. "But, Elinor, surely that is the answer? Tom's father is the proper person to deal with this. He will be as anxious as you to keep it quiet. I think he should be told at once."

Her cousin stared at her. "You don't know Sir Lionel!"

"No. I believe I met him once, but—"

"He would storm up to London and take us both home at once. Everyone would know, and we should never be allowed to forget it. We would both be in disgrace forever!"

"But, Elinor, surely you would not—"

"He would blame me," Elinor interrupted hysterically. "He thinks the family is all the woman's responsibility. I have heard him say so! Oh, Katharine, *promise* you will not tell Sir Lionel."

"Very well. Don't put yourself in a taking. I simply thought that he would be able to deal with the situation far better than we. But if it is impossible, then we shall have to think of some scheme on our own."

Elinor clasped her hands tightly in front of her and gazed at Katharine with huge anxious eyes. "Oh, yes, please, Cousin Katharine," she replied.

Seeing the trust and dazed helplessness in her face, Katharine sighed inaudibly. What could *she* do about this tangle? She had no more idea than Elinor of any "scheme." But the younger girl continued to look at her with such touching relief she had to offer her something. "I must…ah…look over the situation," said Katharine. "Perhaps I will get an idea then. Do you go out tonight?"

"No. But there is Lady Sefton's ball tomorrow. Tom means to go; he said so."

"Lady Sefton? Yes, I have an invitation to that. I refused it, but I shall write a note. I shall see you there, Elinor, and we shall try to make a plan."

"Oh, thank you!" The other girl heaved another great sigh and shook her head. "It is all so horrid. But I feel better now that you are helping me."

"Yes, well, I shall do what I can." Katharine felt very uneasy. It seemed wrong to give Elinor hope when she had no notion how to rescue her.

"Everything will be all right now," answered Elinor, vastly increasing her cousin's discomfort.

At this moment, the drawing-room door opened, and Mary Daltry came in. Elinor rose, saying, "I must go. I promised Tom's great-aunt that I would call. I am sorry to run away, Cousin Mary."

Mary Daltry excused her amiably, and Elinor took her leave. As soon as she was gone, Mary said,

"Whatever has cast you into the dismals, Katharine? You look as if you had lost your dearest friend."

Katharine grimaced. "We are going to a ball, Cousin Mary."

Her despair was so comical that the older woman laughed aloud.

⤳

As she dressed the following evening, however, Katharine could not help but feel a twinge of excitement. She had not been to a ball in more than a year, and though she disliked society, she was very fond of dancing. She surveyed herself in the long mirror over her dressing table as she fastened her mother's amethysts around her neck. Though she was still in half-mourning, the clear lavender of her gown became her, and the trim of silver ribbons was very fine. With the amethysts and matching silver slippers, she looked very fashionable indeed, and she could not resist making a face at her reflection in the mirror before pulling a gauze wrap around her shoulders and starting downstairs to find her cousin.

Mary was waiting in the drawing room, somberly dressed in gray silk, and she smiled when she saw her charge. "You look lovely, dear."

Katharine wrinkled her nose, and her cousin thought, not for the first time, that she really was beautiful. Her pale glittering gown accented her dark hair and warm glowing skin, and her amber eyes lent a piquant flavor to the whole.

"Are you ready for the gauntlet?" asked Katharine. After considering the matter, she had told Mary

Elinor's story, so that the older woman was fully aware of the reason for their outing tonight.

"I am," she replied. "I shall do my best with the chaperones. I don't know any of them well, but gossip never waits for close acquaintanceship. I shall hear whatever is being said about Tom, if anything is." She shook her head. "I cannot help but hope that Elinor has made a mistake."

"No more than I do," was the positive reply, "for all our sakes. But let us go and see."

They arrived at Lady Sefton's town house about ten, threading their way through a great press of carriages and linkboys with flaring torches and ascending the staircase with a crowd of other guests. Their hostess greeted Katharine effusively, twitting her on her avoidance of society since her return to England. Fortunately for Katharine's temper, the crowd was such that she could not keep them lingering long, and in a few moments the two cousins entered the ballroom and looked about them.

"Well," said Mary, "it certainly is lovely. I have never seen so many flowers."

Katharine was suddenly aware of the fact that her cousin had never before attended a real London ball. She felt ashamed of having deprived her of this treat, and almost glad that Elinor's plight had dragged her out. Mary, at least, should enjoy this evening. "It is beautiful," she agreed. "And there is Elinor."

The girl was indeed hurrying toward them, with such a woebegone expression that Katharine nearly exclaimed her annoyance aloud. Did the girl wish everyone to know her feelings? She would cause no end of gossip by looking so unhappy. When Elinor joined them, Katharine could not help repeating these thoughts, and the younger girl hung her head and looked even worse. "I cannot smile," she murmured. "It is all so horrid. Look, they are there."

Katharine followed the direction of her glance and saw Tom Marchington leaning over the back of a sofa by the wall. On it, a glittering figure reclined, and it was obvious that Tom was fascinated by her. Katharine surveyed the Countess Standen with a mixture of curiosity and contempt. She was certainly lovely, tall and commanding with a stunning figure clearly outlined by a clinging gown of green gauze. Her neck and shoulders rose out of this proudly, her blond hair was a cloud of ringlets, and her features were classically perfect. At that moment, the countess looked up and met Katharine's gaze. Her eyes were a brilliant green, visible even across the room. She raised one exquisitely arched eyebrow, then smiled a charming, crooked smile. In spite of herself, Katharine was almost lured into answering it with a smile of her own. She looked away, as if merely scanning the ballroom for acquaintances, but she was far from feeling the unconcern she tried to put in her expression. However was *she* to combat a woman such as this? She had no doubt now that Elinor's suspicions were correct; one had only to look at Tom to see that he had lost his head. But what could *she* do?

"Oh, dear," murmured Mary Daltry, "she is…ah… so very…ah…"

"Exactly," replied Katharine dryly.

"What shall we do?" whispered Elinor.

"For now, nothing. There is nothing we can do at a public ball, and I must think, in any case. Try to at least *seem* to enjoy yourself, Elinor. Dance, or go and talk to some of your friends. The less concerned you appear, the less talk there will be."

"But, Katharine, I *can't*."

"Of course you can. Make an effort."

Ruthlessly she sent the younger girl off to join a group of her contemporaries. Elinor went, but anyone looking at her must have seen that she was extremely uneasy.

"Poor girl," said Mary. "Perhaps you were too hard on her, Katharine."

"No, sympathy would only have caused her to break down entirely. And that would have gone round the *ton* in a trice. How I hate their petty little world! No, Mary, she must try to put on a brave show, and we must do what we can to help her."

"Yes, dear." The older woman sighed. "I shall go sit with the chaperones." Katharine nodded, and Mary walked away, leaving her charge sorely puzzled. What ought she to do? Would a serious talk with Tom Marchington solve the problem, assuming, that is, that she could muster the effrontery to interfere in that way?

"Katharine Daltry!" exclaimed a male voice behind her. "What incredible luck. I can't believe my good fortune in finding you here, and alone." She turned to face a slender young man with brown hair and an impish expression. As soon as she met his dancing eyes, he took her hand and bowed over it. "I kiss your hand. I worship at your feet." He dropped gracefully to one knee for a moment, then stood, grinning.

"Don't be an idiot," said Katharine.

"Alas, is this the way you greet an old friend after years and years? When I think of the way I pined for you, unable to eat or sleep, almost putting a pistol to my head."

"Still telling outrageous bouncers, I see, Mr. Tillston. I had several correspondents in London during my absence, you know. They never mentioned your misery."

"I kept it all locked away in my heart," he replied, putting a hand on his chest. "Too precious for the eyes of the world."

"Oh, Tony, take a damper. You know I hate these transports."

The man grinned again. "Well, I do, but as you were calling me 'Mr. Tillston' in that frigid way, I thought you deserved some punishment." In the corner, the orchestra struck up the first set. "Come and dance," he added.

Katharine hesitated. Though she was not in deep mourning, it had been less than a year since her father's death. But the sound of the music, and the knowledge that her father would have roared at the idea that she should refrain from dancing for his sake, finally made her nod, and Tony led her into the set forming nearby.

She enjoyed the dance. Tony remained, as she remembered him, an amusing, scatterbrained companion. And it was pleasant to move and turn in time to the music after such a long time. When the set ended, Katharine encountered several other old acquaintances, and she was soon the center of a chattering group.

The novelty of her reappearance, combined with her very real charm and others' memories of her earlier success, made her an object of interest for many of the *ton*. Katharine herself was soon feeling bored, but whenever she thought of slipping away, she turned her eyes to the corner where Tom Marchington was now competing with several other gallants for the attention of the Countess Standen, and her chin came up.

The second set had ended, and the third was not begun, when a deep voice behind Katharine said, "Miss Daltry." She turned and looked up, an unusual thing in itself, for Katharine was a tall woman. But the man who stood before her was a good six inches taller. His height alone would have made him striking, but it was combined with a dark handsomeness and a commanding air so pervasive that it nearly obscured his other attributes. His assurance was so complete that many, meeting him for the first time, wondered at it audibly.

He said nothing further, seeming to scorn the platitudes usual in such a situation. He simply held Katharine's eyes with a bland expression in his very dark blue ones.

Katharine, coolly surveying his impeccable evening dress, did not look as pleased as one would have expected a young lady addressed by an extremely attractive man to look. She bowed her head slightly and replied, "Good evening, Lord Stonenden."

He raised one dark eyebrow. "I came to beg the honor of a dance. I see you are not engaged." And before Katharine could reply, he had put an arm around her waist and pulled her onto the floor, where a waltz was just beginning.

His action was so abrupt that she was speechless for a moment. He guided her firmly and expertly down the ballroom as she angrily framed and discarded a number of caustic remarks. Finally she said, "You haven't changed, I see."

Lord Stonenden laughed. "Nor have you, Miss Daltry. Your eyes still glitter when you're angry. I had nearly forgotten those amazing amber eyes. But not quite."

"I withdraw my statement. You *have* changed. You are worse than ever."

"Worse?"

"More insufferably arrogant and, if possible, even less careful of others' feelings."

"Miss Daltry! You can't have forgotten that your feelings, at least, were once of the greatest concern to me."

"Nonsense!" Katharine's reply was so emphatic that a gentleman dancing near them turned in surprise to look at her. "You never cared a straw for anyone or anything but yourself. Why did you force me to dance in this absurd way, merely to be irritating?"

Lord Stonenden's dark blue eyes flickered, but he said, "Of course, Miss Daltry. Have I not said that your eyes are extraordinary when you are angry?"

Katharine looked up at him, an equally sharp retort on her lips, but before she could speak, a picture out of memory intruded between her and the man in whose arms she circled. She saw Lady Eliza Burnham's drawing room as it had been five years ago, and herself, a thin large-eyed girl, sitting on the sofa with folded hands. This man stood before her, looking much the same, and he was saying, "You are everything I desire in a wife, Miss Daltry. Will you do me the honor of becoming Lady Stonenden?" And before she had said a word in reply, he had stepped confidently forward and taken her hand.

He had looked positively stunned when she had pulled it away again and stood up, refusing him in a few curt phrases. "What?" he said when she finished.

"I cannot accept your offer," Katharine repeated.

"What do you mean?"

"I believe I spoke very clearly."

"You are refusing *me*?"

She had merely nodded, very annoyed.

"But why?" Stonenden's incredulity had obviously outweighed his disappointment.

"I do not return your regard," Katharine had begun.

"Nonsense. I can offer you every luxury. And I know myself to be far from repulsive. What is your true reason?"

Goaded by his manner, Katharine had spoken her mind perhaps too freely. "You are the most odiously arrogant man I have ever met!" she had snapped. "I have been trying for weeks to let you see that your proposal was unwelcome, and you have been impervious to the most blatant hints. You care only for yourself, and that is not the sort of husband I look for."

His handsome face had frozen as she spoke, and when she finished, he bowed. "I beg your pardon," he had said then, and left the room without another word, to Katharine's vast relief. As soon as she had spoken, she had been frightened at her own temerity, and at the flash her words had brought to Stonenden's eyes. She might despise his arrogance, but that did not prevent a healthy respect for his tongue. She had seen him give more than one unlucky offender a blistering set-down, for affronts much slighter than hers, and she had expected something of that sort herself.

But to her amazement, Stonenden seemed to blot out the incident entirely. She had seen him again, of course—it was inevitable that she should, in the small world of London society—and she was astonished to find that he acted just the same. He asked her to stand up with him and chatted at parties as if nothing unusual had passed between them. Indeed, he seemed, if anything, more amused by her company. To Katharine, this had appeared a further example of his utter disregard for others. She had no idea what he felt about their changed relation, but she did know that he cared nothing for her embarrassment and awkwardness. This had made the whole affair much worse. She could not have endured it for any length of time, but, soon after, she had left the country with her father, never thinking of Stonenden again until this moment.

The memory fading, Katharine looked up, again wondering what thoughts passed behind those inscrutable dark blue eyes. It was no good asking him, of course. He would not say, and he would take malicious amusement in her curiosity. It was not worth thinking about. Smiling slightly, she shook her head. "In that case, my best defense is to refuse to be angry, is it not? So, I am all compliance." Her smile broadened with false sweetness.

"Bravo! Still an opponent worth one's steel, I see." But Katharine had abruptly ceased to attend and was looking over her partner's shoulder with a frown. Her expression held such unmistakable concern that he glanced quickly back to see what she was looking at. "What is it?" he asked.

"What?" answered Katharine, clearly distracted.

"Whom are you watching with such a black look? I pity the poor soul from the bottom of my heart."

Katharine sniffed. She wished there were some grounds for pity, but she had been looking at Tom Marchington waltzing with the Countess Standen, holding her much closer than was customary or proper, and though she could easily believe that her look had been black, she was only too aware that the countess had nothing to fear from her. She continued to gaze at them, and Lord Stonenden now isolated the subject of her stare. "Are you wondering at Elise Standen's new flirt? We all are, I promise you. He is quite the country bumpkin, and not at all in her usual style."

The condescending amusement in his voice so infuriated Katharine that she snapped, "That country bumpkin happens to be newly married to my cousin!" As soon as she said it, she could have bitten her tongue in irritation. After urging Elinor to be discreet, she herself had just exposed the whole matter to one of the most sardonic critics in the *ton*.

"Ah," replied Lord Stonenden. "So that's it, is it?"

Katharine struggled to cover up her slip. "Yes, isn't it amusing? He is indulging in a bit of light flirtation, quite unlike him. My cousin is delighted to find he has such skill." She looked down as she finished, her excuse sounding lame even in her own ears.

"Is she?" answered her partner dryly. "What an unusual girl she must be, to be sure."

Katharine raised her eyes and tried to frame some light reply.

"Oh, for God's sake, don't look so stricken," he said. "I promise not to tell anyone what you have said, if that is what you are worried about. Do you think me a gossip too?"

Katharine was too surprised to answer him, and at that moment the music ended and they were surrounded by couples moving to the edge of the floor. Lord Stonenden escorted her to a chair and was about to speak when they were joined by Lady Eliza Burnham.

"Katharine!" she said. "The very person I wanted. I must speak to you." She took the chair next to the girl. "Go away, Stonenden," she added, waving him off with her hand. The gentleman smiled wryly and walked away.

"How utterly insufferable he is!" exclaimed Katharine when he was out of earshot. "I truly cannot abide him. And why he asked me to dance, I shall never understand."

Lady Eliza looked surprised. "Stonenden? Don't you like him? Why, he is the chief object of every girl in London. They have begun to call him Stoneheart, you know, because he is never caught by any of our beauties, though he flirts with them all."

"A very good name for him," retorted Katharine, "though 'No Heart' might be even better."

"But I find him quite charming. And terribly attractive, of course. He has such an air of...I don't know what to call it, really."

"Consequence?" offered the other. "Self-satisfaction?"

"You *don't* like him, do you? I shouldn't call it either of those." Her friend suddenly remembered something. "Didn't he dangle after you when you first came out?"

"Some thought so. I was never deceived. He was so full of himself that I don't believe he ever really *saw* me. He must have felt it was time he settled down, and he lit on me as a proper candidate for the immense honor of his hand. I have never understood why. I daresay a hundred other girls would have fallen at his feet in gratitude."

Lady Eliza gaped at her. "You mean he *offered* for you? Oliver Stonenden? Katharine!"

Uncharacteristically, Katharine Daltry flushed crimson from forehead to neck. "I didn't mean to say so much. I was angry. Please disregard it, Eliza."

"My dear, you know I would never repeat anything you told me. And you cannot leave me in such suspense. Did he?"

"Well…well, yes."

"And you refused him? Stonenden! The earldom? And that immense fortune?"

This brought back Katharine's irritation. "Yes, I did. And I pity the woman who becomes his wife, in spite of all those things. He will never care a straw for anything she may think or want."

"Well, but, Katharine…"

The girl's jaw hardened. "This can't have been what you wished to say to me."

"No. Oh, no, but…"

"Well, I would much rather hear what that was. I am sick of the subject of Lord Stonenden."

"But his asking you to dance this evening. He almost never dances, you know. Perhaps he still—"

"Eliza!" exclaimed the younger girl, revolted.

Seeing that she was really incensed, Lady Eliza dropped the subject. "Yes, well, it meant nothing, I daresay. I wanted to speak to you about your cousin, Katharine."

"Elinor?"

"Yes. Or rather, her husband. He is making himself very conspicuous, Katharine. People are beginning to notice the way he hangs about Elise Standen."

"Are they?" replied Katharine bitterly.

"Yes, and I thought I should just give you a hint."

"Hint? Why do you think I dragged myself here tonight, Eliza, after all my efforts to remain quietly at home?"

"You had heard, then?"

"Elinor came to me for help."

The older woman looked doubtful.

"Of course it is ridiculous," said Katharine in response. "I do not see what I can do. But I could not refuse."

"Perhaps his parents?"

"I am assured that that would be the worst possible solution. I am thinking of speaking to Tom myself."

"Katharine, no! That would be extremely improper."

"I don't care about propriety. But I doubt that he would listen to me. I would not, in his position. Who am I to lecture him?"

"Very true, dear. Young men do not like to be scolded, particularly by a female." The two women contemplated the problem in silence for a few moments. "You know," added Lady Eliza then, "I have just remembered that Stonenden is fairly well acquainted with Elise Standen."

"Undoubtedly," replied Katharine.

"Oh, not in *that* way. Though I think it was when one of his friends was… But that is by the by. He does know her, and he is just the person who might be able to help in this awkward situation. People listen to him. He would know how to handle Elise, and all the young men look up to him. Perhaps…"

"I would sooner ask the dustman for help," snapped Katharine.

"But, my dear—"

"Eliza, please. Do not mention it again. It is out of the question. I shall think of something."

Lady Eliza sighed, but her eyes roamed the ballroom until they found Lord Stonenden, talking to a friend in the far corner, and her expression then was not that of a person who has given up hope.

Coincidentally, the two men were talking of Katharine at that very moment. "Did I see you dancing with the Daltry girl?" Mr. Case was asking his friend. "Alvanley was telling me about her earlier. I understand she's quite out of the common way."

"She is that," replied Stonenden.

"Lovely, too." Case gazed across at her. "Say, Stonenden, I seem to remember that you showed quite an interest in her once. I'd forgotten."

"Oh, yes. I sat at her feet with the rest of London's callow youth five years ago. She appeared to find the lot of us quite ridiculous. Rightly, I imagine."

"Got engaged to some military sprig, didn't she? I

recall it now. A great romance, it was. My wife was in alt over the thing. She followed him to India, and he up and died. A sad ending for the poor little thing."

"She evidently thinks so," responded Stonenden, with something like contempt.

"What do you mean?"

"According to the gossip, she is still pining for the fellow. Her heart, apparently, was broken."

"Well, and why not? It's refreshing, when all the young people seem to think nothing of getting engaged and breaking it off again twice in a year. It wasn't so in my day. But the way you talk of the girl, I wonder you danced with her, Stonenden."

"I wonder myself," murmured his companion. He looked across. Katharine had left Eliza Burnham and was dancing again. As he followed her with his eyes, Oliver Stonenden felt a most unaccustomed uneasiness. Before him was the one person he had ever known who disturbed his ingrained assurance. He had not thought of her in some time. Her absence from England had made it easy not to do so. But now she had returned, stirring up a host of unwelcome thoughts and emotions.

Katharine Daltry's refusal of his suit had been the first, and really the only, shock to Oliver Stonenden's self-consequence in the course of his thirty-two years. Orphaned very early in his life, he had been reared by a maternal uncle who was nearly overcome by the honor and responsibility of his task. His mother's family, while genteel, occupied a much lower social stratum than the earls of Stonenden, and his uncle had been only too conscious of this disparity. He

had at first tried to avoid the role of mentor, but
finding that there were no suitable members of the
Stonenden family available, he had then devoted his
life to Oliver's education. Unfortunately, his outlook
had imbued the boy with an exaggerated idea of his
own worth. To Charles Beele, no family was greater
than his nephew's, and no person more perfect than
Oliver Stonenden. His continual reiteration of these
principles had at last produced belief, and by the time
he was fifteen, the young earl unconsciously thought
of himself as far superior to the people around him.
The early possession of a large fortune had merely
compounded this process, giving him the freedom to
do as he liked and an attraction for flatterers and toadeaters of all descriptions. The latter had engendered a
contempt for his fellow man, but they had not taught
him to question his own position.

It was left for Katharine Daltry to threaten his self-
esteem, and even her refusal of his hand had merely
dented it. She acquired an odd fascination for him—he
could not seem to stay away from her—but when she
left the country, Stonenden's old habits of thought
returned intact. He dismissed her from his mind.

But now she was before him again, and some of
the old disturbance welled up when it became obvious
that she thought as little of him as ever. In the four
years of her absence, Stonenden had met no one else
who rated him so low. Indeed, the *ton* flattered and
fawned in an only too familiar fashion; young women
of marriageable age pursued him despite the sharpest
set-downs his ready wit could devise. But now, here
was this girl who called him arrogant to his face and

named him "worse than ever," a girl who had refused the hand that any of the debs would give almost anything to accept. Stonenden felt the old fascination rise once more. The girl was impossible, of course, yet…

Mr. Case had been watching his friend's face curiously during this pause. He was slightly shocked by the look that crossed it now. "Say, Oliver, you're not still piqued that she chose another fellow over you? I mean, if a girl's in love…"

"Of course not. What do you take me for?"

Case begged his pardon. "Not but what there are men who would hold a grudge over that sort of thing. But I should have known you're not that type." He followed Stonenden's eyes to where Katharine was dancing. "But, I say, why did you dance with her?"

"Pure folly, I believe," responded Stonenden musingly. "Or possibly mere boredom."

The other man stared at him. "Beg pardon?"

The earl shrugged. "Come, John, how about a hand of piquet?"

Mr. Case followed him to the card room, a speculative gleam in his eye. Katharine Daltry was not mentioned between them again that evening, but she was much in Mr. Case's thoughts, and he would have wagered a good deal more than he was willing to venture on piquet that she was in his partner's as well, though what place she occupied was wholly unclear.

Four

ELINOR MARCHINGTON CALLED ON HER COUSIN VERY early the following morning. She found Katharine and Mary at breakfast, and before they could even rise to greet her, she blurted out, "You must believe me now. You have seen with your own eyes how Tom—"

Katharine quickly gestured toward the maid, who was putting a fresh pot of tea on the table, and Elinor fell silent, but both the Daltrys could see from her expression that she would not be able to remain so long. She was plainly bursting with chagrin and indignation. Katharine sighed a little—it was clear there would be no painting for her this morning—and dismissed the maid. Elinor sat down, looking from one to the other of her hostesses. "You do believe me now, don't you? You saw how Tom is acting."

Mary Daltry looked grave, and Katharine nodded reluctantly.

Elinor, far from being gratified by their agreement, seemed near tears. "What am I to do? I have tried to talk to Tom, but he won't listen. He has never been like this in his life. We always...we always..."

She choked a little and groped in her reticule for a handkerchief. Mary got up and went to sit beside her, patting her shoulder comfortingly. And both of them looked to Katharine, their expressions full of confidence in her ability to solve this problem and put things right again.

Katharine smiled wryly back at them. Their faith was touching, but quite misplaced, she felt. She had no more idea than either of them what could be done about Tom's infatuation with the Countess Standen. Nothing in her admittedly somewhat unusual life had prepared her for the role of rescuer in such a situation. But the other two women continued to watch her hopefully, and Katharine felt she must speak. She cleared her throat. "Are you certain, Elinor, that we cannot go to Tom's father? I admit I am not well acquainted with Sir Lionel, but—"

"No, no. I told you what he is like! He would never forgive us. He would blame me."

"But surely—"

"Katharine, I tell you, he *would*! And there would be a great row. And Tom would be so angry with me. Oh, no, you mustn't. *Promise* me you won't tell him!"

"All right. If you say we cannot go to Sir Lionel, then we cannot. But has Tom no other relative he respects? Perhaps his mother might influence him?"

"Oh, she is just like Sir Lionel. She would tell him at once."

"Ah. But an uncle, perhaps, or…or anyone else?"

Elinor considered this, then shook her head. "Tom has never mentioned any family member with particular affection. I don't think he is close to his uncles."

"I see." Katharine's heart sank. She could not help believing that this problem would be much better handled by a man. She did not at all doubt her own judgment; she was simply convinced that Tom Marchington would not pay the least heed to the opinion of a woman little older than himself, whom he had met only once a very short time ago. A wry smile touched her lips again briefly. She could not help but add that Tom was probably right.

"Katharine, you must talk to him," said Elinor then. "You must make him see how foolish he is. He will listen to you. You are so knowing."

Staring a little at this description of herself, Katharine met her cousin's anxious brown eyes. "You know, Elinor, I really don't think he will. He barely knows me, and—"

"Of course he will!" protested the other. "You are just the person to show him how dreadful the Countess Standen truly is. You know all about the *ton*. When I try to talk to him, he always says I don't know anything about town life, but he cannot say that of *you*. Oh, Katharine, please!"

The older girl quailed before her cousin's pleading gaze. She was convinced that Elinor was distorting the situation in her desperate hope for a solution. Even she must realize that Katharine hadn't the slightest influence over Tom Marchington. Helplessly Katharine looked to Mary Daltry. "What do you think?" she asked her.

With understanding sympathy in her eyes, Mary shrugged. "I imagine you are right, but what else can we do? Have you some other plan? I do not. And I am unlikely to discover one." She spread her hands in an eloquent gesture of helplessness. Her education had not prepared her to deal with a situation such as this.

Katharine sighed again and shook her head. "I haven't any plan at all. I suppose I must talk to him."

Elinor clasped her hands. "You will? Oh, I knew you would not fail me." For the first time that morning, she smiled. "Everything will be all right now. You will go at once, won't you, Katharine? Tom is usually at home until eleven."

Katharine's amber eyes widened. "Now? But I…"

"Oh, please. I am so miserable. I cannot bear another day of this."

"But I have not thought what I will say, or…or…" Katharine looked to Mary for help.

But she merely shrugged again. "Perhaps it would be best to get it over with," she said. Meeting her eyes, outraged, Katharine read a very different message there. Like her, Mary clearly thought this mission hopeless. The older woman glanced briefly at Elinor, then made a tiny gesture with her hands, and Katharine saw at once that she was concerned about Elinor's false hopes. The girl was transformed, all her despondence dissolved by the belief that Katharine would magically make everything right. The sooner she was forced to face the truth, the easier it would be.

Still, Katharine could not feel pleased about the prospect of confronting Tom Marchington. She rose from her chair slowly and reluctantly. "Very well," she said finally. "I shall go this morning."

Elinor bounced to her feet and came to hug Katharine. "Oh, thank you, thank you, Cousin

Katharine. I knew you would help me. You are my favorite relative in the whole world!"

Katharine tried to return her smile, but when she met Mary's eyes over Elinor's shoulder, she grimaced eloquently.

Katharine did not leave her house until ten. She had, after all, insisted upon a little time to marshal her thoughts. But Elinor had assured her that Tom never left his bed before nine, so she hoped to catch him as he finished breakfast. As she rode the short distance to the Marchingtons' rented town house, she pulled nervously at the fingers of her gloves and rehearsed yet again what she meant to say. It would require all the tact and calm reasonableness she possessed, she felt, to get Tom to listen to her at all. Persuading him to change his behavior would be something else again—and most probably impossible. But she hoped at least to be persuasive enough so that he might think about it once she had gone.

When Katharine arrived at the house, however, she met with an unexpected setback. Tom was out. She had been so concentrated on her argument that this simple problem defeated her for a moment. She stood on the steps before the front door and stared at the fashionable butler who had imparted this news.

"Perhaps you would care to leave a message?" he said. "Will you come in?"

"No. No, I…it is very important that I speak to Mr. Marchington right away. His wife has…that is, do you know where he has gone?"

"He didn't say, Miss Daltry. But I did hear him direct the coachman to the exhibition of Greek statues."

"The Elgin Marbles? Oh, that's all right, then; I shall look for him there."

"Yes, miss. I hope there hasn't been an accident or anything of that nature? Mrs. Marchington is—"

"No, no, of course not. She is perfectly all right. Thank you." Katharine climbed back into her carriage feeling that she had not handled this encounter very smoothly.

By the time she reached the exhibition hall, however, she had gathered her wits once again. And she went in looking resolute. The place was nearly empty at this time of the morning, and Katharine walked quickly through one deserted room after another, hardly glancing at the sculpture that she had more than once spent hours admiring. She had begun to conclude that Tom was not there—indeed, when she thought about it, it was a very odd place for him to come—when she heard the murmur of voices from the chamber ahead of her. She increased her pace, and in a moment was under the archway and face-to-face with the Countess Standen, the sole occupant of the room. Thoroughly taken aback, Katharine stopped short and, regrettably, gaped at the older woman.

Her patent astonishment called forth the countess's crooked smile. And in the brief instant they stood silently facing one another, Katharine's heart sank. Seen so close, Elise Standen was even lovelier than she remembered. Her statuesque figure was flawless, her pale blond hair and clear skin exquisite, and her brilliant green eyes both alluring and intelligent. She wore an elegant morning dress of dark green cloth and had been pulling a matching pair of kid gloves over her fingers when Katharine entered. "Good morning," she said in a cool, amused voice as Katharine continued to stare. "Have we met? I am Elise Standen."

Katharine got the distinct impression that the countess knew precisely who she was, but she said only, "I believe not. I am Katharine Daltry."

"How do you do? You are General Daltry's daughter, are you not? I knew your father years ago."

At this, still spoken in that mockingly amused tone, Katharine's eyes widened slightly. She looked at the countess, thought of her own dashing father, and almost laughed. It was quite possible that the general had known Elise Standen—she was very much in his style—but the countess was too young to have known him "years ago" in the intimate way that her voice implied. The woman was trying to bait her. A glitter appeared in Katharine's amber eyes. "Did you?" she replied sweetly. "I don't remember. Was it before I was born?"

The other woman's head jerked a little as she glanced quickly at Katharine, an arrested expression in her eyes. Then, surprisingly, she slowly smiled her crooked smile once again. She surveyed the younger girl from head to foot, appreciatively. "You *are* your father's daughter, aren't you?"

Katharine had to suppress an answering smile. The woman's humor was contagious. "People seem to notice a resemblance."

"Oh, undoubtedly. I congratulate you."

The remark seemed so sincere, and the countess's expression so clear of mockery, that Katharine was suddenly struck by an idea. Could she speak to this woman about Tom, rather than vice versa? She dismissed the thought at once. She could not broach such a personal matter with a stranger who possessed not even the slender link of being married to her cousin. But even as she came to this conclusion, Elise Standen said, "Did you come looking for Tom?" Laughter was again in her voice.

Katharine was taken aback.

"It was not so hard to guess, you know. You came in with such a determined look, it was obvious you were searching for someone. And when you saw me, you were *so* astonished." She laughed. "It helped, of course, that I knew you were Tom's cousin."

"His wife's cousin," Katharine could not resist replying.

"Yes, of course. His wife's cousin." The countess's green eyes met Katharine's amber ones lazily, and she smiled.

"Won't you stop what you're doing?" blurted Katharine then. This exchange was extremely improper, but she could not let such an opportunity go by.

The older woman's smile broadened. "I could pretend that I don't know what you mean," she answered. "But I think I won't. It is far more piquant."

"Do you *like* hurting people?" said Katharine, at once put off and somehow fascinated by this woman.

"Not particularly." The countess was careless.

"Then you will stop?"

"Oh, no, my dear. I am having far too much fun with little Thomas. And my own amusement is more important than anything else to me. You cannot imagine how bored I was before he came along."

"But that is despicable," began Katharine, appalled by such lighthearted selfishness.

"Oh, la, what a word. It is no more than half the *ton* is doing every day, Miss Daltry. There's not the least harm in it."

"There is," insisted Katharine, thinking of Elinor's face this morning.

Countess Standen shrugged, losing interest in the subject. Katharine was about to go on, to try to make her see the rightness of her request, when there was a slight noise behind them and Tom Marchington hurried into the room.

"Sorry to be so long," he was saying. "The damned groom…" Seeing Katharine, he stopped abruptly.

"Tom," murmured the countess caressingly. The look in her eyes, a mixture of confidence, amusement, and calculation, made Katharine frown. "Your cousin was searching for you, darling. I told her you'd be right along."

Tom and Katharine frowned at one another, he in uneasy annoyance, she in angry disgust. The countess had told her no such thing. "I want to talk to you," she snapped, forgetting all her careful plans.

Tom's frown deepened. "I am just escorting the countess home."

"Oh, don't mind me," put in this lady, drifting toward the door. "I can find my carriage perfectly well. Do have your little 'talk.' This is such an *uplifting* place for one." And with a mocking smile over her shoulder, she was gone.

Katharine was immediately aware of the complete impropriety of talking to Tom in a public place. Why had she followed him here instead of calling at the house again later? She was annoyed with herself, and her annoyance shifted irrationally onto Tom as he started to go after the countess. "Tom! I want to speak to you," she snapped.

He turned back, plainly exasperated. "Well, you've chosen a dashed inconvenient time for it…and place, for that matter. I must go."

"On the contrary, you must stay and hear what I have to tell you," Katharine heard herself retort. As soon as the words were out, she bit her lip. This was no way to persuade Tom Marchington.

A carriage went by outside, and Tom strode to the window to watch it. When he turned back, he looked even more annoyed. "She's gone. What the deuce do you want?"

Katharine tried to stifle her anger and recall some of the very rational phrases she had framed this morning. She took a deep breath. "I want to talk to you about the countess, Tom. Elinor—"

"Oh, yes. I see. Elinor sent you to lecture me on my behavior, is that it? Well, I can't see that it's any business of yours."

Wishing that she had not mentioned Elinor's name, and that she did not more or less agree with his objection, Katharine ventured, "Perhaps it is not, precisely. But I am a member of your family now, and I wanted to urge you to think of what you are doing. It is not only that you are hurting Elinor, though that is very important, but you may cause a scandal that will affect all the Marchingtons." Katharine had determined on this approach after Elinor's remarks about Sir Lionel, and she was gratified now to see Tom's face change. Perhaps being reminded of his father would check him.

But Tom said sullenly, "I haven't any intention of causing a scandal. I can be as discreet as anyone." He stuck out his chest. "And I do think Elinor might be more understanding. *She* always wanted to come to London, too. We often talked of how we wished to try our wings in town. And a man has a right to a few larks before he settles down."

"But you are married already," Katharine replied.

Tom's round face looked rebellious. "Well, I asked them to let me come for a season first, and Father refused. It's not my fault."

Exasperated, Katharine surveyed his mulishly unreceptive face. She could think of no reasonable arguments against his position, because he was being thoroughly unreasonable himself. So she tried illogic. "I suppose Elinor is free to do as she likes also, then?" she asked.

For a moment Tom looked startled, and she hoped; then he shrugged. "Of course. All she wants is to attend balls and that sort of nonsense."

At this flip dismissal, Katharine's annoyance flared into anger. "You are acting like a spoiled child," she snapped. "Don't you care for anyone else's feelings?"

Predictably, this simply angered Tom in his turn. "Whether I do or don't, it's none of your affair," he retorted. "And you can tell Elinor not to send people to preach at me. I am perfectly able to manage my own life—yes, and my wife's, too, if you and the other interfering tattlemongers would just leave her alone."

And with this he turned on his heel and walked out of the room.

Katharine stood still for a moment when he was gone. She was very angry indeed—mostly with Tom, but partly with herself for handling him clumsily. She took several deep breaths, thinking, as she did so, of a number of telling remarks she might have made during the exchange, and finally started toward the door. She had come to one decision during this abortive effort to help Elinor. She would see Tom Marchington separated from the countess and returned to Elinor if it was the last thing she ever did.

Five

ELINOR WAS UNDERSTANDABLY DISAPPOINTED WHEN Katharine told her the outcome of the encounter with Tom. But when she was assured that her cousin did not mean to give up, and indeed was determined to think of some plan, she brightened and went home not too despondent to prepare for a luncheon she was to attend. Katharine, eating her own meal with Mary, was less sanguine. They discussed the problem for some time without hitting upon any plausible solution. And in the end, they were forced to leave the subject, for it was clear that neither had the least idea what the next move should be.

"I am going up to my studio," said Katharine, rising, "and put this whole matter out of my mind for a while. If anyone calls, I don't wish to be disturbed."

"Of course, dear. But you had better tell one of the maids. I am going out this afternoon to visit old Mrs. James."

"All right." Katharine started out of the dining room. "I will see you at tea, and we shall try again to discover some plan."

Once upstairs, Katharine forgot all about Elinor, Tom, the countess, and other annoyances. She had found years ago in India that she could put almost any worry or pain out of her mind when she stood before her easel, and the initial use of this activity as an escape had gradually developed it into a great love. She was finishing her painting of the poppies today, as she would have done yesterday but for Elinor's interruption, and she was soon completely happy, tracing the delicate lines of the petals with a tiny sable brush.

Nearly two hours passed, Katharine heedless of anything but her work. She was just standing back from the canvas and looking it over, trying to decide whether to call it complete or to add a few further touches, when there was a slight noise from the doorway, and a male voice exclaimed, "That is good, really good!"

Katharine whirled to find Tony Tillston walking into the studio, surveying her painting with real interest. "Tony! How did you get in here? I left strict orders that I was not to be disturbed."

Her visitor turned away from the canvas and grinned, his hazel eyes dancing. "I know you did," he replied. "Your maid told me so. But I fear I overbore her with the...er, force of my personality. I assure you she did not willingly reveal your hiding place." He looked around the room. "This is unexpected, Katharine. I had no idea you were interested in painting." He turned back to the canvas. "Or so gifted. I meant what I said, you know. That is really good. And I know something about art."

Katharine was torn between gratification and

embarrassment. She hated to have people see her work before she was prepared, but she was human enough to find his praise irresistible. She put down her palette and began to clean her hands of paint.

"Did you begin this in India?" continued Tony. "You never mentioned it when I knew you before."

"Yes." Katharine kept her eyes on her hands. "There was very little for me to do there, you know, after Robert was killed. I always liked painting, so I took it up again. After a while, I went from watercolors to this."

Tony nodded, examining the painting more closely. "You mean to say you taught yourself to paint this way?"

Katharine shrugged. "I had a great many lessons in watercolors."

"But this is quite different. I really am impressed, Katharine. You should do something with this."

Katharine made a slight derisive sound. "What? Exhibit? I have no wish to be a nine days' wonder, thank you. I have seen what happens to women of my sort who fancy themselves poets or artists. They may be tolerated, but only as freaks, and only while they do not disturb anyone. I am quite happy painting for myself; I don't want anything but time."

Tony laughed. "A telling shot at me. But I will not apologize again for interrupting you, because I think I can do you a service. I understand your feelings about exhibiting, and I daresay you are right. But you might still do something privately. There are any number of collectors who would admire your work." She started to speak, but he held up a hand. "*And* I think you should become acquainted with some other painters. I am told that it is very helpful to be able to talk about one's work with those who can understand it."

"It may well be," responded Katharine impatiently. "But you know quite well that I cannot do that, Tony. I am grateful for your interest, but—"

"In fact," he interrupted, "I should like to take you to Lawrence's this very afternoon. He is always at home on Tuesdays for tea."

"I can't..." began Katharine, then stopped. She stared wide-eyed at her guest "Lawrence? You can't mean—"

"Yes, I do." Tony grinned impishly again. "Sir Thomas Lawrence. I am well acquainted with him. He painted a portrait of my aunt several years ago, and we struck up a friendship."

"You...you *know* Lawrence?" echoed Katharine.

"Come, come, this astonishment is not very flattering. I realize that I am not the weightiest of fellows, but I do have my points. Will you come?"

"B-but, I cannot," stammered Katharine. "I do not know him at all. And...and my gown." She looked down helplessly.

Tony laughed. "I will present you. But I agree that you must change your costume." He eyed her worn muslin dress and voluminous apron with amusement. "Not that it isn't very fetching, of course."

Gathering her wits, Katharine grimaced at him. "But who will be there? Are you certain I may go uninvited?"

"Of course. It is open house on Tuesday, and a great many fashionable people look in, including ladies who want their portraits painted, so you needn't worry about the proprieties." He turned back to her painting. "And you can take some of your work to show Sir Thomas. I suppose you will take his word for its quality, if you won't take mine."

"Oh, no!" Katharine was appalled. "I couldn't possibly do any such thing." She thought of putting one of her efforts in front of the most admired painter of their time and put a hand to her mouth.

"But he's very good about that sort of thing. Says that he wishes to help young painters as Reynolds helped him when he first came to London."

Katharine merely shook her head emphatically from side to side.

"But..." Tony met her eye and paused. "Oh, very well, but I think you are being overnice. Someone is always bringing a canvas for Lawrence to see, and most of them are not nearly as good as this." Katharine made a quick gesture, and he raised his hands. "I say no more. Go and get ready. It is nearly teatime."

She hesitated only a moment. The chance to meet the great painter overcame all her scruples. "I'll be in the drawing room in half an hour," she answered, turning to leave the room. "Are you coming?"

"Yes." Tony followed her, but on the landing outside, he suddenly exclaimed, "What's that?" and bent to examine his gleaming Hessian boot. "Dust! You go on. I shall come down in a moment." And he pulled out his handkerchief as if to brush off his boots.

Shaking her head at this piece of affectation, Katharine went down the stairs to her bedroom. As soon as she was out of sight, Tony straightened. He listened to her footsteps die away, then, with a mischievous grin, turned back to the door of the studio and disappeared within.

Katharine said very little on the ride to Sir Thomas Lawrence's house. She was too excited, and apprehensive, at the thought of meeting the man whose portraits of the rulers of Europe had lately been the talk of London. She had dressed with great care in a quietly elegant pearl-gray gown, and as they rode she wondered to herself what she would say if she had the opportunity to talk with Lawrence. Every phrase she thought of sounded idiotic.

"You mustn't mind if Sir Thomas flirts with you," said Tony when he helped her down from the carriage. "He always flirts with pretty women. He doesn't mean anything by it." As Katharine stared at him, he laughed. "Have I shocked you? I beg your pardon."

They were admitted at once and taken upstairs by a footman. Katharine heard the buzz of conversation before they entered the drawing room, and when they stood in the doorway to be announced, no one seemed to pay any heed. Surveying the group in the room, she was relieved to see several people she knew, and a liberal sprinkling of females. She had retained some small doubts about this call despite Tony's assurances. The latter took her arm and led her forward. "Come," he murmured, "I will present you." They made their way across the room to stand before a tall commanding man with chestnut hair and a full, handsome face. "Sir Thomas," said Tony, "how are you? May I present a friend of mine, Miss Katharine Daltry? She is very interested in painting." He grinned at Katharine and stepped back a little to allow her to come forward.

"H-how do you do?" said Katharine.

"My dear young lady." Lawrence actually bowed a little. "I am enchanted to have you in my house. Will you have tea? Of course." He signaled one of the servants.

Katharine, very nervous, turned to find that Tony had basely abandoned her. He was not to be seen anywhere in the room. She gazed frantically about, but encountered only the sardonic eye of Lord Oliver Stonenden, who was standing some distance away chatting with two men she didn't know. His apparently mocking glance did nothing to reassure her. Indeed, if anything, it increased her confusion. What was *he* doing in Sir Thomas Lawrence's salon, the last place she would have expected to encounter him? With a tiny shiver, she turned back to Sir Thomas. Tea arrived, and she took her cup.

"What sort of painting do you like?" asked Lawrence genially.

"Oh, I...I think your pictures are splendid," Katharine blurted. "They have such...such ease and... and sparkle." Cursing herself for this banality, she strove to gather her wits. "And of course, the drawing is perfect," she added more coherently. "You are so wonderful with the pencil."

The artist bowed slightly again. "You are too kind. But you talk more like a painter than a collector."

"That is because she is a painter," responded a voice behind them. "Here, Sir Thomas, look at these."

Katharine whirled and, to her horror, found Tony holding up one of her own canvases. He had several more beside him, and others in the room were turning to see what was being shown. "Oh, no," she gasped. "You mustn't…Sir Thomas, I did not mean…"

"She didn't want to mention her work," added Tony. "But I went behind her back and brought these because I think they're dashed good. What do you think, sir?" He handed the painting he was holding, a portrait Katharine had done of her native maid in India, to Lawrence, who took it willingly and began to examine it.

Moving closer to Tony, Katharine whispered, "I shall never forgive you for this! How could you bring them when I expressly forbade it?"

But Tony was pleased with himself. "Nonsense. Lawrence does this sort of thing all the time. He likes it, and now you will get an expert opinion."

"I doubt that he sees paintings by *women* 'all the time'!" Katharine hissed. She was torn between anger, acute embarrassment, and a sort of diffident curiosity as to what Sir Thomas would think of her efforts.

Lawrence looked at all of the paintings, slowly, one by one. When he put down the final canvas, he looked judiciously at her. "You have talent," he said, "though you clearly lack training. You studied…?"

"Only watercolors, with my governess." Katharine's reply was choked; she was very conscious of being the center of a critical group.

"Indeed? Very impressive, Miss Daltry." The artist held up the final canvas again. "One might almost say astonishing." He looked around. "Here, Stonenden, you have a good eye. What do you say?"

To Katharine's chagrin, Lord Stonenden approached and took her painting from Sir Thomas. He surveyed it quickly, though not carelessly, and went on to view the others. Katharine watched him with mixed emotions—surprised that his opinion should be sought by Lawrence, nervous of his sharp tongue, and as she watched his expression change, a little pleased at his obvious favorable reaction. Clearly, she was not the only one to be startled here today.

At last he put down the final canvas and turned to look at her. Katharine was struck again by the incongruity of the situation. Stonenden, in his creaseless fawn pantaloons and perfectly cut coat, was the last person she would have thought to meet here, and certainly the last she would have asked about her paintings.

"A definite talent," said Lord Stonenden in a queer tone. He sounded grudging and admiring at once.

"As I said," responded Sir Thomas. "I am glad to see you agree." The artist looked down at Katharine. "Lord Stonenden is one of our most discriminating collectors."

Katharine blinked, surprised yet again. She had known nothing of this. Stonenden smiled sardonically.

"But you know," added Lawrence, "if you are truly interested in becoming a painter, you should make arrangements to study seriously."

Katharine nodded. She had known, of course, that she lacked training. Just as she had known how unlikely it was that she would be permitted to study in any studio. That simply was not done. But this praise from the president of the Royal Academy was more than she had ever hoped for. She felt elated.

"Nonsense. Of course she didn't paint them," said a high, squeaking voice from the rear of the group around them. "No woman could possibly have done these. It is all some sort of unpleasant hoax. You know what Tony Tillston is. He will do anything for a joke."

"Who is that?" snapped Tony, as Katharine stared with outrage at the thin foppish man who had spoken. "Winstead? I might have guessed it. Always pronouncing judgment upon things you know nothing about. If you were twice as knowledgeable about art as you claim to be, you might be able to paint half as well as Miss Daltry yourself."

A titter arose as the thin man bridled. "I must bow to your knowledge *there*, Tillston," he replied. "I'm sure you know a *great* deal more of Miss Daltry than I do." His tone was so offensive that Katharine was appalled. She had never seen this man before. Why should he embroil her in just the kind of brangling, gossip-feeding situation she hated?

A cold, masterful voice cut across Tony's indignant rejoinder. "We are all acquainted with Miss Daltry," said Lord Stonenden, "*and* her family, which is more than one can say for the scaff and raff one is continually meeting in town these days."

His implication was so clear, and so insulting, that several people gasped. Katharine herself, though grateful for his intervention, thought he was being excessively harsh.

"I don't see what that has to do with anything," answered Winstead, his voice squeaking more than ever.

Lord Stonenden stepped closer to him. The contrast was marked. "Naturally you do not."

The thin dandy quailed before him, then looked to Sir Thomas for aid. The artist, who had appeared increasingly uncomfortable during this exchange, shifted from one foot to the other and murmured, "Here, gentlemen."

Lord Stonenden's lip curled. "You are charitable."

Mr. Winstead, routed, turned on his heel and stalked from the room, throwing Katharine a glance filled with such venom that she shivered.

"Don't heed him," said Stonenden, who had returned to her side. "No one else will. He is the veriest worm."

"You were very severe with him," replied Katharine.

"He deserved it. I can't abide toadeaters."

She gazed at him in astonishment, and he laughed. "No, he wasn't toadeating *you*. But he does Lawrence, and he has tried his tricks with me. He is tolerated because he writes a column for one of the artistic journals, but he is a man of no birth and indifferent education. He will not annoy you again. He hasn't the courage."

His tone was so contemptuous that Katharine could not help but feel a twinge of compassion for the wretched Winstead. The man might be exasperating, but surely no one deserved the kind of set-down Stonenden had given him. Katharine would not have spoken so harshly herself, and she was the one insulted. It was just like Stonenden, she thought, to treat him so. Perhaps it was this very attitude that made Winstead so disagreeable.

At this moment, Tony joined them. "I say, Katharine, I am sorry about that. Winstead is abominable. Are you much upset?"

"No, I am all right. But I am still angry with you, so you needn't look relieved."

Tony grinned. "No, come. You must be pleased that Lawrence praised your paintings. And Stonenden, of course. Without me, you would never have shown your things to anyone."

Katharine fought a smile, and lost. "Tony, you really are despicable."

They laughed together.

Lord Stonenden cleared his throat.

Tony turned to him. "You certainly gave Winstead his own again. I felt quite sorry for him." The other man did not look particularly gratified.

Looking away, Katharine noticed that several new arrivals were being taken to see her paintings, which now rested against the wall of the drawing room. "Tony," she exclaimed, "we must gather up those canvases and go. I have had all the 'praise' I can endure for one day."

"Yes, I think we should go. Wait a moment and I'll get them." Tony went over to fetch the canvases.

"An enterprising young man," murmured Stonenden.

"Too enterprising," laughed Katharine.

"Your work shows real talent."

This remark was so abrupt that Katharine blinked. She did not know quite how to respond to a compliment from Stonenden.

"Do you think of selling anything?" he added.

"Oh, no. I paint for myself only."

"I see. And yet, it is important to you."

She raised her eyebrows. This conversation was taking the oddest turn. "It is."

Tony came up with the paintings under his arm, "Ready?"

Katharine nodded and took her leave.

"If *I* can be of any help, you need only say so," responded the other man as they walked away.

"What did he mean by that?" wondered Tony, following her down the stairs.

"I haven't the least notion."

Stonenden, watching them go out together, might have agreed. He really had been much struck by Katharine's paintings. They were good, and he respected her talent. And seeing Katharine more or less under the protection of Tillston had given him the oddest feeling. He had had a strong urge to outdo Tony's half-joking show of her work with some truly stunning service. Yet when he had moved to rescue her from Winstead's attack, he had seen more disapproval than gratitude in her face. Stonenden knew Winstead for an unprincipled social climber, ready to go to any length to establish himself, and utterly unconcerned about who might be injured in the process. He fabricated gossip to make himself interesting, and Stonenden knew of at least one case where he had not hesitated to ruin a respectable man's reputation, quite unjustly, in this cause. Yet Katharine seemed to feel sympathy for the man.

Stonenden shrugged and turned back to the group around Lawrence. But even as he joined the conversation, the picture of Katharine's laughing rapport with Tony Tillston came back to him, and he frowned so darkly that a young woman about to address him thought better of it and backed hastily away.

Six

KATHARINE AND MARY WERE TO ACCOMPANY ELINOR to an evening party that night, and they called for her at nine. "Tom has been out all day," were her first words. And she settled herself across from them with such a woebegone expression that Katharine immediately felt guilty. She had not thought of Elinor's problem all day.

"Well, that may mean nothing at all," she replied, trying to sound cheerfully reassuring. "There are a great many things to fill a gentleman's time in London. I daresay Tom went to a boxing saloon, or to Tattersall's."

"No, he didn't," replied the other dejectedly. "I sent one of the footmen out to search for him. He wasn't in any of those places."

"Elinor! You can't have done anything so foolish."

"What do you mean? Of course I did. I wanted to know where he was."

"But to send a servant! Don't you realize that will cause talk?"

"Oh no it won't," retorted Elinor smugly. "I particularly instructed him to keep it a secret."

Katharine groaned. "It needed only that. *Everyone* will be gossiping about 'the Marchington scandal' by now."

Tears started in Elinor's eyes. "B-but I…"

"Don't cry," continued Katharine hastily. "I didn't mean to sound harsh. I know you are very upset. But you must understand that London is not unlike a small country neighborhood, Elinor. It seems quite large and private, but the circle of society is in fact very small, and all the servants know one another and gossip together. You would not have sent one of your country servants looking for Tom, would you?"

"Oh, no. They all know Sir Lionel's people. He would hear in an instant."

"Well, it is not very different here, though it seems so."

"I won't do so again," answered Elinor in a small voice.

Katharine nodded and tried to smile encouragingly, not telling her younger cousin that the damage was most likely done. Once the *ton* got a whiff of scandal, it had its own ways of finding out more.

Mary Daltry reached across and patted Elinor's hand. "There, now. Everything is going to turn out for the best. And I daresay your footman is quite trustworthy, and no one has heard a word about it."

But when they walked into their hostess's drawing room a short time later, it was immediately clear to Katharine that Mary's forecast had been overoptimistic. The room was already crowded, and there was a noticeable rise in the conversational hum at their entrance, several guests turning to look at Elinor. The avid gleam in their eyes told Katharine the whole, and her heart sank even as her chin came proudly up. It would, she was certain, be a difficult evening. She looked around for some friend that they might safely join, but at that moment the hostess signaled the beginning of the evening's musical entertainment, urging everyone into gilt chairs, with no thought beyond settling and quieting her audience. Thus, the Daltry party found itself placed next to Lady Jersey, one of the people Katharine had most hoped to avoid.

As the others were moving into their seats, Lady Jersey leaned forward and said to Elinor, "Where is your delightful husband this evening, my dear? I was quite charmed with him when we met."

Elinor looked stricken, and Katharine could not help wincing at her inability to disguise her feelings before this notorious gossip. "Oh, Tom won't be dragged to a musical evening," she responded lightly. "You know how gentlemen are, Lady Jersey. They will do anything to be excused from such things."

"Alas. But one *would* expect a newly wed gentleman to make an exception, wouldn't one?" Her tone was so sweetly mocking that Katharine had to grit her teeth to keep back an angry reply. She saw tears swimming in Elinor's eyes and clenched her fists beneath her shawl. "And I do believe you are mistaken," continued Lady Jersey, her voice full of wicked glee. "Isn't that Mr. Marchington now? I believe we have wronged him."

Katharine and Elinor both turned to see Tom standing in the doorway with the Countess Standen on his arm. Katharine had to restrain a groan. Lady Jersey would gloat over this perfect coincidence for weeks. She heard Elinor make a small noise and hastened to say, "Yes, indeed, you are quite right. I shall apologize to Tom for underestimating his interest in music."

"Music?" echoed Lady Jersey. "Yes, of course."

To Katharine's vast relief, the musicians struck up, and they were free to turn away and present the semblance, at least, of listening. Elinor radiated unhappiness, and she could not seem to keep her eyes from turning toward Tom and the countess, but they need not endure any more malicious hints and smiles from other guests.

Katharine barely heard the concert, and at the interval she was one of the first out of her seat. "I think you should take Elinor home," she whispered to Mary, "as soon as the crowd makes it unlikely that your departure will be noticed. She cannot bear this."

Mary nodded, her eyes full of concern. "What about you? Won't you come with us?"

"No. I shall stay and try to smooth things over. It will be impossible with Tom hanging upon the countess, of course, but I shall do what I can."

Mary nodded sympathetically and bent to speak to Elinor. In a few moments, when the room was crowded with groups of chattering guests, they slipped quietly out. But Katharine saw Lady Jersey's sharp eyes follow them. She herself looked quickly around and made her way determinedly over to Eliza Burnham.

Lady Burnham was standing alone in a window embrasure, having just rid herself of a well-known bore, and she smiled happily at Katharine when she came up. "My dear, how splendid. We can have a cozy chat here behind this curtain. I have never properly appreciated the usefulness of drawing-room hangings."

The girl smiled slightly. "We can't go behind it, Eliza. It would be too cramped. And besides, anyone might come up and overhear your confidences from the other side."

Lady Burnham was much struck by this. "Very true, my dear. You are so clever." She looked around the room. "And I particularly wish *not* to be overheard just now. I must speak to you about something, Katharine."

"There is no need. I know about the gossip. If you can tell me what to do about it, I shall be forever grateful."

Eliza looked over to the corner where the Countess Standen was holding court, Tom Marchington a prominent member. "Oh, if only that woman's husband hadn't broken his neck on the hunting field. He kept her much too busy to make mischief."

"I couldn't agree more," replied Katharine dryly. "But, Eliza, what am I to do? I tried talking to Tom, but made an awful mull of it. And the countess wouldn't listen to me either, of course." She shrugged. "There was no reason why she should."

"You spoke to the countess?" Lady Burnham stared.

"Through the merest accident. And it did no good."

"You are the most extraordinary girl, Katharine!"

"Possibly. But that cuts no ice in this case. Have you no good advice for me, Eliza?"

The older woman looked at the countess again. "Well, if there is no male relative you can go to…" She trailed off.

"Evidently there is not."

"Well, then, Katharine, I do not see what you *can* do but ask help."

"What do you mean?"

"Well, my dear, you really cannot deal with a woman like that yourself."

"I have told you that I cannot. I admit it freely. But what sort of help do you mean?"

Eliza eyed her friend; she was fairly certain that Katharine would not like the suggestion she was about to make. "The thing is, gentlemen are more accustomed to these sorts of tangles." Seeing Katharine frown, she rushed on. "I advise you to ask some friend to help you, a man who would know how to handle the countess. It will be awkward, I know, but—"

"Awkward! Eliza, I cannot believe you mean what you are saying. I, to approach some gentleman with this kind of request? Who, pray?"

"Well, but you are acquainted with any number of—"

"Acquainted, yes. But that hardly allows for such a service. No, it is out of the question."

"But, Katharine—"

"No, Eliza. Thank you, but I shall have to think of some scheme myself."

"What sort of scheme?"

"I haven't the least notion," snapped Katharine, "yet." She sighed.

"And now, I must go about the room and try to convince people that all is well with Elinor and the rumors the merest silliness. Do come to see me soon, won't you?" And with this, she was gone.

Eliza Burnham watched her move through the crowd,

smiling brilliantly and dropping an amusing remark here, a compliment there, the very picture of a carelessly happy member of society. She would have been fooled herself, she thought, if she had not just seen the worried look in Katharine's eyes. "Poor child," she murmured to herself, and began to scan the room carefully. Finding what she sought, she hesitated, then walked purposefully across to speak to Oliver Stonenden.

She talked with him for some minutes, at first inconsequentially and then with strengthening purpose. Katharine, seeing the two of them a little later, wondered in passing what she could be saying. She knew that angle of Eliza's head. It meant that she was throwing out hints about some quite important matter even while her constant stream of agreeable chatter continued uninterrupted.

Katharine had seen it often. But what could she be discussing with Lord Stonenden?

She dismissed the question with a shrug, but it recurred later in the evening when she encountered Stonenden himself. This gentleman, attired with his usual somber elegance, greeted her with unaccustomed cordiality. "Quite a different scene from our last meeting, Miss Daltry."

"Indeed, yes." Katharine felt a twinge of curiosity. "Do you go often to Sir Thomas's?"

"Tolerably often. He is an engaging companion. And just now, I am trying to convince him to accept a commission. My Uncle Charles insists that I must have a portrait done to add to the superfluity of family likenesses already in my possession. I hoped Lawrence would do it, but he is much occupied at present."

"He is the best."

"Unquestionably. But I get the distinct notion he prefers painting ladies." Stonenden smiled, but Katharine did not respond. Was he mocking Sir Thomas Lawrence? Did he dare?

"What was Eliza Burnham telling you so earnestly a while ago," she said to change the subject. "I recognized her 'managing' look from across the room."

"Did you?"

"Oh, yes. And I would wager that she was trying to persuade you to do something you haven't the least wish to do. Was she hinting for a contribution to her orphans? Eliza is mad on the subject of orphans. She has helped endow three foundling homes that I know of."

"No, it wasn't orphans." The man's dark blue eyes watched Katharine speculatively. "But you may say it was a sort of charity case."

"I knew it!" laughed Katharine. "You did not succumb, of course."

Stonenden surveyed her sparkling amber eyes and the charming curve of her smile. "You sound very certain of that."

The girl stared at him. "You mean you did?"

"Is it so surprising? Perhaps it is, to you."

Katharine quickly hid her real amazement with a renewed smile. "I warn you, Eliza will mark you down for every sad case she unearths."

Smiling a bit wryly in return, he said, "Oh, I think not. She sees me as rather specialized, I believe." As he spoke, a shadow passed across Katharine's face, and her smile faded. "What is it?"

"Nothing, nothing. So you are to help Eliza in one of her schemes. Famous."

But the bantering note had gone out of her voice, and Stonenden, glancing quickly behind, saw that Tom Marchington and Elise Standen were saying farewell to their hostess. He looked down at Katharine. For a fleeting moment, the public mask had dropped from her face, and it showed a mixture of helpless frustration and anger. Against his will, Stonenden was moved. "It can be stopped," he said involuntarily.

Katharine started. "What? Oh, yes, you were telling me about Eliza's charity case. It is admirable of you to help her. I am sure it is a very worthy cause."

His dark blue eyes unreadable, he replied, "I think, you know, that it is."

She nodded absently, watching Tom escort the countess out the door.

"Miss Daltry, you spoke to me about your cousin Marchington recently," ventured her companion.

Katharine looked up at him, her face suddenly closed. "Tom? Oh, yes. Such a silly boy. He is amusing us all so with this flirtation. Elinor was in whoops only last night." She met his eyes, as if daring him to contradict her. She had been taking this line all evening, and she believed she had had some success in quelling the gossip that had arisen, though many, like Lady Jersey, were clearly skeptical.

"Yes," agreed Stonenden, "he is acting the fool like most young men set down for the first time in London. He will get over it."

"Oh, of course! Why, I would hardly call it anything to 'get over.'"

"But the process can be hastened," he continued, ignoring her light reply. "By one who knows how."

Katharine stared at him. He seemed a good deal more concerned with Tom than she would have expected, or than she liked. What interest could Lord Stonenden have in Tom Marchington, a raw youth from the country? None, unless as a subject for derision, she concluded. "It is not really of the least consequence," she said airily. "Oh, there is Lady Sefton. I must speak to her. Excuse me."

He bowed slightly, and she moved on, completing her round of the party's guests. Stonenden watched her progress for some time, his darkly handsome face intent. And when one of his friends joined him and inquired what was making him so serious, he replied, "I was thinking that a woman can show as much gallantry as any man. More, perhaps," which surprised the other gentleman considerably.

Seven

THE FOLLOWING MORNING, KATHARINE WAS ONCE
again in her studio, struggling unsuccessfully with a
new canvas. She had just stepped back from it, with
a disgusted sigh, put down her charcoal, and pushed
an errant strand of hair back into the careless knot
on top of her head when Tony Tillston burst into
her studio once again, excitedly waving a newspaper.
Katharine was in no mood to be interrupted. And she
had no intention of allowing Tony to come upstairs
whenever he liked; she would never be able to work
at that rate. Thus, before he could speak, she said,
"Tony, I cannot have this. I really cannot. If they tell
you downstairs that I am not to be disturbed, you
must go away and come back another time. Please
promise me that you will."

Her visitor seemed hardly to hear this. "Of course,"
he replied distractedly. "But I had to come today. You
can't think what has happened."

"Something extraordinary is always happening to
you, Tony. And I am happy to hear about it, but not
here and now."

"It isn't me. I have something to show you." He held out the newspaper—it was the *Morning Post*—and met her eyes with a very uncharacteristic anxiety in his own.

Automatically taking the paper, Katharine looked at him more closely. Indeed, Tony was very unlike himself. He had not even spared a smile for her bulky apron or cracked a single joke. "What is it?" she asked. "Is something wrong?"

"You may say so. Look here." He pointed to a column on the second page, which he had turned back.

"'A Morning in the Master's Studio,'" Katharine read aloud. She looked up at Tony with puzzlement.

"Read it all, Katharine. And then you may say whatever you like to me."

Mystified, she cast her eyes down the column. The article was a description of a gathering in an artist's home. As she read, a detail here and a scrap of repeated conversation there made her realize that it was a rendering of the scene in Lawrence's house yesterday. Some of the character sketches were wickedly amusing; she was particularly caught by one which had to be Lord Stonenden. The writer had captured his odious haughtiness to perfection, though he mentioned no names. She looked up, smiling. "What has so ruffled you in this, Tony? I think it is rather well done."

He stared, then moved to point at a paragraph close to the bottom of the page. "You can't have seen this."

Katharine read the heading, "'A Lady Painter?'" and met Tony's eyes, startled.

"Read it," he groaned.

Frowning, she continued aloud: "'The artistic audience in London has in recent years become almost accustomed to the awful spectacle of lady novelists and poets. These literary females have increased to such an extent that one can hardly go out without being plagued by at least one, and more commonly three or four. But we have hitherto been spared the incursions of the "fair" sex in painting, some remnants of sense perhaps warning them that they were neither qualified nor constituted for the palette and brush. Now, however, it is my sad duty to inform you that this laudable reticence has been broken. Yesterday, the Master's inner sanctum was invaded by a pushing female who styles herself a painter.'" Katharine looked up, her amber eyes sparkling with anger. "Who wrote this nonsense?"

"Finish it," replied Tony. "I want you to know the worst."

Katharine now read aloud from scorn, rather than interest. "'This sort of shameless exhibition would be distasteful at all times,'" the article continued, "'but I regret to add that the sin was compounded by the falseness of the woman's claims. The paintings represented as her own, by herself and her male confederate, are obviously not her work. No female is capable of the application and concentration necessary to paint, and I must admit myself shocked and saddened by the vulgarity of the creature's attempted imposture. I will say no more, except to beg my female readers to confine themselves to those homely pursuits and surroundings which they so charmingly grace, and leave their better-qualified spouses to labor in the studios of the world.'"

For a moment after she finished, Katharine

was speechless with rage. Then she sputtered, "Confederate...not capable...charmingly! I should like to show him charmingly." She turned to Tony. "Who wrote this...this rot?"

Tony looked dejected. "Winstead. I am so terribly sorry, Katharine. It is all my fault for taking your paintings to Lawrence. You didn't want to, and you were right."

"Winstead," repeated the girl, "that...that worm."

Tony nodded. "He is certainly that, and worse. He has done this sort of thing before. I cannot understand why Lawrence tolerates him."

"No, indeed. But why should he attack me in this way? I did nothing to him."

"Well, he was publicly humiliated because of you, though of course it wasn't your fault. And Winstead is infernally jealous of anyone Lawrence distinguishes. Sir Thomas is his only link with society, you see. He clings to him like a limpet."

Katharine was calmer now, though she felt a flash of annoyance at Lord Stonenden. "Well, I have never heard of anything so infamous." She threw the newspaper onto a chair. "His opinions are pernicious, but if he is despised, as you say, I suppose the article doesn't matter." She shrugged. "No one will know whom he means in any case."

Tony grimaced. "Well, uh, Katharine, I'm not sure they won't, you know."

She raised her eyebrows.

"There were a good many people present that morning. Someone will more than likely connect you with the article."

Katharine frowned. "Well, let them. It will be annoying, I daresay, to have it talked of. But it can do no real harm."

"No." Tony looked uneasy. "Only, well, people are likely to wonder about your paintings."

"What do you mean?"

"It's not very important, I daresay," continued the other hurriedly. "It won't stop you painting or anything like that, but people are likely to ask if you really did paint the things we took to Lawrence's, you know. I...I just wanted to warn you before someone mentioned it."

Katharine frowned. "But I understood that this Winstead was not received. Surely no one will believe his ridiculous accusations?"

"They shouldn't, of course. But you know the gossips. They are always eager for new tidbits, and Winstead has provided some juicy ones before now. The *ton* doesn't invite him, but it talks about him."

"I see." Katharine walked a little up and down the room. Her painting had always been a very private thing with her, and she had cherished this solitary pleasure. When it was exposed to a few interested spectators at Sir Thomas's, she had winced, then thought no more about it, believing that the sensation would die out at once. Now it appeared that she had been wrong. Moreover, she now faced a much larger notoriety than she had bargained for. She had a momentary urge to stay shut up in her studio until this thing should pass.

Watching her face, Tony grimaced. "You can't think how sorry I am about this, Katharine. It is all my fault." He struck his palms together. "I am always doing some heedless thing without thinking of the consequences."

"It's all right, Tony. You couldn't know how this Winstead creature would react."

"But I might have thought more of your feelings before stealing your paintings."

Katharine waved this aside. It was done now. She looked down at the folded newspaper on her chair, and a spark of anger returned. The article really was intolerable, less so for her, she now saw, than for other women who were perhaps trying to earn their way by writing or by some other artistic pursuit. She would continue to do just as she pleased; fortunately, there was no obstacle to that. But to others, this offensive article might actually be harmful. A feeling akin to that aroused when Elinor begged for her help suddenly filled her. Men like Winstead should not go unscathed. Katharine's jaw hardened as a plan began to form in her mind. She looked up abruptly, meeting Tony's worried gaze. "It's all right," she repeated. "In fact, it may be better than that. Perhaps I can give Mr. Winstead a bit of his own again, Tony."

Her visitor's expression did not lighten. If anything, he looked more concerned.

Katharine smiled. "Wait and see."

Soon afterward, she sent Tony away, still fidgeting over the article and what she meant to do about it. But instead of returning to her painting when he was gone, she took off her apron and went downstairs to her bedchamber. She spent the two hours before luncheon closeted there, very uncharacteristically, and when

Mary came to look for her just before the meal, she commented on this unusual behavior. "Here you are," she said when bade to come in. "I could not imagine what had become of you. I looked in the studio and the drawing room. Are you feeling well?"

"Very well," replied Katharine from the corner of the room. She still wore her old painting gown, and her hair was twisted in the same careless knot, but the writing desk at which she sat was adorned with a tidy stack of written-over sheets, and there was an ink stain on her finger.

"Have you been writing letters?" exclaimed Mary Daltry. Though she was not usually inquisitive, the sight of these pages was unexpected enough to draw the question from her. Katharine hated writing letters of any sort.

Indeed, her cousin often had to beg her to compose the merest notes, and the idea that Katharine had written the pile of manuscript on the desk was astonishing.

Katharine laughed. "Not letters. But you are right to be surprised. I have been writing. I shall tell you all about it over luncheon, but I must change first or I expect they won't serve me."

"Yes, of course, dear," murmured Mary, eyeing the younger girl warily. She had heard that note in Katharine's voice before, and it boded mischief.

The girl grinned at her. "Have you seen today's *Morning Post*?" she asked.

"No, I have been too busy to read."

"Well, I recommend it to you. Go down and look at it while I change. I particularly suggest the article on the second page, right column."

"Katharine, are you up to something?"

Her charge turned wide amber eyes on her and murmured, "I?"

Mary shook her head and turned to go. "I will look at this article, but I expect a full explanation at lunch."

"You shall have it."

When Katharine came downstairs, her hair newly brushed and falling in ringlets over her ears and her old gown changed for a crisp white muslin morning dress, her cousin was sitting on the drawing-room sofa and frowning, the *Morning Post* lying on her knees. She looked up at once. "This is about you, isn't it?"

"I fear it is."

"Well, it is a great piece of impertinence, and I am sorry for it. But, Katharine..." She paused and looked earnestly up into the younger girl's face. "Are you planning some retaliation? I must say I think it unwise. One should never respond to this sort of thing."

"That is what I thought at first," agreed Katharine. "But after a while, I changed my mind." She explained her earlier reasoning to her cousin. "So you see," she finished, "this could be a truly hurtful piece of mischief. I must prevent that."

Mary was frowning. "Yes, I see what you mean. But, Katharine, what do you intend to *do*? I really don't think..."

Katharine dimpled and started to reply, and the maid came in to announce that luncheon was served.

Throughout the meal, Mary eyed her uneasily. Katharine ate heartily, her morning's exertions having given her an appetite, and occasionally chuckled at her cousin's expression. Finally, when the maid had left the fruit and departed, Katharine said, "Poor Mary, I mustn't keep you in suspense any longer. You look so apprehensive. Here." She pulled a folded manuscript from the pocket of her gown and handed it to her cousin. "This is what I mean to do."

Mary took the papers gingerly, as if she thought they might bite, and began to read. Katharine watched her with a smile. A variety of expressions passed across the older woman's face—startlement, concern, amusement—but she did not speak again until she had read the pages through. When she came to the end, she refolded them carefully and put them down beside her plate. Raising her eyes to Katharine's, she sternly repressed a smile and said, "My dear, you cannot. You simply cannot."

"No?"

Mary shook her head firmly. "It is very amusing, Katharine, but…"

"Isn't it? I had such fun writing it."

"I'm sure you did, but—"

"And I should think it will amuse the people who read Winstead's article in the *Morning Post*."

"Katharine!"

She burst out laughing. "Oh, Mary, if you could see your face. I understand your feelings; I truly do. But I must publish it."

"Why?" wailed the other.

"I have told you." Katharine rose and took up the papers. "I shall send it off at once. There will be no problem in getting it printed, I'm sure. The paper will be overjoyed at such a controversy."

"You won't, at least, let them know who you are?" begged Mary.

"Of course not. Don't worry so." And she strode out of the room.

The Daltrys had been engaged to accompany Elinor to the opera that evening, but Katharine cried off, and when Elinor objected, told her that it was just as well for them all to avoid the public eye. "It will deprive the gossips of the opportunity of staring at us," she finished. "And we do go to the Laytons' tomorrow, Elinor."

Elinor was forced to be satisfied with this, but she spent a great part of the evening at the Daltrys' bemoaning her fate and wondering what Tom was doing. So despairing was her conversation, in fact, that she quite tried Katharine's patience. Katharine had great sympathy for her cousin's plight, but she could not bear whining. She sent Elinor home early and declared that she was going to bed.

Mary agreed. "It has been a trying day. I will go up, too." She hesitated, then added, "Did the newspaper…that is…"

Katharine laughed. "Yes, they took it gladly. Indeed, John said that they were positively gleeful when they realized what it was."

"Oh. You sent John, then?"

"Yes, and after I scolded Elinor for employing servants on private errands. But John was with Father for years and years, you know. He would never betray me."

"No, dear." Mary seemed to have other concerns. "I only hope you are not very sorry tomorrow and wishing you had not written it."

"I shan't be. Whatever happens, Mary, I have done something *right*. I shall be glad of that."

Mary nodded feebly, looking unconvinced. "I hope so."

Katharine laughed again. "Come, forget about it and let us go to bed. A good night's rest will make everything look brighter." She took her cousin's arm, and they walked upstairs together.

Eight

KATHARINE HAD HARDLY REACHED HER STUDIO THE following morning when she was once again interrupted. Without so much as a knock, Eliza Burnham burst into the room, the latest edition of the *Morning Post* clutched in her neatly gloved hand.

"No, really," said Katharine, turning from her critical examination of the painting she had started the previous day, "this is too much. Am I never to be left in peace?"

"Katharine," said Lady Burnham commandingly, "I *must* talk to you."

With a sigh, Katharine began to remove her apron. She had the feeling that she would not do any painting today. "Shall we go downstairs?"

"I wanted to come yesterday, but something kept interfering. And then I thought to see you at the opera last night, and you did not come. I am *extremely* disturbed, Katharine!"

"I can see that you are," replied the other more kindly. "Come downstairs. Mary is there, and I am sure she will agree with everything you say." She looked at her visitor sideways from under her lashes.

"You *do* know about this, don't you?" cried Lady Burnham. "I tried to tell myself that it was some sort of joke, but when I read *this* this morning…" She tapped the newspaper.

"I refuse to speak until we go down," answered Katharine. "Come."

They found Mary Daltry in the drawing room, holding her own copy of the *Morning Post*. She was reading with a worried expression, and as they entered, she made a small distressed sound.

"Here is Eliza, Mary," said Katharine as they walked in. "I brought her straight to you so that you can both ring a peal over me at once." Her eyes twinkled.

Mary Daltry and Lady Burnham exchanged a glance. "Let me understand, Katharine," said the latter. "Did you have something to do with the article printed this morning?"

"Yes, Eliza," replied the girl meekly, her amber eyes still dancing.

Their guest sank onto the sofa beside Mary. "Oh, lud!"

Katharine burst out laughing. The two older ladies eyed her helplessly. After a moment, she said, "But did you see Winstead's article, Eliza?"

"Yes. It was grossly impertinent, of course. I meant to come and see you about it."

"So you heard it was about me?"

"Oh, yes. Someone who was there mentioned it, and the gossips made sure everyone heard. But, Katharine—"

"Well, I'm glad I wrote a reply, then."

Lady Burnham gaped at her. "*You*…you wrote…?"

Katharine nodded, suppressing a smile, and Mary Daltry made another small sound.

"Katharine, how could you?"

"Come, come, it's not so bad as that. It's nothing but a newspaper piece, and no one else will know I did it."

"But everyone will be talking. And Winstead…I don't know him, of course, but I understand that he is a very spiteful creature. What will he do?"

"If he has any common sense, he will abandon the subject." Katharine's jaw hardened. "In any case, Eliza, I was obliged to do this; it was only right."

"Obliged?"

Katharine explained the motives behind her action. "We cannot ignore injustice simply because it does not hurt *us*," she finished.

"No, dear," murmured Lady Burnham weakly. She picked up the paper. "But, Katharine, to say, 'the learned gentleman who speaks so kindly of the ladies' proper sphere overlooks the fact that said ladies were never consulted when the label "proper" was put upon it,' or further down here, 'I daresay that a hundred women who have limited themselves to sketching and watercolor might yet paint better than a mere critic.' Really, Katharine!"

"Yes," put in Mary. "It sounds so…so combative, Katharine." She looked down at the paper in her lap. "'I would back those lady watercolorists against any dozen of the so-called painters who frequent the studios of London. Taken generally, they have more taste, more range, and in many cases, better training.' Oh, Katharine, everyone will be so angry with you."

But Katharine was looking a bit angry herself. "Will they? Well, they must be, then, for I have said nothing less than I think, and if that makes people angry…" She shrugged.

"It is not the sentiments," said Eliza Burnham. "They are quite…quite admirable, I suppose. But, oh, Katharine, this will raise such a furor. It will be a nine days' wonder, everyone talking of it, and the newspapers! It just isn't…well, it isn't *done*."

Katharine turned away from them impatiently and walked over to the window. As she looked down, she laughed shortly. "Another voice for your cause is arriving, Eliza."

In the next moment, Tony Tillston was hurrying into the drawing room. He checked briefly at the sight of Lady Burnham, but when Katharine greeted him by saying, "Come to join in the scolding, Tony?" he pulled his own copy of the *Morning Post* from his pocket.

"Katharine, did you—?" he began.

"Yes, yes," she replied impatiently.

Tony looked from one face to the other. "Well, I don't say you should have done it. But it's the sharpest set-down Winstead has had in his life, I daresay." He grinned. Katharine met his eyes with a gleam in her own.

"Tony, you mustn't encourage her," exclaimed Lady Burnham. "Oh, where will this end?"

"Tony, help me convince them that it is not a catastrophe," replied Katharine.

"Well, it isn't," agreed Tony. "There will be a good deal of talk, of course, but it will go off in a few days."

"And no one will have the least notion that I wrote that piece, will they?"

"Shouldn't think so." Oddly, Tony looked almost embarrassed. "The thing is, Katharine…ah…some of the fellows seem to think that *I* did."

Katharine laughed. "No, do they? How *famous* for you, Tony! You will get a reputation as a literary man."

He grimaced. "Well, I wanted to ask you about that. I thought, you know, of telling them that I hired some writer fellow to do it."

"Oh, no," said Katharine immediately.

"Quite right," added Eliza unexpectedly. "It is by far the best thing to claim no knowledge at all. Say you haven't any idea who wrote it, Tony."

Katharine nodded, and Tony's face fell. "But no one will believe me. Dash it, that's just the sort of thing I *would* say if I had written it."

"Precisely," answered Katharine, grinning in her turn.

Tony groaned and sat down.

"So it is settled, then," continued the girl. "Now, if you will excuse me…"

"Oh, no," responded Eliza. "I have a great deal more to say to you."

"We have said enough, dear Eliza. I am not the least sorry for what I did, and you will not make me so. But I have no intention of doing anything more, so you may rest easy. And now I am going upstairs, and I will *not* be interrupted." She turned and walked out of the room.

Lady Burnham sighed. "She is going to fall into a real scrape someday."

Mary Daltry sighed also.

"I'm not so sure," responded Tony. "She seems to know what she's doing. But I say, Katharine has certainly changed since she went away to India, hasn't she?"

The two ladies sighed again.

As they had promised Elinor, the Daltrys accompanied her to an evening party that night. Elinor came to them for dinner beforehand, and whenever there was any opportunity for private conversation, it was all of Elinor's plight and what could be done about it.

"Tom is almost never home now," she told them after the soup had been served. "I hardly see him, and when I do, he brushes me off as if he were thinking of something more important." She shook her head sadly.

Katharine, looking at her younger cousin, thought she seemed tired and subdued, as if the melancholy experience she was going through had altered her, physically. She felt a pang of compassion. She had been almost grateful for Elinor's problem this evening, since it superseded all talk of the *Morning Post* article. Elinor was so taken up with her own concerns that she had heard nothing about the "painting controversy." But now Katharine reaffirmed to herself her determination to help her young cousin. If only she could think of some solution as easy and clear as her response to Winstead. But this seemed a much more knotty issue; involving not some abstract "justice," but her own cousin and her husband. She wanted to say something encouraging to Elinor, but she couldn't think of anything that sounded sincere.

The party that evening included dancing—an

impromptu "hop," their hostess called it when she greeted them, not a formal ball. As they walked together into the crowded room, Elinor wistfully remarked, "I thought I would have such fun going to *ton* parties."

Katharine looked down at her with concern. Despite her fashionable sprig-muslin gown and cropped hair, Elinor was rather like a schoolgirl deprived of a long-anticipated treat. Katharine searched the room, hoping someone would ask her cousin to dance, but a set was in progress, and everyone else was chatting. Moreover, it was obvious that several people, having seen Katharine herself enter, were coming to speak to her. And Katharine had a good idea what they wished to talk about. Thus, she signaled Mary to take Elinor to sit down, and turned to face Lady Jersey and another lady, who bore down on her at that moment.

"My dear," said Lady Jersey, "I was just telling Jane—you know Jane Foster, of course—I was just telling her about your *fascinating* experience at Lawrence's studio. *How* I wish I had been there! And these articles! It is too amusing."

"Isn't it?" agreed Katharine.

"You do think so, then? I didn't know, of course, whether you might be offended."

"Offended?" Katharine was looking particularly splendid tonight. She had finally put off her half-mourning and was wearing a gown of amber silk that exactly matched her eyes, with a glowing set of topazes that had belonged to her maternal grandmother. She now gazed innocently at Lady Jersey.

"Well, being talked of in the newspapers, you know. So…ah…unusual."

"The newspapers?" Katharine was all amazement. "But what have the newspapers to do with me?"

Lady Jersey frowned. "Well, that article described what happened…"

"Oh, I see. I didn't precisely understand you before. I thought you were talking of my visit to Sir Thomas's studio, which I enjoyed immensely. It was a privilege to meet him. But these articles you speak of…" Katharine shrugged.

"But the first told the story of your visit."

"Oh, no," corrected Katharine kindly. "It was mentioned, of course, but the writer goes on to talk of completely unconnected things. It really had nothing to do with me."

Lady Jersey seemed confused by this distinction, and it took her a moment to recover. But then she leaned forward a little and asked, "But tell me, dear, did you really do the paintings, or *was* it a joke?"

A spark of anger showed in Katharine's eyes, but she kept her face impassive. "My daubs? Oh, of course I did them."

"Ah." Seeming satisfied with this piece of information, Lady Jersey moved back to let another guest approach. And Katharine was soon surrounded by a group of eager questioners, whose inquiries she parried expertly.

The dancing had ended, and a new set was forming when Tony Tillston joined them. "Come and dance," he said determinedly to Katharine. "You promised this set to me."

"Of course. Excuse me." Katharine nodded to the others and walked down the room on Tony's arm. "Thank you," she added as they fell in with the dancers.

"Not at all. I thought you looked as if you had had enough."

"It is amazing how avid people are for something to talk about. Haven't they any interests of their own?"

"No," he responded promptly.

Katharine laughed. "Well, I was glad to escape." They began to dance. She looked around for Elinor, who was still sitting beside Mary among the chaperones. "Oh, dear."

Following her gaze, Tony shook his head. "I'll ask your cousin for the next set."

"Would you, Tony? Oh, that would be splendid."

"Happy to; she's a nice little thing." He hesitated, then added awkwardly, "Like to help there, but the thing is, I'm frightened to death of the Countess Standen."

Katharine met his eyes with surprised gratitude. "How kind! But there is not the least need for you to do anything." She looked around the room again. "Are they here?"

"In the corner by the windows."

She looked and saw the countess, as usual leaning languidly back on a sofa, surrounded by her accustomed court. Tom Marchington hovered in the background, and to Katharine's astonishment, Lord Oliver Stonenden sat beside the countess, bent over her attentively. An exclamation of surprise escaped her.

"What is it?" asked Tony.

"Nothing. I was merely surprised to see Lord Stonenden among the countess's entourage."

"That is curious, isn't it? He's stayed beside her

quite half an hour, a thing he never does. And I didn't think he liked Elise Standen above half."

"Perhaps he has just noticed her…ah, attractions."

"Can't have *just* noticed them," replied Tony practically. "And she's not really his style, either. Unaccountable thing."

"Well, it is not of the least consequence," snapped Katharine.

Tony looked at her with raised eyebrows. "No."

Unable to account for her annoyance, the girl tossed her head. "Let us talk of something interesting. Have you heard what Winstead thought of the reply to his article?"

"Have I not? They say he is positively livid. He will do something about it, you know."

"Let him."

"Yes, well, it is all very fine to say that, but Winstead is a nasty customer. There's no telling what he may try."

"We can only wait and see," replied Katharine, dismissing the subject. Her eyes had drifted involuntarily back to the corner where Lord Stonenden was talking so intimately with Countess Standen. If this was his taste, well…

Tony asked Elinor for the next set, and Katharine danced with another acquaintance. As she moved across the floor, she saw Lord Stonenden leave the sofa and bid his hostess good-bye. Tom took his place, but after a few minutes the countess waved him away and beckoned to another young man who had been hovering nearby. Tom, looking thunderous, stalked off just as the music was ending. And when

Elinor and Katharine rejoined Mary Daltry, he came up to them and stood before their chairs, putting his hands beneath his coattails and rocking back and forth on his heels. Elinor looked torn between gratification and doubt.

No one seemed to know what to say. Katharine was far too annoyed—over Tom's cavalier attitude, she told herself—to make conversation. Elinor seemed afraid to speak, and Tom himself appeared to be brooding. Finally, Mary Daltry ventured, "It is growing quite warm in here, isn't it?"

"Yes," replied Elinor eagerly, "quite warm."

There was another pause.

Abruptly Tom said, "Who was that you were dancing with, Elinor?"

His wife stared up at him, then said, "Tony Tillston. He is a friend of Katharine's."

"These town beaus," snorted Tom, "think they're so wonderful. And women are just silly enough to believe them."

Elinor looked amazed, but Katharine, watching Tom's surly expression, was suddenly struck by a stunning idea. She was fairly certain that his remark had originated in pique over the countess's dismissal, but that feeling might, perhaps, be played upon. Katharine's eyes lit as she developed her plan in her mind. Yes, indeed—perhaps she had at last hit upon a way to help her Cousin Elinor solve her distressing problem.

Nine

KATHARINE FOUND NO CHANCE TO SPEAK PRIVATELY with Tony during the remainder of that evening, so the following afternoon she sent him a note asking him to call. He arrived as she and Mary were having tea. "What's happened?" he asked as she poured him a cup. "Winstead not up to any new mischief, I hope."

"No," replied Katharine. "Would you like some bread and butter?"

Tony eyed her. "No."

"A slice of this cake, perhaps. Cook will send us cake, even though she knows that neither Mary nor I eat it in the afternoon."

He shook his head. "What are you plotting, Katharine?"

Katharine looked surprised.

"Oh, I can see that you're plotting something, no need to put on airs for me. And since you asked me to come, I must have some part in it, so you may as well tell me what it is. I warn you that I shan't have anything to do with another slap at Winstead. The man's about to have an apoplexy as it is."

"Is he?" replied Katharine, clearly gratified.

"Yes, he is. Now, let's have it."

Mary Daltry looked from one to the other of them with a slight frown.

"Well, it is hardly a plot. I was only thinking that Elinor enjoyed dancing with you last evening."

"She didn't show it, then," answered her caller suspiciously. "Hardly spoke, and kept her eyes on her oafish husband."

"Oh, well…" said Katharine vaguely. "She is a little uneasy these days, you know. But I thought, Tony, what a nice thing it would be if you would call on her, and just chat a little. Take her mind off herself."

"Yes?" He surveyed her. "Well, I could do that, I suppose."

"Of course. And I thought you could take her for a drive in the park one day. Elinor should get outdoors more. She is accustomed to the country."

"That's what you thought, is it?" Tony was frowning. "Well, I don't mind, but what's behind it? And you needn't say nothing, because I shan't believe you."

"Oh, Katharine," put in Mary Daltry. "You aren't thinking of…?"

Looking from one doubtful face to the other, Katharine said, "Oh, very well, I shall tell you my idea. Tony has heard the gossip about Tom, so I am not revealing any secrets. Elinor is very unhappy over Tom's infatuation with the Countess Standen, Tony."

He nodded.

"And I promised to help her with the problem, but for the longest time I could not think of any way to do so. Then, last night, something Tom said struck me." She hesitated, then hurried on. "And I thought that if we could make Tom jealous over Elinor, he would probably forget all about the countess. I don't believe that he really cares for her. And then I wondered who—?"

"Who would be fool enough to play the ardent suitor," interrupted Tony, "and of course, you thought at once of me."

"Who could be trusted to help," corrected Katharine. "And you were the *only* person I could hit upon."

He looked partially mollified.

"You wouldn't have to do more than squire Elinor about a bit," she added persuasively. "No more than you would do for a dozen other acquaintances. But when Tom sees that Elinor is receiving attentions from another man, he will come running home."

"And probably draw my cork," said Tony wryly.

"Oh, no."

"But, Katharine, is this wise?" sighed Mary. "I don't know. It seems so…well…so underhand and not quite right."

"I daresay it is a little devious," she answered, "but I do not see how else we are to combat a creature like the countess." She turned back to Tony. "Will you?"

Meeting her eyes for a moment, Tony grinned lopsidedly, then shrugged. "I suppose I must."

"Oh, thank you." She gave him her hand, which he raised briefly to his lips, and favored him with a brilliant smile.

And so it was that Elinor drove twice in the park

with Tony Tillston and stood up with him for a waltz at Almack's. Katharine watched them indulgently, part of her attention also on Tom Marchington, to see if he noticed this new development. At first, he did not appear to. And her scrutiny also forced Katharine to note that Lord Stonenden continued to dance attendance upon the countess as well. But this she refused to think of; the man's affairs were certainly none of her concern.

On the following Thursday, Tony invited them all to a play, and Katharine, pleased, asked him and Elinor to dinner beforehand. It was a pleasant party, and they arrived at their box in good spirits, Elinor looking happier than Katharine had seen her in weeks. Their group attracted some attention as they sat down. The *ton* had not yet ceased talking of Katharine's painting. And in the first interval, the box was soon full of visitors. "Everyone is agog to see the subject of the newspaper controversy," whispered Tony as yet another gentleman came through the plush curtains at the back. Katharine grimaced and turned to greet the newcomer. To her surprise, it was Lord Stonenden.

Politely, but inexorably, he dislodged the acquaintance sitting beside Katharine and took his place. Katharine, while admiring the address that allowed him to do so without offending, was also put out. What made Stonenden think he was so welcome that he might dismiss her friends? Thus, she spoke to him coolly. He did not seem to notice, however, but made several remarks about the play, at once so astute and so cutting—for the piece was a melodrama—that Katharine was soon smiling in spite of herself. When Stonenden saw her lips relax, he leaned back a little in his chair. "You know, Miss Daltry, I have just realized that I never asked you about your stay in India. I can't think why not. It must have been fascinating."

"Perhaps because you have no great interest in any but your own affairs," replied Katharine sweetly.

Stonenden's brows came together. "You wrong me. Am I not expressing interest now? Admitting my tardiness—and I suppose I *am* behind every other person you have met in London—won't you tell me of the place?"

"You know, it is strange," answered Katharine, struck again by a thing that had often puzzled her, "no one *has* asked. They all behave as if I had merely gone into the country for a month, albeit at an eccentric time of year, or to an odd place. But none of the *ton* seems to wonder at all about what I have seen or what may have happened to me abroad. I have often been perplexed by it."

He had been watching her face, and now he said, "Well, at least I redeem myself in this, then—that I *have* asked. And I am truly interested."

Katharine met his dark blue eyes doubtfully, as if she did not quite believe him.

"You lived at the army's headquarters, I suppose?" he prompted.

"Yes, Father spent most of the year there. Occasionally he traveled to visit various regiments, and I went with him once."

"It was a great change for you."

"Yes. But I didn't mind that. At first because of...

that is, it was exciting to see a wholly new country. I had never traveled before."

"Tell me about it."

Katharine looked at him doubtfully again. "You aren't bamming me?"

"Not at all."

She continued to frown at him for a moment, then looked down, her eyes growing faraway. "The thing that amazed me at first was the colors. They were so different from those here in England. And then the people, of course. I had an Indian maid whom I used to talk with, and she told me a great deal about her family. It was a revelation. I had never imagined anyone like her." She met his eyes without seeming to notice it. "Do you know, she had eleven brothers and sisters. And they all lived together in what we should call a hovel. Her father was a water carrier, and they were terribly poor. It was a cause for rejoicing when she found work with us." She shook her head. "And yet they were considered far superior to any of their neighbors, who lived in the same houses and had the same possessions, because their 'caste' was higher."

"Just as a so-called 'genteel' family may live in poverty here without giving up any of their pretensions, I suppose."

Katharine stared at him. "Yes! Yes, there is some similarity." She thought about it, then frowned. "Though it is not *precisely* the same."

"Naturally not. But did you have no English friends in India, Miss Daltry?"

She shrugged. "My father sometimes invited officers to dinner, of course. But there were very few

Englishwomen for me to visit. They do not care to travel so far, you know."

"You must have been lonely."

"At first, I was. But later, I found things to do. I began to paint, and that was wonderful."

"It consoled you for your loss."

"My loss?" Katharine looked blank.

"Of your fiancé."

"Oh, yes. Poor Robert." She sounded quite matter-of-fact, and Stonenden frowned at her uncertainly. Katharine fell silent. She had been talking very frankly to Stonenden, she now realized, and this was odd. She did not wish to share confidences with *him*. "At any rate, I was quite content," she finished.

Seeing that her mood had changed, her companion nodded. "I think you should be thankful for the chance that took you there. You have had experiences that few women can have. And discovered something you care about doing; that is important."

Katharine looked up at him, startled. "Yes, it is. Of course, here in London, my painting has only created a nine days' wonder."

"Much of that is envy, I daresay, and the rest arises out of boredom. Our contemporaries"—he gestured contemptuously at the audience around them— "haven't enough to do, and so they search out new fads and sensations. They are hardly worth deploring."

Though she had herself thought something similar, Katharine found his supercilious tone offensive. She looked down.

Mistaking her reaction, Stonenden added, "This

furor about your painting will die down, you know. Does it pain you?"

"Pain? No, of course not."

"Good. You must do just as you choose and not allow others to dictate your behavior."

"As you do?"

"Of course."

She eyed him. "But you must offend many people."

"One can't care for that. By and large, the opinions of others are not only irrelevant, they are dangerous. If one began to worry about them, it would destroy one's independence forever."

"Opinions, perhaps. But what of others' feelings?"

"Are they not one and the same?"

"Good heavens, no! You cannot really think so. How often do we not see someone express a certain opinion and then behave in precisely the opposite way."

"That is mere hypocrisy."

"Sometimes. Sometimes it is simply that what they feel is at odds with what they believe they *should* feel."

Stonenden pondered this.

Katharine, realizing that their conversation was once again becoming serious, shook her head and tried to think of some light remark. But before she could do so, there was a disturbance at the entrance to the box. Two of their visitors who had been going out were pushed aside by a man coming in. The newcomer's hat was knocked off in the process, and Katharine was astonished to see that it was Winstead, with whom she could not even be said to be acquainted.

"Here, you, pick up my hat," snapped Winstead to one of the men he had jostled.

"Pick it up yourself," was the reply.

"You knocked it off, you ruffian, and you shall pick it up."

"I did no such thing. It was your fault, shoving in here."

Winstead flushed ominously and clenched his fists. For a moment, Katharine was afraid he would strike the other man. But Stonenden rose, towering over both of them, and said, "Enough."

The challenged gentleman, abashed, continued his exit from the box with a muttered apology to the ladies. Winstead at first swelled with wrath, but then, with an obvious effort, controlled himself. All of the occupants of the still-crowded box stared at him.

"Did you want something?" asked Tony from the corner, his tone discouraging.

"I did," replied Winstead. His overloud, dramatic response caused several people in the audience to turn their heads. "I did indeed."

"Well, what is it? I suppose you know you are intruding here." Tony sounded at once annoyed, and a bit nervous.

"Intruding, am I? I'll have you know that—"

"What do you want?" asked Lord Stonenden, who still stood over Winstead.

Winstead was daunted, but he answered, "I want justice." The sound of his own voice seemed to give him courage, and he added, "Justice!" very loudly. More of the audience was turning to watch now, despite the imminence of the third act. Whispers were spreading through the crowd. Winstead, seeing this, seemed very pleased.

"What do you mean by that?" said Tony belligerently.

"Oh, I think that's obvious. Yes, I think that's quite obvious," Winstead sneered, and though Tony continued to frown at him, he appeared unwilling to go on.

"Not to me," said Stonenden.

Winstead flushed. "I have been called a liar!" he shouted. "I demand satisfaction!"

"What has that to do with any of us?" asked Stonenden coldly.

Winstead pointed at Katharine with a great flourish. "I challenge you to prove that you can paint anything like the pictures you used to hoax Sir Thomas Lawrence. I dare you to try!"

Katharine, astonished and extremely annoyed, stared at him.

"Get out," said Stonenden.

Winstead looked uneasy, but he stood his ground. "She cannot do it," he continued, still in a voice that could be heard yards away. "You all know she cannot, and you are protecting her. *I* may be slandered and called a liar in print, but *she* is not even to be spoken to. *She* is not to be called a bold-faced liar, even when she is one."

Stonenden advanced purposefully on him, and Winstead backed away.

"You are afraid," he squeaked. "You are afraid to put her to the test. You have all concocted this story between you, to discredit me and ridicule art, but I shan't let you get away with it."

The whispers in the audience had risen to a murmur, and the stage manager had been forced to delay the curtain until the disturbance should die down. Several theater employees were making their way toward the box. Katharine, scarlet with embarrassment, was also angry. So the idea that she painted was a ridicule of art, was it? Suddenly she heard herself speak in a clear, ringing voice. "I shall be quite happy to prove that I can paint. But I won't have a crowd around me. Choose a trustworthy witness, Mr. Winstead."

The intruder seemed utterly astonished at this, and Katharine realized that he really had not believed she painted the pictures. "Ah…I…ah…" he stammered.

"Not yourself," added Katharine. "We must find a neutral party."

There was a pause; almost the whole audience was now staring at the drama in the box, play forgotten. And in the sudden silence, Lord Stonenden abruptly said, "What about me?" Hundreds of pairs of eyes swiveled to stare at him. "I want a portrait of myself. Let Miss Daltry paint it." He looked at Winstead. "I suppose you will take my word? I am thought to be a tolerably good judge."

The little man quailed before his eye, moving back toward the doorway.

"Well?"

Winstead seemed to collapse upon himself. Murmuring brokenly that it was quite all right, he backed through the plush curtain and out of the box.

"I shall show you the portrait when it is done," called Stonenden after him.

The noise in the theater rose to a roar. Those who had heard this final exchange were besieged by those who had not caught it, and the story of Winstead's challenge and Katharine's acceptance ran round the audience like lightning. "Oh, dear," murmured Katharine, "perhaps I should *not* have written that article."

"*You* wrote it?" exclaimed Stonenden, who still stood near her.

Startled, Katharine looked up at him; she had spoken without thinking. "Shh. Yes, but please do not tell anyone."

"You! I thought it was Tillston."

Katharine shrugged. The stage manager signaled the orchestra to begin and glared around the audience until people began to settle back in their seats.

"I suppose I'd better go," added Stonenden. "I shall call about the portrait."

"You meant it!"

"Of course. I never say what I do not mean."

"But it will be...that is..."

"You do not mean to play faintheart now, I hope?"

"No, but—"

"Good." And with that, he was gone.

Katharine heard nothing of the rest of the play; she was too preoccupied with her own emotions. Embarrassment was paramount; she hated scenes such as had just taken place, and she hated exposing her painting to strangers, as had now abundantly been done. She was also astonished at Lord Stonenden's very uncharacteristic action. When he had first intervened this evening, she had admitted a moment of gratitude. It had become clear to her that Winstead required an uncompromising response, and he was more capable of it than anyone else she knew, certainly than herself. But when he had gone on to suggest the portrait, she had been amazed. Lord Stonenden administering a blistering set-down was a familiar figure; going out of his way to support her, he became a stranger.

But even her surprise was overborne by excitement. Katharine had never had the opportunity to paint a real portrait. Her Indian maid had sat for her, and she had once attempted a likeness of Mary, but she had never tried a male figure, and she had never done anything public. The chance was daunting and thrilling at once. Could she paint a creditable portrait, one that Stonenden would wish to hang in his house? This uncertainty outweighed all other concerns, and Katharine began to plan just how she would set to work. Her companions, after unsuccessfully addressing her several times, abandoned her to her thoughts, no doubt concluding that she was upset by the evening's occurrences.

Ten

On the following morning, Elinor was at the Daltry house before breakfast, and she joined the ladies at the table when they came down. She seemed very agitated, quite unlike last night, but as long as the servants were in the dining room she kept to unimportant topics. Katharine, watching her closely, was impressed with the way the younger girl controlled herself. Elinor had clearly learned a great deal since her arrival in London.

When they had finished their meal, Elinor leaned forward and said, "Oh, Katharine, I must talk to you."

"Of course, let us go up to the drawing room, where we can be private."

Mary made as if to leave them, and Elinor added, "You come too, please, Mary. I did not mean that I didn't want you."

When the three women were seated upstairs, Elinor pulled a sheaf of papers from her reticule and exhibited it. "I found these in our library," she said dolefully. "They were lying open on the writing table. I did not look in Tom's pockets or anything low. He didn't care whether I saw them, I suppose."

"What are they?" asked Katharine.

"Bills. He has been spending amazing amounts of money. I don't know what his father will say, though Tom has an income settled on him, of course. But he is buying things for...that woman."

"He is not paying her bills?"

"No. It is presents, I think. But, oh, Katharine, what am I to do? He is so irritable now, I can hardly talk to him. And he is never home. I don't know what he does or where he goes. My life is ruined." She drooped in her chair.

"Now, Elinor."

"Of course it isn't, dear," added Mary. She patted Elinor's hand. "This will pass, you'll see."

"I don't know. Tom has started railing against Lord Stonenden now. He is mad sometimes, I think. I am so afraid he may actually call him out. What a scandal that would be! And Stonenden is a leader of fashion."

"Stonenden!" exclaimed Katharine so abruptly that both the others stared.

Elinor nodded. "He has been seeing the countess also, and Tom is in a rage over it. Last night when he came in, he raved about town beaus and their insinuating ways until I thought he should have an apoplexy. And if it came to a duel—"

"Well, it won't," snapped Katharine. "Stonenden would never accept such a challenge even if Tom were addle-brained enough to offer it."

Elinor drew back a little in the face of her vehemence.

"And in any case," continued the other, "I believe the plan I have set in motion will end this thing soon."

"What plan?" replied Elinor eagerly, and Katharine

realized with a start that she had neglected to tell her young cousin about her scheme to make Tom jealous. She flushed a little.

"Tony," she said.

Elinor frowned, then, surprisingly, flushed slightly herself. "What do you mean? Did you know I wished to talk to you about him, too?"

"Talk about him?"

"Yes." The younger girl's flush deepened. "He has been coming to see me quite often, and I...I have been wondering...that is, I know he is a friend of yours, Katharine, and I thought you could tell him for me that I am not—"

"Tony is my plan," interrupted Katharine.

Elinor stared.

"I asked him to take you driving and pay you attentions in order to make Tom jealous. I'm sorry I forgot to tell you, Elinor. I don't know how I came to be so heedless."

"To make Tom jealous," repeated Elinor slowly. She sat for a moment taking this in, then smiled brilliantly. "Then he is not...and Tom will think...oh, Katharine, how splendid!"

Katharine could not help laughing a little.

"You must think me such a ninnyhammer," continued Elinor. "I was worried that Mr. Tillston was truly interested in me. I didn't know what to do. But if it is all a hoax..." She contemplated this beatific vision. "What a grand idea! I wonder if Tom has noticed? I shall go out with Tony every day. I wonder if I should order a new pelisse for driving in the park?"

Katharine laughed again, but Mary said, "My dear.

Should you be so happy with a scheme that is, however necessarily, based on deceit?"

Elinor paused, frowned, then tossed her head. "I don't care. Tom is being abominable, and he *deserves* to be deceived. It is not as if I were doing anything wrong."

"No," said Mary doubtfully.

Elinor rose. "I must go. Oh, Katharine, thank you! I knew I could count on you to help me, and you *have*."

"Wait and see how it comes out before you thank me."

"I know it will be all right." She sighed. "Tom, jealous—only think of it!" She started to turn away, then looked back and added, "And you are certain it will be all right about Lord Stonenden? He would not fight Tom?"

"I shall forbid him to." Katharine looked grim for a moment, then smiled thinly. "How can I paint his portrait if he is fighting duels?"

Elinor laughed. "Will you really paint him? I thought it was a joke. How famous." With a wave of her hand, she hurried out. Katharine watched her go with a smile.

But when she turned back to Mary, the older woman was looking at her very seriously. "Do you mean to go forward with the portrait, Katharine?" she said. "I don't think it wise."

"Why not?"

"It will merely keep the whispers alive, dear. You would do much better to ignore them."

"But then everyone would think that odious Winstead told the truth."

"I doubt that. But even if they did, it would be

better than exposing yourself to public notice this way. Admit that you were cruelly embarrassed last night."

Katharine nodded. "It was very unpleasant."

"And you hate being gossiped about, particularly your painting."

"Yes."

"Well, then?"

"All that is true, Mary. But it is also true that this portrait would be my first chance to do a *real* painting. One that might be hung and seen. I have stacks of canvases upstairs that no one will ever look at. At first, I preferred it that way, I admit, and I was furious with Tony when he showed them. But now, I don't know. If I am to get any better, I must have criticism, I think. And this seems a perfect way—"

"Katharine. You could show your painting to a number of people without doing this portrait."

The girl looked down. "Yes, well…the truth is, I want to do it, Mary. It is an interesting challenge, and I want to try it."

Meeting her cousin's eye, Mary Daltry sighed. "But having Lord Stonenden in your studio for hours at a time…"

"Oh, you will sit with us, of course," replied Katharine eagerly.

"I?"

"Yes. I cannot be closeted with Lord Stonenden day after day. You must be there."

Mary frowned.

"You can sit in the corner with your workbasket, Mary, and it will be quite all right."

"I suppose I could."

"And it will only be for a short time. I can do a portrait in two or three weeks, I daresay."

Mary sighed. "You insist upon doing it?"

Katharine met her eyes and nodded.

"Well, then, I suppose we must do our best." The older woman shook her head.

Katharine jumped up and went to hug her briefly. "You *are* wonderful. And now I must go look over my paints and see if I need anything. I shall see you at luncheon." She was out of the room before Mary could reply.

In the afternoon, Mary went out to pay a call, and Katharine sat down in the drawing room to write some long-overdue letters. Her hatred of letter writing arose out of its impersonality. She got no sense, from a sheet of pressed notepaper, of the other person's presence. Yet if she did not write, she had no contact with them at all. So, at long intervals, she forced herself to sit down and pen something, however unsatisfying; but she faced such occasions with loathing.

Thus, when one of the maids came in to announce a caller, Katharine jumped up from the writing desk at once and said, "Oh, whoever it is, send them in!" But she was a bit taken aback a few moments later when Lord Stonenden strolled into the room.

Clothed with his usual quiet elegance, in a dark blue coat and yellow pantaloons, he smiled and nodded. "Good day. I have come as promised."

For some reason, Katharine felt a bit flustered. "Promised?"

He raised his eyebrows. "To discuss the portrait."

"Oh, oh, yes! Please sit down." Katharine did so

herself, on the sofa, and he took the armchair across. "What…what sort of portrait do you want? A full-length, or only a bust?"

"Oh, a full-length, to be sure. You do mean to paint it, then?"

She cocked her head. "Of course."

"I thought you might have changed your mind."

"Not at all. Why should I?"

Stonenden smiled slightly. "I can think of several reasons."

He did not elaborate. Katharine met his dark blue eyes and saw both amusement and challenge there. Her chin came up. "Of course, if you have changed *your* mind, Lord Stonenden, you need only say so. I shan't hold you to your word."

"On the contrary, I am eager to begin. When is it to be?"

Katharine had not thought quite this far ahead. Once again, she was disconcerted. "Well…oh… perhaps tomorrow?"

"Certainly. I have never before sat for a portrait. What must I do?"

Katharine took a breath and gathered her wits. "Nothing, really. Simply come here in the morning. Do you mind beginning early? The light will be best then."

"I am completely at your service."

"Eight o'clock?"

"Very well. And how long do you expect to work? Not that I mean to hurry you in any way, but I must put off some engagements."

"Say…two hours?" Katharine was not at all sure

how long she would wish to work on a formal portrait. This would be very different from drawing her native servants in India.

Lord Stonenden nodded. Katharine expected him to take his leave now that their business was concluded, but instead he leaned back in his chair and said, "Your talk of India interested me greatly, Miss Daltry. Might I perhaps be allowed to see some of your paintings of native subjects tomorrow, or sometime?"

"I…suppose so." Katharine's eyes dropped from his. She remained oddly uneasy, not sure how to deal with this new Stonenden. His interest seemed sincere, and the genuine attention in his dark eyes was hard to meet calmly. It confused her. He continued so assured. Several things she had meant to say to him fled her mind.

"You don't like showing your work?"

"I never did. But I am trying to learn to now. Sir Thomas made me see that I need objective criticism if I am to progress."

"I am sure he would be happy to give it."

"Oh, I shan't ask him again; I shouldn't have the courage. But I think I shall show some things to friends, perhaps."

"You don't sound very certain."

Katharine smiled, then shrugged. "Well, it is difficult for me. For a long time, my paintings were such an important, private thing, not to be shared with anyone. It is hard to change that." Even as she spoke, Katharine was surprised. She was revealing more than she meant to, and she could not understand how it happened.

He was nodding. "Yes, I can see how that might be."

Katharine stared at him, her amber eyes full of astonishment and doubt.

"You don't believe me?" he responded with amusement.

"What? Oh…I…"

"But I assure you I can understand wanting to keep some favorite pastime from society's eyes. I have wished many times that I could do so."

"H-have you?"

"Indeed."

"But what pastimes…I mean…" Katharine stopped abruptly.

"What are these mysterious activities?" He laughed a little. "Ah, but they are secret."

Katharine met his eyes and laughed also. "I see. But if I show you my paintings of India, you must reciprocate by telling me."

"It seems a fair bargain." They smiled at each other. "I had hoped to meet your companion today," continued Lord Stonenden then. "Miss Daltry is out, I take it?"

"Yes, Mary is paying calls. I am sorry she is not here to greet you."

"And how are your other cousins, the Marchingtons?"

Katharine's momentary contentment evaporated. The mention of Tom and Elinor brought a rush of associations. "They are well," she replied stiffly.

"You are less worried about him, I hope?" He smiled at her with what Katharine felt to be odious superiority.

"Yes," she snapped before she thought, "no thanks to the Countess Standen."

"Ah, Elise can be irritating."

"*Some* people find her the reverse, seemingly."

"She has her attractions, of course."

Thinking that Stonenden knew more than most about these attractions, Katharine rose abruptly to her feet. She was not going to sit here and discuss the man's paramour, though he and the countess would no doubt think that a fine joke. "If you will excuse me now," she said. "I have an appointment."

Stonenden, rising also, looked surprised. But he said, "Of course. I did not mean to keep you."

She rang the bell for the maid.

"I hoped to reassure you about Tom Marchington," added Stonenden as they waited for the girl to appear.

Unable to imagine how he had hoped to do that, Katharine merely continued to look at the floor. In a moment, the maid entered.

"Good-bye," said Katharine.

Lord Stonenden gazed down at her as if he expected she might offer her hand, then said, "Good day. I will be here tomorrow promptly at eight."

"Y-yes." She had almost forgotten about the portrait.

He bowed slightly and followed the maid out of the room. Katharine went to fling herself back on the sofa. Had she, she wondered, made a mistake after all? Her desire to paint this portrait had suddenly waned. What had seemed an exciting and important chance now looked more like drudgery. Should she try to cry off? Katharine stared blankly at the wall for a long moment; then, with an impatient exclamation, she got up and went back to the writing desk and her unfinished letter.

Eleven

LORD STONENDEN ARRIVED AT THE DALTRY HOUSE ON the stroke of eight the following morning. Katharine and Mary had already breakfasted and were prepared for his arrival, so they all went directly upstairs to Katharine's studio to begin the portrait. Katharine wore her customary old gown, and after a quarter hour of indecision she had determined that she would wear her apron, whatever Stonenden might think of it. Her studio was not a ballroom. But she had made the concession of dressing her hair more fashionably than she usually did to paint.

Upstairs, the women had provided an easy chair and worktable for Mary in the corner, and she sat down there. Katharine had draped one wall in blue cloth in an effort to provide a background for her painting, and now as Stonenden looked at her, she gestured toward it. She was extremely nervous, she found, in this new situation. Other concerns aside, she had never tried to paint anyone like Lord Stonenden, and she began to be afraid that his interested, knowledgeable gaze would prevent her from doing anything.

"How shall I stand?" he asked, moving in front of the draperies.

Katharine looked at him helplessly for a moment, then tightened her jaw and told herself to stop behaving like an idiot. "What sort of portrait do you want?" she asked, her voice sounding amazingly assured to her own ears.

Stonenden smiled, "The usual sort."

This made the girl laugh. "In that case, you should put one hand on your hip and one foot forward and look straight ahead."

Still smiling, he did so.

"That is it. Now we require only a worshipful spaniel to complete the composition."

"Alas that I left mine at home."

"Well, we shall simply have to get on without it. But I think we will use another pose." Katharine lost all her self-consciousness as she studied the problem. "There is a stopped-up fireplace behind the drape. Do you feel the mantelshelf?"

He tried. "Yes, here it is."

"Rest one elbow on it and lean back a little." He did so. "Yes, that is it. I think that will do. What do you say, Mary?"

Her cousin looked up from her sewing, startled at being consulted. "Oh, yes, very nice, dear."

"No, but, Mary, does it look right?"

Thus appealed to, Mary Daltry surveyed Lord Stonenden more carefully. "It does, you know. It seems…characteristic."

"Labeled as a drawing-room lounger," exclaimed the man. "Unfair."

Mary looked taken aback, but Katharine laughed. "That is what happens when you request a portrait. Your innermost character is revealed. Now, are you comfortable? Can you remain so for a while?"

"Certainly."

Katharine got out her sketching block and began to do some preliminary drawings from various angles. In each, she noted some particular detail, the line of Stonenden's neck and shoulders, the precise position of his bent knee, the way his hand rested negligently on the mantel, trying to catch the essence of her subject. She grew more and more pleased and excited as she worked. The sketches were good, and Stonenden an admirable model. For the first time, Katharine began to see him as a man, apart from any flaws of character he might possess. He really was extremely attractive, less because of the arrangement of his features, though this was pleasing, than the strength and confidence he automatically projected. She suddenly saw that these were not affectation, but an integral part of him. Even standing perfectly still, he compelled attention in some undeniable way. One might glance past other men idly, but never Stonenden.

"May I move a little now?" he asked finally.

"What? Oh, of course! I should have let you rest before now. Are you very stiff?"

"Not unbearably, but I admit I shall be glad to stretch." He suited his actions to his words, moving his arms back and forth.

"I am nearly finished for today," said Katharine. "You can walk about or go downstairs. Would you care for some refreshment? The servants will get it for you."

"No, thank you. But I believe I will walk about the room."

He proceeded to do so as Katharine filled in detail with the charcoal. To her relief, and gratitude, he did not come round behind her and watch her work, a thing she hated. After a while, during which she had been lost in her drawing, she turned to find him chatting quietly with Mary in the corner. "Can you do a bit more now?" she asked. "I want to make one more sketch, and then we will stop."

He came back to stand as before, and she sat down in front of him to draw his face. This was the most difficult preliminary, and Katharine had left it for last; her other studies held only a blur. Now she gazed at him intently and began to outline his features on her pad—the firm jaw, straight nose, and broad forehead, marked by two dark curls from his fashionable Brutus. Once again she was struck by the power of the man— not in the sense of physical strength, but strength of character. His face clearly reflected the magnetic personality behind it. The effect was so marked that she paused for a moment, charcoal suspended, and simply gazed. He pulled at some deeply buried part of her, making her wish to speak, to move, to somehow shake that massive confidence.

Taking a breath, Katharine looked down and resumed her drawing. She had come to the hardest area, the eyes.

She looked into his; there was none of the harshness she had thought part of his personality. Stonenden appeared serious, interested, and something more; she could not define the last. But the expression in his eyes made her falter again, until she shook herself and shut out everything but the idea of the portrait.

After another half hour she leaned back and looked over the sketch critically. "Yes, that will do for a beginning," she said. "We will block in the canvas tomorrow. You may go if you like. I daresay you are very tired of standing."

"Not particularly." Katharine was afraid then that he would ask to see her drawings, but he did not, merely adding, "I shall come tomorrow…at eight again?"

"If you please." She was so grateful for his restraint that she punctuated this with a brilliant smile. There was nothing worse than an observer who hung about and insisted on seeing each stage of a painting. Katharine hated showing anything that was not complete.

He smiled back at her. "Very well."

"I will go downstairs with you," said Mary, rising.

"Tomorrow, then." And he followed her out of the room.

Katharine, feeling suddenly very tired, went to sit in the armchair. Her sketches were good; they captured a real sense of the subject. Now, if she could just do the painting as well, it would be a fine portrait. She smiled a little, stretched her arms, and got up, feeling extraordinarily happy about her new project.

৵৹

Stonenden was prompt again the following morning, and Katharine was prepared for him. She had spent the afternoon setting up her canvas, and beside it, another easel holding the preliminary sketches she had made.

By a little after eight she was hard at work, blocking out the figure in charcoal on the clean canvas and adding suggestions of the background she had decided to use, an actual fireplace.

She worked in silent concentration for half an hour, allowed Stonenden a short rest, and then continued. By nine thirty she was generally satisfied with the initial design. "There," she said, putting down the charcoal. "I must put in a few more details before we stop, but that is a fine beginning. You may rest. Tomorrow, I can begin to paint." She stood back and gazed critically at what she had done so far.

"Splendid," replied Stonenden, moving his limbs to relieve the stiffness. "It goes faster than I expected. Do you think I might see…"

Katharine stiffened as he spoke. Why could no one resist looking at things before they were ready?

But he finished, "…some of your other paintings? Remember, you promised to show me your work from India."

She laughed from relief and said, much more cordially than she would normally have done, "Of course. They are here." She walked to the far corner of the studio, wiping her hands on a rag. "All of these."

Stonenden looked impressed. "You did a great deal of work there."

"I had a great deal of time." She turned to one row of canvases that were a little separated from the rest. "These are the only ones worth showing, however. Most of the others were disappointing." She turned the first in this row and held it out to him. It was a portrait of a man in loose white clothes and a white turban against a background of green leaves.

He took it and studied it carefully. "One of your servants?"

"Yes." Katharine's heart beat faster, and her breath was uneven. It really was difficult to show her work. She dreaded others' opinions, yet longed for reactions, preferably favorable ones.

"It's good," said Stonenden finally. "The line is sharp. The composition is well done, particularly the way this branch curves downward behind the figure here. And you have captured the light; that is very hard. It seems to have been an odd light, too."

"It was," replied Katharine eagerly. "It came through a thin awning and was very diffuse. I worked on it for days." She bent and took up another painting. "Here, look at this one." And she almost snatched the first to thrust it into his hands.

Smiling a little, he looked down. "Ah, a garden."

"Yes, it was part of a temple compound. You can see the beginning of the pillars there."

"Yes. The color is splendid."

"Do you think so?" Wholly engrossed, she leaned farther forward. Her shoulder brushed Stonenden's, and she put a hand on his arm. "They were lovely."

He looked down. Katharine was so close that her deep brown curls nearly brushed his cheek. "Lovely," he echoed, in such a changed tone that she raised her eyes to his. For a moment, they remained so; then Katharine drew back abruptly.

"Here is a portrait of my maid, Mali," she went on in a breathless voice. "She is lovely also."

Stonenden exchanged pictures silently, but it was a moment before he could focus attention on the new work and offer an opinion.

They looked over the whole row together, one after the other. Stonenden's comments revealed both knowledge and discrimination, and Katharine was very glad to have such expert criticism. She did not always agree with his evaluations, and they argued heatedly over two of them, but this too she enjoyed, seeing her pictures through new eyes. Indeed, she was astonished to find that nearly an hour had passed when they put down the last canvas in the row.

"Oh, my! We must get back to work. You will be wishing to leave for your other appointments. How did it get so late? Mary, you should have told us."

"You were enjoying your discussion so," answered Mary.

"And I am completely at your service this morning, Miss Daltry," added Stonenden. "I have no other appointments."

Katharine went back to her canvas. "Have you not? That is fortunate. Will you take your pose again, then?"

He did so, and she finished outlining in another half hour, putting in as much detail as was necessary at this stage.

"There," she said again. "I will start to paint tomorrow morning." She took a deep breath and suddenly felt exhausted.

Lord Stonenden seemed to see it. "You are getting on very well," he replied. "It is fascinating to see. Shall I come at the same time?"

"If you will."

He bowed his head, straightened, then, to Katharine's intense gratitude, took his leave. She felt more in charity with Stonenden than she ever had in her life, but she was tired. She rubbed her face with both hands, transferring a smear of charcoal to her forehead.

"Are you all right, dear?" asked Mary.

"Oh, yes. But I think I will rest a bit before luncheon."

"Why don't you. And I shall move about a little. I have done nothing but sit."

Katharine smiled at her, only to find her cousin's pale eyes intent on her face.

"It is going well, isn't it?" said Mary then. "You are happy?"

A bit puzzled at the seriousness of her tone, Katharine nodded.

"Good," responded the other with a sharp nod. She turned to leave. "I shall see you at luncheon."

Katharine stood alone in the studio for a moment, frowning; then she followed her cousin down the stairs and went to her bedchamber for a half hour of quiet reflection.

❧

That evening, Katharine and Mary were engaged to accompany Elinor to Almack's. Katharine, in unusually good spirits, dressed happily after dinner in a silk gown of deep, soft red trimmed with Mechlin lace. It was a lovely dress, and she whirled before the mirror to see the skirt bell out, laughing at her own enjoyment of the sight.

Their party arrived at the assembly rooms at nine thirty, and Elinor immediately joined a group of lively young people. Tony Tillston had drawn her into this circle, and Elinor was very pleased to be a part of it.

Though most of its members were unmarried, she was still so young and inexperienced that she fit in perfectly. A set was just beginning, and Tony asked Elinor to dance. Seeing it, Katharine smiled.

She herself was soon surrounded by people eager to gossip about her painting. The scene at the theater remained very fresh, and it seemed that everyone was discussing it. Repeatedly she was asked if she would *really* paint Lord Stonenden, and though she had resigned herself to this onslaught before coming in, facing it turned out to be more annoying than she had expected. She had planned to say merely that she *would*, and no more, but the twentieth time the question was put, she found herself snapping, "Yes, I am. I have already begun, and you may tell everyone that I mean to say nothing more about the painting until it is finished."

This, not unnaturally, caused a sensation, and Katharine soon found that instead of silencing the gossips, she had encouraged them. The story went around the room in a flash. The girl looked for rescue and, providentially, saw Eliza Burnham just coming into the ballroom. Hastily excusing herself, she made her way across and joined the newcomer before she was pulled into any of the chattering groups.

"Eliza! You must save me," she said.

Lady Burnham smiled. "Must I?"

"Yes, you do not know what the last quarter hour has been like."

"Oh, I have a fair idea, Katharine. You know, when I urged you to come to my ball at the start of this season, I hadn't the least notion that you would set the *ton* on its ear when you *did* join its activities. I wonder if I would have insisted so if I had," she added meditatively.

"I did no such thing," retorted Katharine. "They set themselves on their ears; they like nothing better." She looked around the room disgustedly. "They positively *search* for things to be scandalized over."

"Well, of course they do, dear. They lack occupation. But there has to be *some* basis for their talk, you know."

"They would be much better off helping you with your hospitals and orphans," said Katharine.

"Undoubtedly. But they do not find them amusing, I fear. Really, Katharine, I do want to talk to you about this portrait scheme. It seems a bit unwise."

"Why?"

"Well, to paint Stonenden, just as if you were an official portraitist—it will only increase the gossip."

"It already *has*." Katharine laughed shortly.

"Has? You mean you have begun already?"

"Yes."

"Oh." Lady Eliza sighed. "Well, I suppose it is no good arguing with you if you have actually started. I had hoped to persuade you not to do it."

"But why?"

"Well, obviously, because it will keep this whole silly story alive so much the longer. I think it would be far better to let it drop. The *ton* would soon be onto something else, and it would be forgotten."

"I shouldn't forget," replied Katharine, her jaw firm.

"Is it so important to you, dear? Why?"

The girl raised her amber eyes and met her friend's squarely. "For two reasons, I think. First, of course, I resent being accused of pretending to paint, of hoaxing Sir Thomas Lawrence. I am proud of my painting. But more important, this article was so unfair, and in the most *sweeping* way. Winstead does not want any woman to have a chance. And only think, Eliza, there could be someone who paints much better than I who would never get anywhere because of him."

Lady Burnham, who had been watching her closely, nodded. "Yes, I see. Well, you must do what you believe right. Though I must tell you, dear, that one person can do very little in this world. I have found that in my charity work. It is very frustrating."

"But it is not an excuse for giving up."

"No." The older woman smiled. "Did I ever tell you, Katharine, what a sensation it caused when I took up my orphans?"

"No!" The girl smiled delightedly back. "Did it?"

"Society was appalled that I should wish to involve myself with lower-class brats. They are all accustomed to it now, of course. I am pointed out as a curiosity, nothing more."

"You are no such thing," laughed Katharine. "But thank you, Eliza."

Lady Burnham nodded and looked about the room. "What a crush. I must go and speak to Mary. And there is Elinor. How is she?"

"Much better since I told her my scheme for making Tom jealous. She thinks it splendid."

"Poor child. But is it working?"

"Not yet, apparently." Both women looked across the room to where the Countess Standen was sitting, Tom Marchington in his usual position. As they watched, Lord Stonenden came up to the countess and bowed slightly, clearly asking her to dance. Tom eyed him with patent hostility.

Lady Burnham raised her eyebrows. "Well, that is certainly an unexpected sight. Oliver—"

"Yes, I know," interrupted Katharine. "He very seldom dances. If you will excuse me, Eliza, I must speak to Mary about something." And she strode off, her friend looking after her with mild surprise.

❧

Later in the evening, as Katharine was walking across the room, she heard her name and turned to find Lord Stonenden approaching. "May I have the pleasure of this next set?" he asked. "It is a waltz, I believe."

For some reason, Katharine found this unexceptionable request irritating. "I'm sorry," she said, "I…I'm already engaged." She had noticed Tony Tillston nearby, and now she beckoned him unobtrusively. "Tony, this is our dance, I think."

Tony, showing only a brief flicker of surprise, came over and bowed slightly. "Of course."

"I am sorry," repeated Katharine, not sounding particularly so. Stonenden shrugged, and she and Tony walked out onto the floor.

After a moment, the music began, and they danced in silence for a while. Finally Tony said, "I'm quite a useful sort of chap, aren't I?"

"What? Oh, Tony, I am grateful. You took my hint splendidly."

"Always at your service. Not that I get much chance these days. I have hardly seen you since I began bear-leading your cousin about town."

"Tony!" Katharine repressed a smile.

"Not bear-leading, then, escorting."

"Well, it is excessively kind of you to help," responded the girl warmly. "I only wish I could be sure it was working."

"Oh, I've seen Marchington glaring at me more than once."

"Have you?"

"Yes. The thing is, he can't seem to decide whether to scowl at me or Stonenden. I'd say the race was about even just now."

"Oh."

Tony looked down at her. "I can't understand myself what Stonenden is at. You wouldn't have any notion, would you?"

"I? Of course not."

"I thought you might. You and he are so thick these days, what with portraits and so on."

"We are no such thing. We are the merest acquaintances."

"Coming it too strong."

"What do you mean? We are. Professional acquaintances. I am painting his portrait, nothing more."

"Not on your side, perhaps. But a man like Stonenden don't offer himself up to the gossips in this way without some reason."

Katharine frowned up at him. "I don't know what

you mean. Lord Stonenden is only helping me prove Winstead wrong, and getting a first-rate portrait which he has wanted for some time."

"Come, Katharine! What does he care for Winstead? And he might have any painter in England do his portrait."

"Well, and if he might? Is it so astonishing that he should wish me to do it?"

"Yes, it is," replied Tony bluntly. "And you would see it if you stopped to consider. I don't like the whole business, Katharine."

"You are being ridiculous." She stared out over his shoulder stonily.

Tony looked down at her, grinned, and shrugged. "I suppose I am. It is another thing I'm good at. Perhaps I'm simply angry that I did not think of offering to be painted."

Katharine's expression softened, and she smiled. "What would you do with a portrait?"

"Oh, I don't know. Give it to my club, perhaps, for darts. But really, Katharine, you are determined to go on with this painting?"

"Absolutely. We began yesterday."

"I heard. Well, I suppose there is nothing I can do about it. But do be careful, Katharine."

She laughed. "You make it sound as if I were embarking upon some dangerous adventure, Tony."

"I wouldn't go that far. Not dangerous. But—"

"Oh, do stop. Let us talk of something amusing, as we used to."

Tony smiled wryly. "Alas, for the first time in my life, I am caught without an amusing anecdote."

"Well, we shall simply dance, then."

They did so, and when the set ended, Katharine sought out Mary to see if she was ready to go home. But before they could depart, Katharine was accosted by Lady Jersey, whom she had successfully evaded all evening.

"Not going, darling?" she said. "Why, I haven't even spoken to you!"

"Yes," answered Katharine unencouragingly.

"But surely you can delay one little minute. I simply *must* ask you about your fascinating painting. I know you began yesterday."

"Then you know everything."

"Oh, my dear! Not at all." Lady Jersey leaned closer. "Tell me, what is it like to spend a whole morning alone with Oliver Stonenden? Such an *attractive* man."

"Not alone," put in Mary Daltry firmly. "I sit with them, of course."

"Oh." Lady Jersey looked a bit disappointed, then rallied. "But still, it must be…ah, stimulating." She eyed Katharine speculatively.

But Katharine disappointed her by laughing. "If you could see me covered with paint in my ragged old apron, I doubt you would say so, Lady Jersey."

The other raised her eyebrows. "Indeed? Well, my dear, I can only say that if Oliver Stonenden had made such a gesture for *me*, I should take care to look ravishing when he came round."

Katharine, furious, strove to control her temper. She knew that Lady Jersey was on the watch for any reaction, however tiny or unexpected. And she would twist it to fit her own quite mistaken idea. She met the other woman's eyes. "Perhaps you should take up painting, then, Lady Jersey," she replied. "Now, we really must go. Please excuse us." And she turned away without another word.

Twelve

But Katharine found it difficult to forget her conversation with Lady Jersey, part of it an echo of what Tony had said. In fact, she had trouble falling asleep that night, pondering its implications. The more she considered the matter, the odder it seemed that Lord Stonenden should ask her to paint him. Her own astonishment from the night of the play, submerged until then in the excitement of actually painting, flooded back. She had never known Stonenden to exert himself for any other human being. Why, then, had he offered to help her confound Winstead without so much as thinking it over?

Katharine rejected the answer to this question that Tony and Lady Jersey had seemed to espouse. She had seen where Lord Stonenden's romantic interest lay. But why, then, had he done it? Katharine tossed and turned in her bed for an endless time without discovering any satisfactory answer, and only when she had resolved to ask the man at the first opportunity did she finally fall asleep.

This came the following morning. Stonenden

arrived at eight, and Mary Daltry had gone downstairs to speak to the cook when he was brought in. Thus Katharine had a few minutes alone with him in the drawing room. She wasted no time, but as soon as they had exchanged good mornings, said, "Lord Stonenden, I have been wondering why you asked me to paint your portrait."

He raised his eyebrows. "I thought that was obvious."

Katharine shook her head, determined to give him no help.

"But we are proving, are we not, that you are a painter?"

"Why should you care about that?"

The man studied her a moment, his eyes unreadable. "I am interested in painting. And the things you showed Lawrence were good. Do you rate your ability so low that such an explanation is insufficient?"

This stopped Katharine briefly; then she said, "No. No, I rate my skill as it deserves, I hope. But you…" She hesitated again, then, summoning her courage, continued, "Frankly, Lord Stonenden, I know you are not a philanthropic man. I find it difficult to believe that you exposed yourself to the gossip of the ton merely because you are 'interested' in art. I know you hate gossip; you have said so."

"Indeed." He looked a bit amused. "Why do you think I did it, then?" His dark blue eyes rested on her face expectantly.

Katharine was immediately very annoyed with herself for giving him this opening. The thing she had above all *not* wished to do was be forced to guess his motives. "I haven't the slightest notion," she snapped.

"Oh, come. You must have some idea."

She eyed him with loathing. Stonenden was always so sure of himself. "All right. I have two. Either you were amused by my pretensions and hoped to puncture them, or you thought to get a passable portrait for free. If it was the latter, I can assure you you made a mistake. I intend to charge a reasonable fee."

Stonenden's brows came together, and he looked startled and angry at once. "Is this what you truly think, then?" he asked. "This is how you see me still?"

Though Katharine was a little daunted by his reaction, she met his eyes squarely. "What should I think?"

He held her gaze, his own eyes hard, until Katharine felt she could hardly breathe; then, abruptly, he laughed. "I shall certainly pay you for the portrait. I am not clutch-fisted, at any rate. But let us say I began this thing through misjudgment. I see my mistake now."

Katharine found that she was for some reason very shaken. "You…you are withdrawing?"

"No indeed. I always perform what I promise. And I *do* want a portrait. Unless you wish to cry off? I take it this scene was due to the gossip about the portrait. Are you turning cow-hearted?"

"Of course not!"

"Good. We are agreed, then. It is a simple business transaction."

Katharine agreed somewhat halfheartedly, and at that moment Mary came into the room, putting an end to the conversation.

The painting did not go particularly well that morning. Lord Stonenden was unusually silent, it seemed to Katharine, and instead of allowing her to concentrate more closely upon her work, this seemed to distract her. She twice painted over the beginnings of his face, and finally abandoned this difficult area and turned to the coat. At ten, she laid aside her brushes, saying, "I think that is all today."

"I am quite able to go on," replied Stonenden.

"Thank you. I am not."

He shrugged, inquired whether he would be wanted tomorrow, and upon hearing that he would, nodded and took his leave. As the door closed behind him, Katharine dragged off her apron and threw it into the corner of the room, exclaiming, "Damn!"

"Katharine!"

"Oh, I'm sorry, Mary. But nothing is going right this morning."

The other watched her for a moment. "Did you quarrel with Lord Stonenden?"

"Quarrel? What should we have to quarrel about? We haven't anything in common but this stupid portrait." Her tone was so savage that Mary blinked. "I shouldn't dream of quarreling with a man I positively despise!" She began to put her painting tools away with hasty, violent movements.

Mary started to speak, then changed her mind. She began to gather up her sewing things. When she was ready to leave the room, she said, "You are always unhappy when your painting goes badly. Why not go for a walk in the park? You need to get out."

"I mean to walk, though perhaps not in the park."

"If you are going into the streets, you will take someone with you, Katharine?"

"Yes, yes. I'll take James. He keeps quiet."

She nodded and turned to go out.

"Mary?"

"Yes, dear?"

"I didn't mean that the way it sounded."

"I know, dear."

"I'll see you this afternoon."

Mary nodded again and went out.

❧

Katharine took a long walk, so long that James, the footman, nearly protested. She went nowhere near the park, keeping to quiet residential streets and lanes, and when she finally looked around about one o'clock, she found herself near Westminster Abbey. She could just see the clock tower above a row of houses on her right. Smiling a little, she turned in that direction, and in a moment was standing before the great church, looking toward the Thames.

"Hadn't we better be getting home, miss?" asked James.

"In a little while. I am going into the abbey."

"Yes, miss." The footman's lack of enthusiasm was patent.

"You may wait out here. I shan't be long."

"Yes, miss."

She walked into the church through the great doors at the end and strolled slowly down its length. It was empty and quiet, and the sun threw bars of color from the stained glass across the flagged floor. Motes of dust danced in the beams. Katharine looked at the tombs of the kings and queens, which she remembered seeing many years ago when her mother brought her here. They still lay in neat effigy, hands clasped, crowns straight. She felt calmer after her walk, and she considered her situation dispassionately. This morning, she had nearly decided to give up the portrait and, in fact, go back to the way she had been living when she first came home. She had done all she could think of for Elinor, so that problem need no longer take her away from home. She could easily retreat into solitude and forget the excitements of the previous weeks.

But as she walked, Katharine had changed her mind. The portrait was a great challenge, and she would probably never get such a chance again. She couldn't throw it away. And as she considered further, she realized that she had enjoyed going out once or twice this season. Many times it was wearying, but not always. She would not give it up entirely again.

A sound from the doorway heralded another visitor, and Katharine slipped out of the abbey to return home. She had missed luncheon, but she felt much better, and she greeted Mary with a cheerfulness that made the older woman's expression lighten visibly.

The Daltrys spent a quiet afternoon. Katharine went up to work on the background of her painting, and Mary wrote letters in the drawing room. They had no engagement that evening and were looking forward to reading some new volumes from Hookham's after dinner. When the maid brought in the tea tray, Katharine came down, and the two sat together in perfect harmony across the low tea table.

"I was just writing Elinor's mother," said Mary.

"Yes? What can you find to say to her? Is she very uneasy?"

"Well, she is not happy, of course. She wanted very much to come to town herself, though I believe Elinor asked her not to. But the younger boy is still ill, and she could not leave him."

"That is George, is it not? He is very sickly."

"Yes. Poor little thing."

"Well, I think it may be best that she could not come. Indeed, I am glad now that I did not write Tom's father. He and Elinor must have this out themselves. Their parents cannot solve the problem for them."

Mary looked over at her, smiling slightly.

Katharine laughed. "And no more can I. I don't think so, I promise you. I have done my utmost; now it is up to them."

"I think it *is*, you know."

"Absolutely."

"I think…I hope it will all turn out well."

Katharine nodded.

At this moment, the maid came in to announce a caller. But he had followed close on her heels and burst into the room even as the girl was saying, "Mr. Thomas Marchington has called, miss."

"What the hell do you mean setting my wife against me?" bellowed Tom. The maid gaped at him as the two Daltrys stood.

"That will do, Phyllis," said Katharine, and the maid scurried from the room. "Hello, Tom."

"You won't put me off with your town airs, so you needn't try," replied their visitor. "I'm sick of 'em, you understand."

"Really, Thomas!" said Mary.

"I don't understand you at all," answered Katharine. "But I am ready to do so if you will sit down and speak in a reasonable tone." She sat herself and motioned for Mary to join her.

Tom clenched his fists and frowned; then a tremor went through him, and he sank down in an armchair across from them and put his head on his hands. He looked the picture of despair.

Katharine suppressed a smile. "Would you like a cup of tea?"

"No!"

"Very well. Now, what is wrong? You know quite well that I did not set Elinor against you. If anyone has done that, it is you yourself. We have talked about this before."

Recovering some of his belligerence, Tom said, "I suppose this Tillston fellow isn't a friend of yours, then?"

"Indeed he is." Katharine exulted a little to herself. So Tom had noticed Tony. Things were moving as she had hoped they would.

"Well, why is he hanging about Elinor? I can't turn around lately but he's underfoot."

"Hanging about?" Katharine looked at Mary with bland surprise. Her cousin frowned at her.

"That's what I said. You needn't pretend to be so astonished."

"All right, then. I am not astonished. Elinor is left alone much of the time. I daresay she is bored. What could be more natural than that she should find friends to occupy her time?"

"Friends!" Tom's round face was flushed, and he clenched his hands once more. "She shouldn't be friends with a man like that. These town beaus are all the same—can't be trusted. They're too smooth by half. They inch themselves in where they're not wanted, and before you can blink, they've taken over. And when you try to speak to them about it, they won't face you and have it out like men. They talk and talk until you don't know where you are, and everyone is laughing at you, and then they shrug and turn away as if you didn't matter a rap. They should *all* be soundly thrashed."

He sounded so absurdly young as he said this that Katharine felt a momentary twinge of sympathy for him, but she suppressed it. "Are you talking of Tony Tillston?" she asked. "It doesn't sound as if you are. He is not at all like that."

Tom Marchington's flush deepened. "They're all alike, I tell you. And Elinor should not be seeing the fellow."

"Well, I don't agree. But what has it to do with me, Tom?"

"You introduced them."

"She met Tony in my house, yes."

"Well, then, you're responsible. You must warn him off."

"I shall do no such thing. And I suggest that if you do not like the way Elinor is spending her time, you fill it yourself. I am sure she would be happy to go about with you."

"I can't!" He seemed genuinely upset.

Katharine shrugged.

"You…you don't understand."

"Indeed?"

"No! You cannot know what it is like."

She looked at her nails. There was a silence; Tom fidgeted in his chair. After a while he said, "You know all the nobs. Are you acquainted with this Stonenden?"

A little surprised, Katharine nodded.

"I suppose he's rich?"

"I…I believe so."

"How old a man would you say he is?"

"Oh…about thirty. Perhaps a bit more."

"Huh. He's almighty pleased with himself, isn't he?"

"I really wouldn't know."

"How can you not? The man is insufferable."

"Do you find him so? Perhaps you misunderstood something he said."

"No fear of that. He makes himself plain enough. But if he thinks I'm going to slink off like a whipped hound simply because he comes on the scene, well, he's mistaken, that's all."

For some reason, this allusion to Stonenden infuriated Katharine. "I don't know what you're talking about, Tom, but if you have nothing more pertinent to say, you may as well go."

"What? Oh." He rose. "So you won't speak to Elinor?"

"You and Elinor can deal with your own problems."

"Ha. It's high time someone thought *that*. Very well. Good day." And he strode out of the room before they could ring the bell.

When he was gone, Katharine rose and began to pace about the room.

"Poor Tom," said Mary.

"Tom is a fool!"

"Well, yes, he is being foolish. But he does not seem to be enjoying himself."

"Good! Perhaps he will come to his senses, then. How I should have liked to shake him. Young men like that should not be set loose on the town."

"No, I think his father should have brought him when he was a little younger and introduced him to gentlemanly pursuits."

"No doubt. But he did not. It would appear he is as great a fool as his son. I have no patience with any of the Marchingtons."

Mary eyed her. "Well, I daresay it will be all right. Tom seems to be worried about Elinor."

Katharine made a derisive noise. "Pure dog-in-the-manger. He is at least as worried about Sto…himself."

Mary continued to watch her. "I suppose he is."

"Why are men such fools?"

"I fear my experience is limited on that head. But Father always said that foolishness led to wisdom if one allowed it to."

"Allowed?" Katharine laughed shortly. Then, before her cousin could speak again, added, "I am going upstairs. I shall be down to dinner."

Thirteen

SEVERAL DAYS PASSED WITHOUT INCIDENT. EACH morning, Katharine worked on the portrait of Lord Stonenden while he posed impassively and Mary sewed silently in the corner. The painting began to go better the day after her walk, and in the following sessions she almost forgot she was not alone in the studio. When she had the brush in her hand, Stonenden seemed nothing but a subject, more challenging than a bowl of poppies perhaps, but no more distracting. When she wondered at this in free hours, she put it down to the fact that her canvas had now gone far enough to absorb all her attention. It was good; she knew it. And that fact was so stimulating that she could think of nothing else as she worked.

The Daltrys did not go out much during this time. They attended one concert with Elinor, but the latter had by now made a number of friends, and she did not require their company. She remained grateful to Katharine, however, and had no doubt at all that her plan would succeed. "I went driving with Tony again yesterday," she said as they rode home in Katharine's town coach. "I am positive Tom has noticed. Indeed, he said something yesterday that makes me think he is becoming jealous." She gave a great happy sigh. "I know he will give up that woman before long."

Katharine and Mary exchanged a glance. They had not told Elinor about Tom's call, since he had said nothing to the purpose, but now Katharine felt that she should say something to temper her younger cousin's ecstasies. "Tom still dances attendance on the countess," she ventured.

"Yes. But he is not so fierce about it. Indeed, I think it is a lucky thing that Lord Stonenden has lost interest in Countess Standen, for Tom is much better off without a rival. He always fights much harder when he thinks someone else wants a thing."

"What do you mean?" asked Katharine.

"Oh, he has always been so. Since we were children. If he is hunting or shooting he is much more determined if he has a friend to match against. It is silly."

"No, I mean…" Katharine coughed slightly. "You were worried at one time that he might challenge Lord Stonenden, I know."

"Oh, yes, but that is all over now. Kitty Drew says it is a great pity, but I don't think so."

"What is a pity?"

"Oh, that Stonenden has stopped flirting with the countess. He was, you know, outrageously. But now he isn't. Last night, at the Harridons' ball, he didn't even stand up with her. Kitty says that is too bad, because he might have cut Tom out, but I think Tom will be more likely to lose interest if he has no competition."

"But why has he stopped?" Katharine spoke as if to herself, and she seemed startled when Elinor answered.

"Kitty says he is always doing such things. He will flirt with a woman prodigiously one evening, then pretend not to know her the next. He is never sincere. They call him Stoneheart, you know."

"I...think I did."

"Oh, yes, the matchmaking mamas have given him up. He never shows the least interest in debs, only older women. And even then, he sometimes treats them shamefully. Kitty says he is very bad."

"Kitty seems remarkably full of opinions," replied Katharine dryly.

"Well, she knows a great many people. And she is engaged to Lord Tremont."

"Ah, that explains it."

Elinor turned to look at her cousin. "Are you bamming me? It is just that Kitty is the first *particular* friend I have made in London. I suppose I do talk of her too much."

For some reason, Katharine laughed aloud. "It is all right, Elinor. I was roasting you a little, but I didn't mean anything. And I am very glad you have made some friends."

"Well, it is much more comfortable. Parties are not very amusing when one knows no one."

"No, indeed. Quite the opposite."

"Did *you* feel that, too?" Elinor seemed astonished by this idea.

"Of course, goose. How should I not? I remember the first *ton* party I attended, when I was coming out. I hated it. I couldn't remember the names of half the people introduced to me, and I didn't know what to say to anyone, so I went and hid in a window embrasure, behind the draperies, for an hour."

Elinor burst out laughing. "Katharine, you did not!"

"Oh, yes. But then Eliza Burnham found me and dragged me out again. She was so annoyed."

"I can't imagine you not knowing what to say. Do you think everyone feels that way at first?"

"Everyone. And I cannot imagine why you think me never at a loss. I am, often."

"Well, you never *seem* so. And that is the important thing, I suppose. Here we are already." The footman handed Elinor down at her front door. "Good night. Shall I see you tomorrow at the duchess's masked ball?"

"I think not."

"But, Katharine, you must come! It is the most exclusive event of the season."

"Is it? I wouldn't want to miss that, would I?"

Elinor cocked her head, then laughed. "You are an original, Cousin Katharine. Everyone says so. Good night."

She ran up the steps and into her house, and the Daltrys' coach started again. "Am I an original, Mary?" asked Katharine, half-amused, half-nonplussed.

"Yes," responded Mary placidly. And when the other turned sharply to look at her, added, "You know very well that you are. In society's terms. You enjoy it."

Katharine laughed. "Merciless Mary. And do I indeed seem never at a loss?"

"Oh, no. Elinor is simply too young to see beyond your surface manner. Few do, I believe."

"You?"

"I think I do, more and more. But we have spent a great deal of time together."

Katharine was smiling wryly. "You are always so quiet, Cousin Mary, that sometimes one forgets how very wise you are."

"I? Oh, no. And I do wish I could talk more. That was the one thing dear Father always lectured me about. But I never could get the knack of light conversation. It is one of my failings."

"On the contrary. You do not know how refreshing it is to have a companion who speaks only when there is something important to say. I call it a rare gift."

"Thank you, dear. But you wouldn't say so if you were seated beside me at dinner like poor Admiral Cushing last week. I fear the poor man was dreadfully bored."

Katharine laughed aloud. "Bother Admiral Cushing. He is an awful old bore himself. Here we are. You climb down first."

"It is pleasant to be home again. I feel quite tired out."

"Yes, the concert was tedious. You go straight up, and I will bring you a glass of hot milk."

"I will get it," protested Mary.

But Katharine shook her head. "I insist. You should encourage my benevolent impulses, Mary. They are so rare!"

Mary smiled and started up the hall stairs, pleased to see her charge in such spirits again.

"Get into bed," called Katharine after her. "I will send Phyllis to you."

"You needn't—"

"Mary!"

"Very well. But please, Katharine, do not send up a hot brick. It is quite warm this evening."

The younger girl burst out laughing again. "I promise. Now, go."

❧

Katharine's high spirits persisted the following morning. At breakfast, she kept Mary smiling with a stream of amusing nonsense, and when Lord Stonenden arrived, she hurried him upstairs almost before he had time to take off his hat, she was so eager to get to work.

The portrait was nearly finished. It had gone very fast, but Katharine's best work always did so. Either she painted surely and quickly, or the picture did not succeed at all. Today she took up a very small brush and prepared to put the last touches on the face. She had been saving this difficult task for a day when she felt confident. The background was completed, and the rest of the figure nearly so.

The detail went smoothly, and after a time, Katharine began to talk to the others in the room. Usually she was silent when she worked, but at rare intervals she felt an irresistible urge to chatter. She had once told her Indian maid all about her London come-out as she painted her portrait.

Now, her amber eyes sparkling, she began without thinking, "When I first began to work with oils, in India, it was very exciting. I knew nothing about it, of course. I had done only watercolors, and that unsystematically. But I was determined to learn. I sent to England for the materials; they couldn't be gotten where we were. And it seemed a weary time before they arrived. I was ready to begin, but could not. I made sheaves of sketches and nearly drove poor Father mad teasing him about the mail." As she talked, Katharine continued to paint with great concentration, so that she did not see Lord Stonenden look at her with surprise, then interest, or Mary let her sewing fall into her lap.

"When the paints finally came," she went on, "I was so eager to try them that I hardly waited to learn how. I simply began to daub. I did some dreadful botched canvases and used a vast amount of pigment before I settled down enough to study properly. It was wonderful to watch Father try to find some praise for them. They were terrible, of course, but he so wanted me to be happy that he didn't dare say so."

"What did you paint at first?" asked Stonenden when she paused.

"Oh, the things I had seen painted—bowls of flowers, the English countryside, that sort of thing. I worked from my memory, you see." She laughed a little. "How ridiculous I was."

"But then you began to do native things?"

Katharine hardly seemed to notice the questions, though she answered them readily. "Yes. One morning I was struggling with a landscape that was all wrong. I didn't know what to do; I couldn't remember just how it had looked, but I knew that what I had was not it. As I was puzzling over it, one of the maids came in with a cup of tea for me. She made some sound, I suppose, because I looked up just as she was walking through a shaft of sunlight. There was a beautiful rug on the wall behind her, and the picture she made was dazzling. I knew at once that I must paint it, and when I began, I saw my mistake."

"Mistake?"

"Yes. In trying to paint when I could not look at my subject. I cannot understand now how I could have been so foolish. But I was rediscovering the simplest rules for myself. After that, I got on better."

Lord Stonenden opened his mouth to ask another question, but just then Katharine said, "Hold very still for a moment, please. I am at a difficult place."

He did so, and there was a prolonged silence. Katharine lost all awareness of her surroundings. The others watched her, fascinated.

Finally she straightened, drew a deep breath, and put down her brush. "There," she breathed. She looked at what she had done, smiled a little, then looked up and said, "Do you want to see it?"

"Is it finished?" replied Stonenden, surprised.

"I think so. I must look again tomorrow. Perhaps I shall add a bit here and there. But it is generally finished, yes."

He came forward, and Katharine stepped back. "You too, Mary," the girl added when her cousin made no move, and Mary Daltry joined Lord Stonenden before the easel. Katharine turned away from them. There was silence.

"It's good," said the man in an odd voice. "It's very good indeed."

"I think it's the best thing you have ever done, Katharine," said Mary.

Turning back, the girl scanned their faces carefully. "What is it?" she said to Stonenden.

"What do you mean?"

"You look…well, disconcerted. Is there something wrong with the painting? I should much rather you told me if you see a flaw."

Slowly he shook his head. "I do not. If I am taken aback, it is probably because it is a strange experience, seeing oneself in a portrait." He gazed at it again. "Is that really how I look to you?"

"You think I have distorted your features?" replied Katharine anxiously. She was frowning at the painting now.

"No, no. You are misunderstanding me. It is a wonderful likeness and a thoroughly professional job. But like any portrait worthy of the name, it is revealing. And I feel…somehow exposed. A novel emotion."

Katharine gazed at him, then smiled. "If that is all—"

"All!"

She laughed. "Then it is all right." She took a deep breath, threw back her head, and executed a sudden pirouette. "It *is* good, isn't it? Oh, I feel as if I could fly!"

The other two smiled at her.

"Come, this calls for some sort of celebration," continued Katharine. "Let us all go downstairs and have…"

"Champagne," suggested Stonenden.

She laughed. "I am not quite so extravagant at eleven o'clock in the morning, but we might bring out Father's good Madeira. You go on, and I will come as soon as I wash my hands."

Mary obeyed, and Stonenden, after a lingering

look at the portrait, followed her. Katharine let them go, then walked over to look at her handiwork once more. It was good. She thought she had caught her subject perfectly, leaning carelessly against the mantelshelf, a slight smile on his lips. As she turned away to go downstairs, Katharine gave a little skip of joy, and she shut the door of the studio as if some living person remained behind.

When she entered the drawing room a quarter hour later, she found Mary and Lord Stonenden sitting on either side of a tray containing the Madeira, stemmed glasses, and a plate of festive cakes. "Cook made them for tea," said Mary in answer to her glance, "but I thought we should have some now." She poured out the wine and handed it around.

"I propose a toast," said Stonenden, holding up his glass. "To an artist." His dark eyes met Katharine's as he spoke, and she felt a thrill.

"An artist," echoed Mary. "Oh, my dear, it is a good portrait."

The man nodded. "We must decide how it is to be shown."

"Shown?" Katharine turned quickly back to him.

"Of course. I shall hang it at my house in Kent with the other family pictures, but we must show it in London first. The odious Winstead must be confounded."

"Oh." Katharine sat back a little, wondering at herself. In the pleasure of doing the painting, she had almost forgotten Winstead. And now she was no longer certain she cared what he thought. "I don't know that I want to exhibit it," she said.

"Indeed?"

"I began it to prove something, of course. And I have, to myself. It seems unnecessary to go any further."

Stonenden gazed at her with mingled surprise and admiration. "Does it?"

Katharine nodded, but at the same time, she remembered some of her other reasons for undertaking this project. "Still, I suppose I must show it. I wanted to prove to Winstead that a woman could paint, and if I do not produce a painting publicly, he will always say that I couldn't."

"Yes."

Katharine sighed. "Very well. But how shall it be managed? I will *not* exhibit it here."

"No," agreed the man. "I believe I should do so."

"You? You mean, hang it in your house?"

He nodded.

"And allow crowds of people to troop through to look at it? Not that I am so vain as to think there would be crowds if it were not for this stupid controversy."

"No, that would be insupportable," replied Lord Stonenden. "I think the best plan would be for me to give a party to show the portrait. I shall hang it in the ballroom where everyone may see it, and they can all come at once."

Katharine considered this. "Well, I suppose that will do. It's very kind of you. I shan't come, you understand."

"Not come?"

"Oh, no, I couldn't bear it."

"You don't want to share the admiration?" The man seemed amazed.

"If there is admiration, it should be for the painting, not for me." Katharine dimpled. "And there may be none, you know. In which case I shall be very glad to be absent."

Stonenden was still gazing at her. "You are an extraordinary woman, you know. I never get your limits."

She flushed a little. "I don't see that it is so extraordinary to avoid being gawked at and gossiped about." He continued to watch her, and Katharine shifted uneasily. "Would you, in my place, attend such a party?" she asked finally.

"I cannot imagine being in your place. I have no such abilities."

Now Katharine stared at him. She had never heard him admit any inferiority, and his tone had been both sincere and distinctly respectful. Their eyes held for a long moment. She tried to speak, but could think of nothing to say.

Finally he added, "You leave it to me, then, to arrange the event?"

"I…yes."

"And when should it be? You said you might wish to work on the portrait a bit more."

"Yes. I don't know that I will, but if so, it would be the merest touches. It must dry, of course, but I think it could be shown in, say, a week's time."

He nodded. "I shall set it for the week after this, then."

"Very well." Katharine looked down. "How strange it will be."

"I shall also think of some means for you to attend without being gawked at," he added with a smile. Katharine started to protest, but he held up a hand. "If you could observe without being seen, would you not like to hear what was said about your work?"

She smiled. "Who would not?"

"Well, I shall try to arrange it."

"But how?"

"Leave that to me." He put down his empty wine-glass. "And now I should go, I fear."

"I will walk down with you," replied Katharine, rising. They went down the stairs together and stood waiting while a footman fetched Lord Stonenden's hat. "Will you ask Winstead to your party?" inquired Katharine.

"I must."

"Well, I should like to see his face when he sees the painting."

"I shall ensure that you do."

She smiled. "You are very kind."

"Do you think so indeed? Your opinion was very different not so long ago." He looked intently down at her.

Katharine flushed. "I said too much that day. I apologize."

"You needn't. You spoke your mind, and I prefer that. But if you could alter your view…" He paused, seemed as if he might take her hand, then added, "I was overhasty myself that day." She met his eyes, still more astonished. Their gaze held as he said, "I often am, and I often regret it. But I promise you now that I mean to perform the service I tried to do you."

Katharine frowned. "The portrait, you mean? But you *have*."

"No, the other matter."

Mystified, Katharine stared up at him. He said nothing, but he moved a step closer and again reached for her hand. Taking it, he held it to his lips. Then the footman brought his hat, and after a brief hesitation, he took his leave. She remained in the hall for some time puzzling over his remark and recalling, more pleasurably, the look in his eyes when he had made it.

Fourteen

THE FOLLOWING AFTERNOON, JUST AFTER LUNCHEON, Lord Stonenden unexpectedly called at the Daltrys' again. Mary had gone upstairs to lie down, so Katharine received him alone in the drawing room. She was both puzzled and intrigued when the visitor was announced, for Stonenden had never called upon them except to sit for his portrait.

When he came in, he was smiling, and Katharine smiled in answer. "What is it?" she asked. "You look very pleased with yourself."

"I am. I can stay only a moment, but I had to come to tell you that I have discovered a way you may observe the exhibition of your painting without being seen."

"You are roasting me. I didn't take that suggestion seriously."

"Why not? It is extremely logical. You do not wish to face a gaping crowd; I understand that only too well. But you would not mind seeing how your work is received. Well, I have found a solution." His smile broadened, and his dark blue eyes twinkled mischievously.

Katharine laughed. "Out with it, then."

He drew a sheet of paper from an inner pocket. "I have laid it out so that you can see what I mean." He put the paper on a small table and gestured for her to sit down beside him. "The ballroom in my house has three doorways," he went on. "The large double entrance doors, the passage to the supper room, and this small one." He pointed to a diagram on the sheet. "It leads to a corridor that runs to the kitchen, and it is a recessed door. I propose to move one of the large tapestries a few feet to the left, covering this small doorway. That will leave a niche behind the cloth where you can put a chair. You can peek around the tapestry and see and hear everything. I will hang your painting nearby. And if you get tired, you can simply go out the door and leave the house through the back premises." He looked up, still smiling. "Is that not a first-rate plan?"

Katharine laughed again. "You look like a little boy who has discovered how to escape his nurse."

"Well, I feel rather like one. I can't remember having such fun since I slipped away from my tutor and spent the day with the gamekeeper's son poaching the neighbors' pheasant run."

"You didn't! I can't believe it of you, Lord Stonenden." Her amber eyes brimmed with laughter.

"Oh, yes. We had a famous time. I have always thought it was worth the whipping I got for it. But what do you think of my idea?"

"I think it is wonderful. Easily worth three whippings."

He looked down at her, startled, then began to laugh. "It won't come to that, fortunately. But you will do it, then?"

"Assuredly. I would not miss it for anything."

"Splendid. I'll have the tapestry moved at once." He looked down at his diagram with manifest satisfaction.

"I have never seen you so pleased," said Katharine. "Why is this so important to you? It is kind of you to think of me, but…"

"It is only partly that," he admitted. "Of course, I think you should see people's reaction to your painting without enduring their stares. But it will also give the party a unique piquancy for me, to know you are there secretly observing."

"Ah. I might have known it was something like that. You are merciless, Lord Stonenden."

His smile faded. "I don't mean—"

"I was bamming you. I think it a very good joke."

"It is, isn't it?" He grinned again. "Do you think we might tell one or two trustworthy people? To share it."

"I should like that above all things, but I have observed that telling even one or two usually lets a secret out. One's trustworthy confidants tell another one or two, and so on, until finally some quite untrustworthy person is told, and then all is lost."

"I suppose you are right. Indeed, I know you are. It shall remain our secret, then."

Katharine nodded. "And thank you."

He rose. "I cannot stay. I should have met Alvanley a half hour ago. But I wanted to tell you face-to-face rather than writing a note."

She nodded again, understanding the impulse.

"I will inform you about the party. It will be an odd gathering—both Sir Thomas Lawrence and Mrs. Drummond-Burrell have consented to come."

"You have asked them already?"

"Merely preparing the way for my invitations. I wanted to make sure of a few leading lights beforehand."

"How efficient you are."

"Of course." They exchanged another smile before he bowed and took his leave. Katharine, watching him ride off from the front window, did not realize until sometime later that she had forgotten to ask him what he had meant the previous day.

Katharine had put the final touches on the portrait that morning, signed it, and thrown a cloth over it to keep off the dust while it dried. Nothing remained to be done, and she found that she did not want to begin painting anything else just now. Thus she spent the next few days catching up on neglected reading and seeing some of the friends she had abandoned for her work. She received one note from Stonenden reporting on the plans for his party and the sensation its announcement was creating, but she did not go out to see that sensation for herself, preferring to observe it secondhand. Others were only too ready to report. When her picture was dry, she had it carried to Lord Stonenden's house, taking elaborate precautions to keep it secret. And then she sat back and awaited the day of the showing with a mixture of trepidation and eagerness.

Two days before it was to occur, Katharine and Mary sat in their drawing room in the evening reading quietly. When the bell rang below, Katharine looked up at once, however, for she was rather bored with her book and welcomed the idea of company. And when the maid ushered Tony Tillston into the room, she stood and held out her hand with a pleased smile. "Tony! I haven't seen you in an age."

"I know it," he answered, bowing over her hand and greeting Mary. "I have come to complain about it."

"To me?"

"Yes, it is all your fault, you know. Since you saddled me with your cousin Elinor Marchington, I haven't had a moment to call my own."

"Not 'saddled,' Tony."

"It's becoming something very like that. I didn't mind at first, but the thing is going on a long time, and I'm beginning to be very uneasy about Marchington, I must tell you. I joked about his calling me out, but after last night, I begin to wonder if the man ain't unstable."

"Last night?"

Tony stared at her. "You mean you haven't heard the story yet? It's all over the *ton*."

"No, I haven't seen anyone today. Elinor called when we were out shopping, I believe."

"I daresay she did!"

"Well, come and sit down and tell me."

"All right, but if I had known I would be the one to bring the news, I might not have come tonight."

"Is it so very bad?"

"Well, Marchington made a public fool of himself. But let me tell you, and you may judge. It happened at Covent Garden; there was a masquerade last night, you know."

"I didn't."

"Well, no, you wouldn't. I...er, chanced to escort a friend there—"

"*Not* Elinor?"

"Of course not! It was…uh…that is…"

Katharine laughed. "Go on, Tony. I think we know what you mean."

"Yes…well, at any rate, Marchington was there before me. He came alone and, from what I could see, more than half foxed. I didn't notice him particularly at first, though I understand he was noisy and abusive even then. But it wasn't until Countess Standen and Stonenden came in that he began to shout."

The smile on Katharine's face appeared to freeze. "The countess and…?"

"Stonenden. Yes. Everyone thought that affair over, but apparently Stonenden was simply tired of the crowd. I had it on the best authority that he told her to dismiss the puppies if she wished to see him, and the countess complied." Tony looked meditative. "Though if I know her, she will have done it in a way to keep them dangling."

Katharine, sitting very still, said nothing.

"At any rate, when they came in, Marchington went absolutely wild, started shouting insults and threatening Stonenden. I mean, the man must be mad, trying to call out the best shot in the country. Stonenden refused, of course, but I wonder he had the patience to do so. Marchington was dashed offensive. And of course, the gossips got hold of it at once; they're talking of nothing else."

"Oh, dear," said Mary. "Poor Elinor."

"You may say so. And poor Tony as well. I wouldn't be surprised if Marchington decided to take out his spleen upon me. He's not overfond of me, you know. That's one of the reasons I called. I think I'd best sheer off your cousin a bit. I shouldn't like to face a scene like that myself. I haven't Stonenden's address."

"What...what did he do?" asked Katharine, her tone odd enough to make both the others look at her.

"Who? Stonenden? Oh, he tried to shame him into keeping quiet at first. Whew! I've never heard such blistering set-downs. But Marchington wasn't having any. Some of his friends finally took him away."

"I see."

"If it hadn't been so close to me, I should have enjoyed seeing the countess's face, though. She was livid."

At this moment, the bell was heard to ring again, and soon after, Elinor Marchington came running into the drawing room. "Katharine! Have you heard?"

Katharine nodded.

"Oh, my dear," said Mary.

"Kitty told me this morning. I came here, but you were out. What am I to do?"

"Do?" Katharine looked at her but did not seem to really see her.

"Yes. Tom is getting worse and worse. I was sure your plan would stop him, but it does not seem to be working. What shall we do?"

Slowly Katharine shook her head.

"Nothing you can do," answered Tony. "Better to leave the thing alone now."

Tears started in Elinor's eyes. "But...but...I thought it was all settled. I was sure..." She choked.

"Yes, well...er..." Tony looked at Katharine, but she was staring at the floor.

"Mr. Tillston is right," said Mary Daltry then, in a tone which made him turn to gaze at her hopefully. "You have done everything you can, Elinor. Everything that a woman of character may do. Now you must let things take their course."

"You mean, just give up?"

"Not exactly, though I do not see that there is any further *action* you can take. You must wait now. That is very hard, I know, but you must do it. And, perhaps, pray. Things will come right in the end, I am sure."

Elinor, wide-eyed, turned to Katharine, but she did not seem to be listening. Elinor's shoulders slumped. "I was so sure it would work. I did not even think of anything else." She bowed her head.

"Perhaps you should go home and lie down now," added Mary kindly. "Mr. Tillston, would you escort Elinor home?"

"Oh, but I—"

"Please."

Tony blinked, then rose and held out a hand. "Of course. Will you come, Mrs. Marchington?"

Elinor stared blankly up at him, but Mary bustled over and gathered her things, urging her to her feet. "There you are, my dear. A good night's rest, that is what you need. Try not to think of any of this. I will come and see you first thing in the morning." As she talked, she draped Elinor's shawl over her shoulders, hooked her reticule over her unresisting wrist, and put her arm into Tony's. Almost before Elinor realized what was happening, she was being escorted down the stairs and out to her carriage.

Mary turned back with a sigh. "There." She looked at Katharine with concern clear in her eyes. "My dear, are you—?" But she was interrupted by another peal of the bell and footsteps on the stairs. Before Mary could intercept the new caller, Eliza Burnham walked into the room.

"I met Elinor outside, so I suppose you have heard the story. Katharine, something must be done about that boy. He is becoming a London spectacle." Lady Burnham smiled at her friend; then her brows drew together. "Katharine, what is the matter!"

The girl started. "What?"

"You look...I hardly know what. Haggard. Is something wrong?"

Katharine put a hand to her forehead. "Nothing. I am tired."

"She was just about to go to bed, actually, Eliza," put in Mary.

"At eight o'clock? I was doing nothing of the kind." Katharine sat up straighter and motioned Lady Burnham to a chair. "What can I do about Tom, Eliza? I can think of nothing. I shall be glad of your advice."

"It is difficult. I own I haven't any ideas. But really, he has created a scandal."

"Yes. The gossips must be in ecstasies."

"Well, they are." Eliza sighed. "It's no good talking to him, I suppose?"

"None. At least, if you mean that I should talk to him. I think it may be time to write his father."

"Yes, indeed. Past time."

"Well, I would have done it long since, if Elinor

had not protested so. She is convinced it will ruin her life."

"Well, Tom himself is doing that."

"Yes."

"Of course, Stonenden may—"

"We needn't bring Lord Stonenden into this," interrupted Katharine icily, and Eliza stared at her.

"I have another idea," said Mary. "I shall write Tom's mother. I have nearly done so several times, but I held off in the hope that the thing would come right. We are not good friends, but we are acquainted. I think that she could be a great help."

"Fine," replied Katharine. "Let us do that, then."

Mary nodded. "I shall write tonight."

A silence fell. Katharine stared at the floor. Mary watched her anxiously, and Eliza Burnham, following her gaze, was again shocked by the look on the girl's face. The ticking of the mantel clock seemed loud.

Finally Lady Burnham ventured, "Everyone is talking of your painting, in spite of Tom's antics. I'm desperately anxious to see it myself, and I must say I haven't forgiven you for not giving me just a glimpse beforehand."

"My painting!" Katharine laughed shortly.

Eliza exchanged a look with Mary. "Do you still mean to stay away from the party?" asked Eliza. "Nothing could keep me from going."

"Oh, yes. It is impossible that I should go now."

Lady Burnham cocked her head and examined Katharine as if she were a worrisome puzzle. "Do you go, Mary?" she said absently.

"Indeed, yes," replied the older woman firmly.

Katharine turned to stare at her, and Eliza followed her gaze.

"I am very proud of your painting, dear," added Mary, "and I mean to be there when everyone is praising it. I shall praise it myself."

Her cousin's expression softened slightly. "Thank you. But you needn't—"

"I am determined to go."

"As are we all," added Eliza.

Katharine shrugged.

"Lawrence is coming, you know," Lady Burnham went on. "It will be the oddest collection of people ever gathered at a fashionable party. They say Mr. Winstead is so pleased with his invitation that he no longer even cares about the painting. And Sally Jersey has asked Fanchon to make her an 'artistic' headdress to throw all the rest of us in the shade. She can't bear to have anyone else admired, of course. I daresay she will look a shocking quiz."

Abruptly Katharine rose. "I am tired," she said. "Forgive me, but I think I must go up to my room. You will excuse me, won't you, Eliza?" And before the older woman could answer, she strode out of the room.

"What is it, Mary?" asked Lady Burnham. "She is burnt to the socket. It is quite unlike Katharine. Is it this painting?"

"Partly. But mostly…you will treat this as a confidence, I know, Eliza…mostly it is Lord Stonenden."

"Stonenden! You don't mean…? Katharine?"

Mary nodded, and, unexpectedly, Eliza Burnham began to smile.

Fifteen

THE FIRST THING KATHARINE DID THE FOLLOWING morning was write a note to Lord Stonenden telling him she had changed her mind about attending the showing of her painting. She composed it hastily and left it on the hall table to be posted when she went down to breakfast. However, five minutes later she left her meal and went to retrieve the envelope, crumpling it in the pocket of her gown as she hurried back to the breakfast room. Her mind was in a turmoil, and had been all night. She was certain of only one thing—she never wanted to see Oliver Stonenden again—and this note would probably lead him to call. She would simply not go, she decided then. He could do nothing about that.

But when the night of the party arrived, Katharine wavered. Mary put on her best lavender silk and left the house at nine, very excited about the event, and when Katharine sat down with a novel, determined to read quietly and go to bed early, she found she could not concentrate. She could not help but wonder what society would think of her work. Stonenden was making a real show of it; the canvas was covered, and he would unveil it at ten precisely. Could she let pass a chance to see everyone's reaction?

"No," said Katharine aloud. "I will go. It is so late now that I can slip in unnoticed, and I will leave early. I needn't speak to anyone." Stonenden's housekeeper had shown her the back entrance one day last week.

Katharine hurriedly pulled on a dark dress, which would be harder to see in the unlikely event that someone should glimpse her hiding place, and took a hack to Stonenden's town house. The back door was unlocked, as arranged, and she went in very quietly and walked along the corridor past the kitchens. All the servants were busy, and none seemed to notice her as she moved warily along the hall behind the ballroom to the small door at the side.

She removed her bonnet and shawl there, and then, taking a deep breath, slowly opened the door. At once she could hear a babble of conversation. But only a dim recess about three feet square was visible, nearly filled by a straight chair. Letting out her breath, Katharine slipped in, hung her shawl on the chair back, and sat down, shutting the door behind her. She remained still for several minutes, getting accustomed to her position and listening.

She could hear very clearly. Someone just on the other side of the tapestry that hid her was talking about horses, and farther off a woman was telling someone else about a dressmaker she had found. Katharine looked at the watch pinned to her bodice. It was a quarter to ten; she had arrived in time.

Very carefully, she leaned forward. The tapestry had

been arranged so that its edge hung just over the edge of the doorway. Thus, by pulling it very slightly to the side, Katharine could obtain a view of the ballroom in front of her, and it was very unlikely that anyone would notice this tiny slit.

It was a strange sensation, watching the crowd from her hidden vantage point. Katharine had often been an observer of society, standing aside and cataloging the foibles of its members. But even then, she had retained some feeling of belonging; she had been a part of the scene she observed. Now she was completely detached from it. No one could turn and stare at her as she did at them. She found herself at once more critical and kinder in these circumstances. She could see the flaws in her various acquaintances more clearly, but she also discovered more compassion than she had previously had for them.

Suddenly Katharine saw Lord Stonenden walking directly toward her. It was her first sight of him this evening, and something about the purposeful way he approached made her heart hammer in her chest. It almost seemed that he might expose her hiding place to the crowd.

But he merely threw a speaking glance in her direction, then turned and held up a hand for silence. After a few moments, the noise died down and the guests began to gather round him. When everyone was as near as possible, he said, "You all know, of course, the purpose of this entertainment. I am about to unveil a portrait of me painted by Miss Katharine Daltry. There has been some controversy associated with this undertaking, and for that reason I now assure you all that

Miss Daltry did indeed paint the picture. I watched her do it, as did her cousin Miss Mary Daltry." He turned to where Mary was standing and added, "Is that not right, ma'am?"

"It is indeed," answered Mary in a clear voice.

Stonenden nodded. "Where is Mr. Winstead?"

There was a disturbance in the crowd, and then that gentleman emerged. Katharine nearly giggled when she saw him, for he was dressed in the most extreme fashion of the dandies, with padded shoulders, wasp waist, a collar so high and stiff he could not move his head, and a profusion of fobs and ornaments on his florid waistcoat. "Here I am, your lordship," he called, preening himself before the crowd. Katharine saw more than one member of the *ton* exchange an amused glance with a friend.

Stonenden nodded to him. "I assume, Mr. Winstead, that you will accept the assurances of Miss Daltry and myself about the origins of this painting?"

"Oh, certainly, my lord. Of course." The little man was obviously so overcome with pleasure at being present that he would have accepted anything at all.

Lord Stonenden suppressed a smile. "Good. Then I think we are ready." He signaled, and one of the footmen pulled on a rope that would raise the cloth covering the painting. It was hung on the wall above Katharine's head, well outside her field of vision, but she could see the faces of the guests very clearly, and she watched them as they gazed upward.

Most looked curious, then impressed, then approving. She heard murmurs of "It looks like him, all right," and "One can see at once who it is meant to be." These made her smile. She also overheard several compliments to herself. An old gentleman exclaimed, "The girl's done a demmed fine job of it." And a woman replied, "Yes, Katharine Daltry is certainly accomplished, though a bit odd, you know."

Winstead himself scarcely glanced at the canvas. He looked up briefly, said, "Yes indeed, very competent," and turned back to scan the crowd for notables. Katharine shook her head. Clearly, the opinions he had expressed in his offensive article had really meant nothing to him, beyond a venting of momentary spite. He didn't care whether she painted or not, or whether any woman did; he wanted only acceptance from society and would do anything to gain its attention. Having done so, he promptly forgot everything else. For a moment, this depressed her spirits. She had proved a point, only to have her opponent shrug off the whole question. But then she realized that she had actually proved it to herself, and no one else, and she felt happy again.

Just then, she saw Stonenden bringing Sir Thomas Lawrence closer to the wall where the painting hung. In fact, he escorted him right up to the place where Katharine sat, obviously so that she could better hear his opinion. "It is well done, is it not?" he asked the painter.

"I could see better from farther back," objected Lawrence, "but, yes, I think it is. She has caught something vital, as any good portraitist must. In fact, Lord Stonenden, I hope you will pardon me for saying that she has been very kind to you. You seldom look quite so genial as you do in that painting."

His host laughed. "I must try to model myself on my likeness, then."

Sir Thomas smiled in return. "You might do worse. The girl has seen something of the charm you seldom reveal. Either she is an acute, and kindly, observer, or..." Lawrence's smile broadened, and he shrugged.

Stonenden gestured noncommittally. "Some champagne, Sir Thomas?"

"Indeed."

As they walked away, Katharine sat frowning behind the tapestry. So she had made Stonenden look charming, had she? She couldn't imagine how or why. She certainly had not done it on purpose. As she was fuming, Eliza Burnham came forward, arm in arm with Mary. "It *is* good, isn't it," she heard the former say. "Katharine is talented."

"Very," agreed her cousin.

"And one can see what she feels very plainly. I hadn't realized before what a portrait could show. Though this is an unusual case, I suppose."

"Yes. Shall we get a glass of ratafia?" Mary spoke quickly and started to turn away.

"Oh, no, I want to look a bit longer. You know, if Stonenden looks like *that* to Katharine, I cannot see that there is any obstacle—"

"Elinor!" interrupted Mary. "Hello, dear. Over here." Katharine, still frowning in her recess, was surprised at the vehemence of Mary's tone.

Elinor joined the other two ladies, bringing Tony Tillston with her. She greeted them despondently.

"Do you like Katharine's painting?" asked Mary.

"Oh, yes," murmured the younger girl. "It is...very nice, isn't it?"

"It's first-rate," added Tony. "And the rest of us may as well go out and shoot ourselves now, I suppose."

"Shall we get some refreshment?" blurted Mary Daltry in a high, uncharacteristic squeak. "I am quite thirsty."

Tony shrugged, and Elinor nodded listlessly. Mary took Eliza Burnham's arm and urged her away. Katharine watched them leave with a scowl. Whatever had they been talking about? And why was Mary acting so unlike herself? Did she not like the painting after all? But no, she had liked it.

Before she could reach any conclusion, another group approached, Lady Jersey and two of her cronies escorted by several of the dandy set. "But, my dears," Lady Jersey was saying in a penetrating voice, "it's perfectly obvious to *me*. She has to be in love with him. No one could see Stonenden so otherwise. I mean, only *look*." She gestured grandly toward the painting.

"Well, but, Sally," replied one of the men, "I don't see what you're getting at. The thing looks like him."

"Does it? When have you seen that expression on Oliver Stonenden's face?"

"Expression?" The dandy held up his quizzing glass and peered at the picture. "Ha. See what you mean. He looks uncommon pleasant, don't he? Not sneering or bored."

"Precisely. And look at the eyes, that smile. I tell you, Katharine Daltry is in love with him. I would wager my last guinea on it. Isn't it too funny! And he bedding Elise Standen. I always said Katharine Daltry was overproud. Now we shall see."

"Pity," replied the dandy. "She's a taking little thing."

Lady Jersey gave a silvery laugh. "Well, if you truly think so, Edward, you may have your chance quite soon. I daresay she will be ripe for anything when Oliver drops her, now that he has got his painting."

The dandy looked frightened. "No, no, just a figure of speech, you know. Nothing to do with me."

Lady Jersey laughed again. "Come, let us go and ask Stonenden about his posing. He must see how it is, of course. It will be amusing to rally him about it."

The group moved away again, leaving Katharine sitting bolt upright in her chair, her eyes wide with horror. She could not even think at first, such was the turmoil into which Lady Jersey's careless words had thrown her. She only heard, over and over again, "She has to be in love with him." It seemed to ring in her ears, and she felt dizzy and almost sick. Every member of the *ton* would hear those words before this evening ended, and they would talk of nothing else. Her painting, which she had worked on with such dedication and hope, would come to mean only this in the heedless eyes of society.

Katharine realized that she had been holding her breath, and she released it in one great sigh. She folded her shaking hands tightly and tried to regain control of herself. Lady Jersey was a venomous, hateful creature; she longed to slap her. Everyone knew how she loved to gossip. Surely her silly imaginings would not be taken seriously. Then, abruptly, Katharine remembered Eliza Burnham's cryptic remarks earlier in the evening, and her cheeks flushed crimson. It was clear now that Eliza had seen something of the same thing in the portrait. How could this be?

Putting her icy hands to her hot face, Katharine tried to examine her feelings. She had always disliked Oliver Stonenden. She had! Ever since she first met him. He was a selfish, unfeeling man, completely wrapped up in himself. When he had offered for her, she had known that he did so with no thought of *her*. He had been attracted, perhaps, by the superficials of her appearance and manner, but he neither knew nor cared what she was really like. She had not hesitated for a moment over her refusal. She couldn't love such a man! They were mistaken about the painting; it showed her love of the work, not the man.

Katharine found this explanation very satisfying, for nearly two minutes. But then a vision of Stonenden's laughing face on their last day of work arose, and she realized that it was only partly true. She did love the work. But the man seemed to have changed a great deal since that long-ago proposal. She could not say now that he cared nothing for her true self. Indeed, he seemed to have turned right about. He no longer wanted to marry her, but he treated her as a respected friend. He had inconvenienced himself to help her over the portrait, and he had arranged this whole evening, with evident enjoyment, for her sake. These were not the acts of a selfish man.

Katharine slumped in her chair. She had changed, too. Her feelings toward Lord Stonenden were quite altered by his recent behavior. She did not love him, of course, but she did respect and esteem him more than most gentlemen of her acquaintance.

She flushed again. She had revealed these feelings to the world in the most shameless way. And it was no good saying she hadn't meant to, because the effect was the same. Everyone would interpret it as Lady Jersey had, and they would laugh at her behind their hands for succumbing to a man who had rejected scores of women and was even now known to be involved with someone else. And this mockery would be more bearable than the pity of her friends.

Utterly undone, Katharine stumbled to her feet and groped for her bonnet and shawl. She must get away from this place. She pushed open the door and stepped into the blessedly quiet corridor. Jamming her hat on her head, she hurried along it, but before she had reached the turn to the kitchens, a figure appeared in the archway there. Katharine stopped with a gasp and put a hand to her mouth.

"Did I startle you?" said Oliver Stonenden. "I am sorry. I had to slip out for a moment to see how you were liking the exhibition. Did you hear Sir Thomas?" He smiled at her eagerly.

Katharine tried to speak, but no words would come out. She could not tear her eyes from his. Desperately she nodded.

"Good. I brought him up expressly for that purpose. Your painting is a distinct success. I congratulate you with all my heart." He came forward, still smiling, as if to take her hands.

With a strangled sound, she pulled her shawl more closely around her. How could she escape?

Stonenden's smile faded abruptly. "What is it? Is something wrong? Are you ill? It is stuffy in that doorway, I know. I hope you left the door a little open. Do you feel faint?"

Making a herculean effort, Katharine managed to croak, "I must go."

"You *are* ill! Let me call someone."

"No!" In her turmoil, she nearly shouted. "No, let me alone. I must go home." Shaking off the paralysis that had kept her rooted to one spot, she moved toward him.

Stonenden again put out a hand. "Of course you shall go if you desire it, but let me get someone to accompany you."

"No. Please." She was nearly upon him now; she edged along the wall past him.

He turned with her, his eyes full of concern. "Katharine..."

"Let me alone!" And she broke into a run—past the kitchens and out into the welcome emptiness of the street.

Sixteen

OLIVER STONENDEN CALLED AT THE DALTRY HOUSE not long after breakfast the following morning, but when he was ushered into the drawing room, he found only Mary Daltry sitting there. "Good morning," he said pleasantly. "Have you recovered from the excitements of last night?"

Mary raised her eyebrows a little at this, then nodded.

"And Miss Katharine Daltry? I hope she is better."

"Better?"

"When I saw her last night, she seemed…" He paused, looked at Mary, then added, "Look here, is she ill?"

"Katharine? Why, no, she isn't ill." Mary gazed at him in her turn. "What makes you think so?"

"She was not herself last night. Is she in this morning?"

"Well…well, no, not precisely."

Lord Stonenden smiled. "She is imprecisely in?"

Mary met his eyes, and her lips twitched involuntarily. "She is here, but she will not see anyone. She has shut herself in her studio."

"Ah. Well, of course I mustn't disturb her, then. But is she all right?"

Mary eyed him uncertainly.

"I am concerned; she was upset last night. Did she overhear something at the party which annoyed her? Did someone criticize her painting?"

"Oh, no. I…I really don't think there was anything."

"No?" replied Stonenden gently. "I believe, on the contrary, that you do."

She raised her eyes, startled, to his.

"I can be trusted, you know," he added.

Mary looked a bit flustered. "Well, of course, Lord Stonenden, but…that is, I haven't…"

"Tell me," he said. "Please. I shall treat anything you say as an absolute confidence. My interest in this is not trivial."

She looked at him again. Her unease seemed to lighten, and when she spoke, all trace of embarrassment was gone. But she still appeared undecided. "Is it not?" she asked.

"No. I cannot think of anything more central to my life at this moment."

"Ah." Mary looked at her folded hands. "There was a good deal of talk last evening."

"At the party? There was indeed. Did someone say something offensive?"

"You did not hear what they said about the painting?"

"I heard it praised." Stonenden sounded a little impatient now. "I was told it was a good likeness. Sally Jersey began some nonsense about my eyes, but I was called away."

"I see. You didn't hear, then. Lady Jersey was the source."

"I beg your pardon, Miss Daltry, but the source of what? I don't know what you mean."

Mary took a breath. "A...a number of people at your house last night saw things in the painting that I had not noticed. I thought at first that they were mistaken, but as I looked more closely and listened to them, it...it seemed there might be something in it. Lady Jersey was the most outspoken. Of course, one wouldn't pay much heed to her; she lives on gossip. But others, more reliable, thought the same. Everyone was discussing it. I'm certain Katharine heard."

Stonenden was frowning. "And what did these people profess to see in the painting?"

Mary looked perplexed. "You really did not hear?"

"I did not. I never listen to gossip. And I imagine guests in my house would not be overeager to criticize the portrait to me."

"Oh, it was not the portrait, precisely. It was..." She drew a breath and went on in a rush. "They said that the picture showed great...great feeling. Lady Jersey in particular insisted that it demonstrated that Katharine..." She trailed off in embarrassment.

Stonenden looked at first startled, then intent, then amused. "I see. I believe I can complete that sentence, knowing Sally Jersey only too well."

Mary nodded. "And so, you see, it was very uncomfortable."

"Yes." But her companion's anxious look had disappeared. He seemed almost pleased by her news. "Yes, I'm sure it was quite unpleasant to hear such things gossiped about publicly. But Katharine, Miss Daltry, will get over that, I should think."

Mary's eyebrows drew a little together.

"I think it would help if I spoke to her," he went on.

"Oh, I don't believe she would see you."

"But why not?" He leaned forward. "Miss Daltry, tell me, what do you think about Lady Jersey's conclusions?"

"Why, they are grossly impertinent," retorted Mary.

"Yes, of course." He brushed this aside. "But…do you see any truth in them?" Mary started to protest, but he hurried on. "It is very important to me. I would not ask you such a question otherwise. Any woman would be incensed at such a rumor, but is Miss Daltry merely incensed? Surely not. Anger would not cause her to shut herself away."

"I really cannot discuss this with you, Lord Stonenden."

"Not even if your cousin's happiness depends upon it? I say nothing of my own."

Mary looked extremely uncomfortable. "Are you suggesting…?"

"I think I am doing a bit more than that. Do you know how Katharine feels toward me, Miss Daltry? I do not. I know how she once felt, but I have some hope that she has changed her opinion. If I thought for a moment that Lady Jersey was right, I wouldn't hesitate to burst into Katharine's studio and say what I feel." Mary's folded hands twisted.

"I have done what I could to win her regard," the man added. "I need to know if I have succeeded. Will you not give me a hint, at least?"

Slowly and reluctantly, Mary met his eager gaze. She did not at all know what she should do. She would not betray Katharine's confidence, but in this matter, she did not have it. She had only her own observations and conclusions, and it was so easy to make a mistake. Yet if she refused to say anything, might that not bring even more unhappiness? She sighed. "I…I know nothing of what Katharine feels," she answered finally. "She has not told me. But I have noticed…"

"Yes?"

"I…I may of course be quite mistaken, but it seems to me that Katharine is often upset when someone mentions that you and the Countess Standen…that is…" She stopped, unable to complete this sentence.

Lord Stonenden looked puzzled. "Elise Standen? But Katharine knows all about that. It was practically her suggestion."

Now Mary looked perplexed. "I beg your pardon?"

"The countess and young Marchington—she knows about that. We've spoken of it."

"About…? I'm sorry, I don't understand you."

"Has she said nothing to you?"

Mary stared at him.

"I wonder why." He retreated into his own thoughts for several minutes; gradually, his brow darkened. "Look here," he continued finally, "has Katharine said nothing to you about a scheme to separate the countess and Tom Marchington?"

"Yes, of course," replied Mary, bewildered. "She asked Tony Tillston—"

"Tillston?"

"Yes. I should not tell you about it, I suppose, but under the circumstances… Katharine asked Mr.

Tillston to squire Elinor about, to make Tom jealous. Unfortunately—"

"She had another plan!" Stonenden seemed astonished.

"Yes, we worried for such a time before we could
think of anything."

"But I spoke to her. And Eliza Burnham clearly
requested my help."

"Eliza?" Mary sounded utterly mystified.

Her companion stood abruptly. "There has been a
terrible misunderstanding. I must speak to Katharine
at once!"

Mary rose to face him. "But I don't... What do
you mean?"

He looked impatiently down at her, then straightened and seemed to get control of himself again. "I see
how it is," he said. "What a damnable tangle."

Mary watched his face. "I don't understand. Were
you also trying to separate Tom from the countess?"

"Am," he corrected. "And I believe the only thing to
do now is to finish the process. Explanations are always
less convincing than actions. I shall *show* Katharine that
I had only her interests at heart." He turned away.
"Good day, Miss Daltry. And thank you!"

"What are you going to do?" she began, but he was
already out of the room.

❧

Katharine came downstairs to luncheon, looking pale
and rather tired. Asked how her painting had gone,
she merely grimaced, and the two women ate their
meal in nearly unbroken silence. Afterward, when
Katharine would have retreated to her studio again,

Mary said, "Come into the drawing room for just a moment, dear."

"Mary, I really don't—"

"Only for a moment."

When they had sat down, Mary said, "Lord Stonenden called this morning."

Katharine looked up, startled, then quickly dropped her eyes. "Did he?" she replied coolly.

"Yes. He seemed very concerned about you. I think now that I should have asked you to come down."

"Indeed not. I am very glad you didn't."

"But you know, Katharine, I think there may have been some misunderstanding between you and Lord Stonenden. He was telling me—"

"Really, Mary, I do not care to hear what he was telling you. Please." She got up and walked over to one of the front windows. "Oh, dear, here is Elinor. I suppose I must see her." She laughed shortly. "Her faith in me is so touching, and so misplaced. I do not understand why she keeps coming here. I have done as little for her as for myself."

"Katharine…" But the servant came in to announce their caller, and in the next moment Elinor was with them.

Though she wore a very fashionable fawn morning dress, lavishly trimmed with dark green braid, Elinor looked wan and red-eyed. She sat down with them despondently and gazed from one to the other of them with wide brown eyes. Katharine moved uneasily in her chair.

"How are you, dear?" asked Mary.

Elinor shrugged. "Your painting is very nice,

Katharine. I wanted to tell you. Everyone admired it excessively."

"Thank you, Elinor," said the older girl, touched.

There was a silence.

Finally Elinor heaved a great sigh. "I know I am horridly tiresome, and I do beg your pardon, but I am so worried about Tom. I cannot think of anything else, and I…I don't know what to do." Her voice broke on the last word, and she groped in her reticule for a handkerchief.

The other two watched her helplessly.

"I w-wish I could b-be more s-sensible," sobbed Elinor, "b-but I don't know how."

"You are being very sensible," answered Katharine. "Indeed, I have the greatest admiration for your fortitude."

"Y-you *do*?"

"Oh, yes. In your place, I would have murdered Tom with a hatpin by this time. Or, at the very least, thrown things."

Elinor chuckled shakily at this absurd picture. "Perhaps I should have. Perhaps I will. Nothing else has done the least good."

"Perhaps you should," agreed Katharine.

The others stared at her.

"Well, Elinor is right. Nothing else has worked. And I begin to think we have let Tom off too easily. Why should Elinor wait quietly while he does what he pleases and creates a scandal? It may be time for you to kick up a dust, Elinor."

The younger girl's eyes were wide. "I don't know if I *could*. He hardly speaks now. And when he does, he is sullen and so ill-tempered. He boxed Chivers's ears yesterday."

"Well, he wouldn't dare box yours!"

"No." Elinor sounded doubtful. "He did once, though, when I lost his pet turtle."

Katharine laughed. "I think he takes you far too much for granted. That is what comes of marrying a man one has known all one's life. But if you made a great fuss, I wager he would listen."

"Do you think so?" Elinor frowned.

"I do."

"But I have never—"

"Precisely, Elinor. You have always allowed Tom his way. Perhaps it is time you stopped."

Her younger cousin eyed her uneasily. "I always felt so sorry for him, you see. Sir Lionel and Lady Agnes never let him do anything he wanted to do."

"I understand that," began Katharine, when, as if summoned by Elinor's remarks, another visitor strode into the room as the maid announced, "Lady Agnes Marchington."

The three women turned and stared, Elinor with almost ludicrous apprehension. Lady Agnes stood before them, arms akimbo, looking from one to the other truculently. She was a large woman, taller even than Katharine, with a massive, tightly corseted figure and piercing blue eyes.

Her traveling costume was not the height of fashion, but her air of consequence easily outweighed this slight disadvantage.

"Well, Elinor," she said in a deep commanding voice, "they told me at your house that I should find you here."

"L-Lady Agnes," stammered her daughter-in-law, rising hurriedly. "What a...uh, pleasant surprise."

"Is it?" Lady Agnes surveyed the others. "Hello, Mary. Katharine."

The Daltry ladies greeted her, Katharine with a slight smile. "Will you sit down?" Katharine invited.

"No. I haven't time for that. I came only to fetch Elinor and to ask one question." She fixed them each in turn with a ferocious glance. "*Where* is my son?"

Elinor gave a little squeak, and Katharine had to press her lips tightly together.

"He is not at home," Lady Agnes went on, "and the servants seem astonishingly unable to tell me where he *is*, so I ask you, Elinor."

"I...I don't know...that is, I'm not sure. He went out this morning. He never tells me where he is going." Elinor ended on a gasp.

"Does he not? Well, that is your own fault, my girl. He would tell you if you asked properly. And if you had given him a proper home, he would not be making a fool of himself and his family as I understand he now is. Come along, we shall wait for him at your house."

"I have my carriage," blurted Elinor.

"Hah. Well, you must follow me, then. Don't dawdle. Mary, Katharine, I shall call again when this unfortunate matter is set right. Good day." And she turned and swept out of the room.

"Whew!" remarked Katharine. "She is a tartar, isn't she?"

"Oh, how did she find out?" cried Elinor. "We are lost now."

"I fear I wrote her," admitted Mary. "I had no idea she was so... When I met her before, she seemed quite charming."

Elinor groaned.

"But, Elinor, this is just what we wanted," said Katharine. "You did not want to scold Tom. Well, here is someone who will, soundly." She smiled at her cousin.

"No, no. It will make him wild," protested Elinor. "He hates being lectured by his mother."

"Elinor!" came a stentorian call up the stairs. "The carriages are here. Come along."

Elinor wrung her hands. "Oh, dear…oh, dear. Katharine! You must come with me. I cannot face her alone."

"But—"

"You must! Please, please."

"All right, all right. Do not fall into a fit of the vapors. I will come."

"I knew you would not desert me now."

"I must get my bonnet. You go and tell Lady Agnes you are coming."

"Yes. You *will* come?"

"I have said so, goose. Go on."

Elinor turned to walk downstairs as Katharine started up to her bedchamber to fetch her hat. "Oh, this will be dreadful," murmured the former, "*dreadful!*"

Seventeen

LADY AGNES REACHED THE MARCHINGTON TOWN house before Elinor and Katharine, and she was awaiting them in the drawing room, arms folded over her formidable bodice, foot tapping. Elinor positively cringed when she entered, and Katharine, though somewhat amused, still wished herself elsewhere.

Lady Agnes was surprised to see her. "Katharine?" she said with raised eyebrows. "What are you doing here?"

"I thought I might be of some assistance, Lady Agnes."

"Assistance?" The other appeared astonished.

"I begged her to come," exclaimed Elinor. "She has helped me all along, and I wanted her here when I told you—"

"Helped you?" Lady Agnes looked Katharine up and down. "Can it be that I have you to thank for the way this affair has been botched? I thought it was Elinor, which was only to be expected, of course. But I had been told that you were a young woman of sense."

Elinor made a strangled sound.

"You were obviously misinformed," replied Katharine. "My presence here is evidence of that."

Glimpsing the twinkle in her amber eyes, Lady Agnes snorted. "If you think this is amusing, I don't wonder you botched it. I do not, I promise you. My only son disgracing the family with a highborn trollop! If this escapade reaches my husband's ears, you will all be sorry for it."

"You haven't told him, then?" gasped Elinor.

"I have not." Her mother-in-law glared at her. "Yet."

"Thank heavens. But Lady Agnes, I beg you not to scold Tom. He hates it so, you know that, and he will only—"

"Scold? I mean to do far more than that! I shall drag him back home by his ear, like the naughty boy he is behaving as, and administer the hiding of his life."

Katharine tried to imagine the beefy Tom Marchington being "hided." As she looked at his mother, she could.

"But, Lady Agnes," pleaded Elinor. "He won't come. He won't listen to anyone. And I am afraid you will only drive him to do something worse!"

"He will listen to me! But where is he?" She stalked over to the bell rope and pulled it vigorously. When the butler came in, she ordered, "Bring me Chivers, at once!"

"Who is Chivers?" whispered Katharine to her cousin. "I know only that he had his ears boxed."

"He is Tom's valet," murmured the other girl miserably. "He has been with him forever."

After a few moments, a slender, ruddy man entered the drawing room. Though he was dressed as a gentleman's gentleman, Katharine thought he looked more like a groom. He also looked distinctly frightened when he saw Lady Agnes.

"So, Chivers," said her ladyship. "What have you been at, allowing Tom to run wild? I seem to recall telling you to keep watch over him and not let him fall into any of his distempered freaks." She lowered her voice awfully. "But perhaps I am mistaken."

"No, your ladyship. I have done my best, but Master Tom doesn't heed me any longer."

"Why not?"

"I...I couldn't say, your ladyship."

"No? Well. I can venture a guess. You always indulged Tom shockingly, given half a chance, and I daresay you have done so again." She glared around the room. "You have *all* done so. And I am here to put an end to it, Chivers! Where is Tom?"

The little man had jumped at his name, and now he seemed to shrink into himself. "I don't know, your ladyship."

"You don't *know*?"

Chivers quailed. "No, ma'am. He went out in his town dress."

"Were you not instructed to monitor Tom's activities in London and keep us informed?"

"Yes, your ladyship, but—"

"But of course he could not," snapped Katharine. "A man's valet cannot be spying after him all the time. And you should not have asked it, Lady Agnes."

Tom's mother spun to face her. "I do not see that this is any concern of yours, Katharine. I think it would be best if you returned home. The Marchingtons can deal with their own problems."

"Can they? I have seen very little evidence of it."
Katharine put her hands on her hips and faced Lady
Agnes, in spite of Elinor's inarticulate whimper behind
her. "I must say I think Elinor is right," she continued.
"I was of the opinion that Tom needed a sound rating,
but if you speak to him as you have been here, you
will do nothing but drive him to greater excesses. Any
man would rebel at that sort of language."

"You know nothing whatsoever about the matter,"
snapped Lady Agnes. "I am a plain woman, and I have
always spoken plainly to my son. And," she added
triumphantly, "he has always done as I told him."

"Precisely. And that is why he is behaving like an
idiot. He has never had the chance to try his own wings.
You kept him so hemmed about with rules and orders
that he was bound to break out. And now that he is
doing so, a thundering scold will simply inflame him."

"Young woman! I am at least twenty years your
senior, and I believe I know rather more about how to
handle my son than an impertinent chit who has not
even managed to get herself a husband, though well
past the age for it. Kindly refrain from interfering. If
you won't go home, sit down and hold your tongue."

Katharine's eyes had snapped with anger at the
beginning of this speech, but as it went on, amusement struggled with outrage in her face, and by the
time Lady Agnes finished, she was manfully battling a
giggle. Seeing that she could do nothing to alter the
woman's behavior, she turned away to hide her smile
and, obediently, sat down.

"Good," responded Lady Agnes with a sharp nod.
"Now, then. Chivers!"

But before the little man could answer, the door opened and Tom Marchington walked into the drawing room.

Katharine thought her cousin's husband looked distinctly the worse for wear. He was no longer the cheerful ruddy country squire he had been on his arrival in town. His blue eyes were bloodshot, his round face thinner, and his sensible, serviceable garments exchanged for a costume that reflected some of the worst excesses of the dandy set. Moreover, when the young man saw his mother, he went utterly ashen and his mouth dropped open in appalled astonishment. Lady Agnes's reaction to his entrance did nothing to increase his composure. She fixed him with a baleful eye and cried, "Aha! So here you are at last."

"M-Mama!" Tom cast an anguished eye in Elinor's direction.

"I didn't send for her, Tom," the girl cried. "I didn't!"

"Silence." Lady Agnes looked them both up and down; Tom and Elinor instinctively moved closer together. "You have both, as far as I can see, acted like complete ninnyhammers. You are coming home with me today." She turned to Tom. "You are most at fault, of course, and I shall see to it that you regret your foolishness to the utmost."

Tom had quailed at the beginning of this speech, but now he straightened. "You can't make me go home, Mama, and I don't mean to. I'm tired of being treated like a child. A man must have a bit of freedom, a chance to look about him. I'll settle down as happily as the next—"

"You dare!" interrupted his mother. "You dare to speak so to me?"

Katharine saw Tom's hands tremble a little, but he said, "Yes, Mama. You may as well go back home yourself. I intend to stay here for the rest of the season." His jaw hardened. "And then go to Brighton, perhaps, for a while. Elinor may go with you if she likes."

"Tom!" exclaimed his wife, outraged by this betrayal.

"Or she may come with me, of course," he added hurriedly.

"I see," replied Lady Agnes in menacing tones. "You still have some interest in your wife, then, despite your carryings-on with this Standen woman?"

Tom, avoiding her eye, looked around the room. His gaze passed over Katharine with mild surprise and lighted on Chivers. "What are you doing here?" he roared.

Chivers began backing toward the door. "Her ladyship—"

"Get out!" The valet scurried from the room, and Tom turned back to his mother, seemingly refreshed by his victory in at least one area.

"Did you hear me, Tom?" said Lady Agnes.

"Yes, Mama. And I would like to say that I do not believe this is a proper subject for public conversation."

"You have made it a subject of public scandal. I don't see why I shouldn't talk about it."

Her son's face reddened slightly, and he clenched his fists.

"Well?"

"I am simply enjoying a bit of flirtation," he burst

out, goaded. "No more than any man might do. Of course I am interested in my wife and family. I shall settle down quite happily when we go home. Why can no one understand that?"

"You are a married man, Tom. This sort of behavior, if it *must* occur, should cease upon marriage."

"I know that," shouted her son. "But you and Papa never let me out of your sight. I had no chance to see anything of the world before I married, and by God, I mean to do it now. No one shall stop me!"

"You think not? If you refuse to listen to me, Thomas, I shall tell your father the whole. We shall see what you say then."

Though Tom looked apprehensive at this threat, he retorted, "Go ahead. Do what you like. Only leave me alone!"

Lady Agnes appeared astonished at his obstinacy. It was obvious that Tom had never defied her before. But rather than moderating her position, she unwisely became even angrier. "We will cut you off without a shilling," she said. "See how your countess feels about you then. You will have to come home."

Tom scowled alarmingly, and Katharine shook her head. And Lady Agnes had accused *her* of botching things! "Do whatever you like," retorted Tom. "I can't stop you. But I'm damned if I'll come home, now or ever!" And he turned his back on his mother and slammed out of the room.

"Ohhh," murmured Elinor from the corner.

Lady Agnes stood rigid for a long moment, then said, "I shall return home immediately. My husband must hear of this as soon as possible." And she too walked out.

Elinor put her face in her hands. Katharine went over to sit on the sofa beside her, though she could think of no comforting words to offer.

"What do you think Tom will do?" asked the younger girl in a muffled voice.

"I don't know. I hope he has gone somewhere to calm down."

"No. He always rushes out to *do* something after a quarrel. It relieves his feelings."

"I daresay."

"Do you think I should go after him?"

"You wouldn't find him, Elinor."

"I know." She sighed. "If only Lady Agnes had listened to me."

"She isn't the sort of person who listens to anyone, I fancy," replied Katharine dryly. "None of this is your fault, Elinor."

"I know. But sometimes I can't help feeling that it must be."

"Well, it isn't, so put that out of your head."

Elinor sighed again and straightened. "What should I do now, Cousin Katharine?"

Their eyes met, and Katharine shook her head. "We must simply wait and hope that Tom does nothing *too* rash."

The younger girl slumped. "I wish we had never come to London."

Eighteen

LADY AGNES ACCORDINGLY DEPARTED. KATHARINE stayed with Elinor for some time, finally succeeding in calming her a bit. Tom did not return. And when Katharine at last went home in the early evening, she and Mary discussed Elinor's situation with great concern, but without discovering any solution. They were preparing to go upstairs to bed when the bell pealed violently in the ball, heralding a late visitor, and they looked at one another anxiously.

"It must be Elinor," said Mary. "Oh, I hope nothing is wrong."

But when the caller came hurrying into the drawing room, it was not Elinor, but Tony Tillston. He looked harried. "Thank God you're still up," he said. "Your idiot cousin has done something disastrous."

"Tom?"

"The very same. He has challenged Oliver Stonenden to a duel."

Katharine had trouble drawing her breath for a moment, then she gasped, "He accepted?"

"He had to. Marchington knocked him down in

one of the card rooms at White's. The man must be mad!"

"Knocked him...?"

"Yes, I tell you. Completely mad."

Katharine gathered her wits. "What happened, exactly? Were you there?"

"I should say I was. I was playing piquet with some friends. Stonenden and his party were at the next table but one. Everything was peaceful, when suddenly Marchington came roaring in. He wasn't even foxed. He began shouting insults at Stonenden, saying the crudest things. No other man would have stood it for a moment, but Stonenden is such a fine shot that no one could think him afraid. But then that young fool actually went over to the table and hauled at Stonenden's arm, pulled him out of his chair. There was nothing for it then, but Stonenden was so startled that Marchington got in the first blow. He never would have done so if he hadn't taken him by surprise; Stonenden's remarkably handy with his fives. However, the idiot knocked him flat, in front of everyone, and then challenged him. Stonenden had to accept."

"Indeed? If he is so good with his 'fives,' why could he not just thrash Tom and leave it at that?" Katharine looked both angry and apprehensive.

"This was at *White's*, Katharine. That would have been more insulting than you can imagine."

"Insulting! Well, I should by far rather Tom were insulted than killed."

"Oh, Stonenden won't kill him. He's a superb shot. No, I'm more worried about him than about Marchington."

"What do you mean?"

"Marchington is behaving like a madman. He might very well kill Stonenden. Is he good with a pistol, do you know?"

Katharine obviously had not thought of this; she went white. "Kill Stonenden? But…"

"Yes, and have the law after him and create an even greater scandal. He'd have to flee the country, of course."

"Tony, we must stop him!"

The man looked disgusted. "Why do you think I'm here? To gossip? I came to tell you so that you could do just that."

"Yes, yes, of course." Katharine put a hand distractedly to her brow. "But what shall I do?"

"Talk to your cousin. Drag him out of London, if necessary."

"He won't listen. His mother tried that today."

"Did she? Well, what about his wife?"

"Whose wife?" said a quavering voice from the doorway. They all whirled, to find Elinor standing there. "I couldn't stay home," the girl added. "Tom has not come in, and I was so worried. You are talking about Tom, aren't you? Oh, what has he done?"

Katharine and Tony looked at one another.

"You must tell me," insisted Elinor. "I shall hear. And it is worse *not* knowing."

Acknowledging the truth of this with a nod, Katharine told her what had occurred. Elinor sank into a chair with a groan. "A duel? Sir Lionel will kill him!"

A little amused by this reaction, despite the

seriousness of the matter, Katharine replied, "He need not find out, Elinor."

"Lady Agnes is bringing him to town, and someone will tell him. What are we to do?"

"You must talk to your husband," answered Tony, leaning forward. "You must make him understand his folly."

"But Tom will not listen to *me*," said Elinor piteously. "He does not admit that I know anything about town life. Whenever I have tried to talk to him, he has only become angry with me."

Tony looked nonplussed. "Well, then, Katharine or perhaps Miss Mary Daltry should try."

"I have tried," responded Katharine. "I did no good at all. And Mary…" She looked at her cousin.

"I am quite willing," said the older woman. "But I cannot think that Tom will be swayed by my opinion, when he refuses to listen to his own wife and mother."

"No, I don't think he will," agreed Katharine. "Oh, if there were only someone whose views he respected!" She frowned, considering, then looked up. "Tony, I know it is a great favor to ask, but could you not speak to Tom? You are known to be a man of fashion. Perhaps your arguments would have some weight with him."

Tony looked uncomfortable. "No they wouldn't, Katharine. Not after the way I have squired his wife about. I count myself lucky he did not challenge *me* as well."

"But, Tony—"

"No, Katharine. It wouldn't do any good, I tell you. And besides…" He paused, shifting uneasily in his chair. "Well, I think I've done enough, you know. I tried my best to help, but now, well, I've done all I can."

Katharine looked at him for a moment, then nodded "Of course you have. I shouldn't have asked more. I'm sorry."

Tony grimaced. "The thing is, Katharine—"

"You need say no more. I understand."

"You don't, actually." Tony stood. "You don't know a thing about it. And that's the worst of it. You might have asked the world of me, but you never did. And I…" He stopped, laughed a little, then finished, "And I must take my leave now. Forgive me for bringing such unwelcome news."

"On the contrary, we were glad to get it," answered Katharine, standing and giving him her hand. "We are grateful for all your help."

He laughed again, bowed slightly, and went out. Mary Daltry watched him go with compassion.

But Elinor was too engrossed in her own misery to think of Tony. She pulled at Katharine's sleeve, saying, "We must go to Lord Stonenden, Katharine. It is the only answer. We must beg him not to meet Tom. You can speak to him. You know him quite well."

Her cousin looked down at her, aghast. "I? But I don't."

"You painted his portrait. Everyone says you are great friends. Please, Katharine, I would do it myself, but I have hardly spoken a word to him in my life. He will listen to you!"

Katharine seemed to shudder.

"I will see him," offered Mary. "We are not *well* acquainted, perhaps, but I have chatted with him several times. Indeed, he seems a pleasant, just man. I am sure he does not mean to harm Tom, only to teach him a lesson. And when he knows—"

"I beg your pardon, Cousin Mary, but I think it would be much better if Katharine went. She knows Lord Stonenden well." Elinor gazed at the other girl. "You cannot refuse to do this small thing for me, Katharine. Why should you? In a quarter hour of conversation, you can relieve me of this dreadful anxiety." She fixed her brown eyes on Katharine's face.

The object of her pleading gaze sank into an armchair and leaned back. Small thing, indeed. Elinor had no idea how difficult this small service would be. She *couldn't* face Stonenden again. Katharine turned to tell Elinor so, and again met her tragic eyes. "All right," she heard herself say. "I shall speak to him as soon as possible."

Elinor jumped up and ran over to hug her. "Katharine! I knew you would. You are the most wonderful creature in the world. When will you see him?"

Smiling ruefully, the other glanced at the mantel clock. "Not tonight. It is too late. Tomorrow morning, first thing."

"But what if they fight tomorrow?"

Katharine looked vexed. "How stupid we were not to ask Tony when it is to be. But tomorrow is very soon. Surely they could not arrange it so fast. No, I believe I shall be in time."

Elinor clasped her hands before her. "You must be!"

ৎৎ৯

Katharine slept very poorly that night. Elinor could not be persuaded to leave them until very late, and when the Daltrys did finally get to bed, all the worries and awkwardness of her situation kept Katharine tossing and turning for hours. Repeatedly she cursed Tom Marchington and wished him at the other end of the earth. Then she wished that she herself had never come to London. She wondered how she could possibly face Lord Stonenden on the morrow, and at that point she realized that she had made no plan as to how this was to be accomplished. Under normal circumstances, if she wished to speak to a gentleman of her acquaintance, she would have written a note asking him to call on her. But somehow, she did not want to write Oliver Stonenden; it would only prolong her embarrassment.

Katharine sat up in bed and rubbed her eyes wearily. If only it were possible to encounter him as if by accident, quickly speak, and then escape. But this could not happen in time. She would have to seek him out, either by letter or in person. She squared her shoulders; she would call upon *him*, unconventional as that would be. It seemed infinitely easier to take action than to wait at home for a reply to a letter.

This decided, she lay back once more and tried to think what she would say. Nothing sensible occurred to her. She could ask him, of course, to withdraw from the duel. Perhaps he would do so. But then she would be obliged to him yet again, an intolerable position. She did not want to owe Oliver Stonenden anything. Why had she succumbed to Elinor's pleas? At this point, sleep finally overcame her, and thus

Katharine still had no idea what she would say when she awoke at eight the following morning.

As she dressed and tried to eat her breakfast, she continued to frame and reject various sentences in her mind. Nothing sounded right. And as she rode in her town carriage toward Lord Stonenden's house, she was still unprepared. She would trust to the pressure of the moment, she decided, to bring phrases to her lips.

It was not a lengthy journey. Long before she wished to be, Katharine was climbing down in front of the house, her footman knocking on the door. Almost before he finishing rapping, it was flung open. But instead of the servant she expected, Katharine found herself facing the Countess Standen, magnificently arrayed in a walking dress of pale green cloth and a towering hat trimmed with peacock feathers.

The countess seemed equally taken aback for a moment; then she smiled lazily and walked down the two steps to the street, shutting the door behind her. She stopped directly before Katharine and looked her up and down. Katharine immediately wished she had not worn her old gray morning gown.

"Why, Miss Daltry," said the countess. "What a *very* odd place to meet you."

Katharine was too shaken by the other woman's open exit from Stonenden's house at this early hour to answer her.

"Do you visit Oliver?" continued the other. "I fear he does not rise so early. You may have to wait." She smiled again, so insolently that Katharine nearly slapped her. But the intimate implication of her words had frozen her in one spot.

"Perhaps," continued Elise Standen, "you might even wish to reconsider your visit. Oliver is never in the best of tempers at this hour, and in any case, I'm not certain he is eager to see *you*." She looked sidelong at Katharine. "Have you come about your amusing painting? That was a clever ploy, really, but I fear Oliver was not overpleased by the gossip it caused. Sally Jersey does have a malicious tongue, doesn't she, the naughty creature."

"And a false one," Katharine managed.

"Oh, yes. But many others said the same. You know, Miss Daltry, it is always a mistake to pursue a man publicly. They hate it so, poor dears. And Stonenden more than most. You must hit upon a more subtle scheme if you want to take *him* in. Indeed, I don't know if that is possible."

Katharine was by this time trembling with rage. That anyone, and most of all the countess, should think her portrait had been an effort to captivate Stonenden was monstrous. And if, as the countess suggested, Stonenden himself now thought so, she had nothing but bitter contempt for the man.

"But I am keeping you," purred the other woman, moving a little aside. "I beg your pardon." Katharine was too angry to notice the subtly uneasy calculation in her green eyes as she spoke.

"Not at all," she choked. "I...I was mistaken. My business is not urgent. Pray excuse me." And she turned and ran blindly back to her waiting carriage.

Elise Standen, watching her with a complacent smile, thought how stupid young women were. The girl had never thought to question her statements;

she had believed every word, including the suggestion that the countess had left Lord Stonenden in his bedchamber. As if she would be so indiscreet! In fact, she had not found him home; he had gone off to an early race meeting outside London. She had been able only to leave a note and depart again. Still smiling, Elise Standen turned away, blessing yet again the luck which, since childhood, had helped her out of innumerable scrapes. If she had not been coming out the door at the very instant that knock sounded… She shrugged and hailed a passing hack.

In her own carriage, Katharine was struggling with tears and raging at herself for it. She would not cry, she insisted, over a man like Oliver Stonenden. If he was besotted by the Countess Standen, let him be! It was no concern of hers; she didn't care a rap. Indeed, her only wish was never to see him again as long as she lived.

It was at this point that she remembered Tom Marchington and the duel. Her encounter with Elise Standen had driven it right out of her head, but now her promise to Elinor resurfaced. How could she keep it?

Katharine sat up straighter and dried her eyes. She couldn't, not in the way she had said. It was impossible now for her to speak to Stonenden or to ask anything whatsoever of him. She would have to find another way of aiding her cousin, one which did not involve these things. She sat back in the seat to try to think.

Nineteen

By the time she reached home, Katharine had a plan. She went directly to her writing desk and dashed off a note, then sat down in the drawing room to await results. Mary was out, and she spent a restless hour before the bell was finally heard to ring below and the maid ushered in a guest.

"Hello, Tony," said Katharine then. "Thank you for coming so promptly. Sit down."

He did so. "What's happened? You sound grim. Is something wrong? Something new, that is?"

"No, nothing new. But I need some information from you."

Tony grinned, though his eyes remained wary. "Oh, information. I'm full of that."

"I want to know when and where this ridiculous duel is to take place." Knowing her request to be unconventional, Katharine fixed him with an unwavering gaze.

Tony frowned. "Why should you want to know that?"

"Never mind why. Just tell me, Tony."

He shrugged. "I'm not involved, you know. That sort of thing is settled by the seconds."

"Yes, but you know every secret in London. Stop being evasive, and tell me."

He looked at her. "What do you mean to do?"

"You needn't be concerned about that."

"I dashed well am concerned. I shall feel responsible if I tell you and then you get into some scrape."

"So you do know!"

Tony looked vexed.

"Tell me," repeated Katharine. "It is very important."

"You must say what you are going to do, first."

"No. Come, Tony, I am not a schoolgirl. I don't indulge in distempered freaks. You can trust me with this terrible secret."

He grinned in earnest this time. "Yes, that's what you think, but in your calm way you do far more unconventional things than any hoyden." Under her answering glare, he capitulated. "Oh, very well, I suppose it can't do any real harm. They are to meet tomorrow morning, out on the Heath."

"What time, precisely, and where?"

"Katharine—"

"Tony, I am asking your help in this small thing, and nothing more. I could find out what I want to know elsewhere, but it is far easier and pleasanter to ask you."

He acknowledged the truth of this with a sigh. "All right. At six. And I can direct you to the place, if you must know it."

"Thank you."

"But what *are* you planning, Katharine? I don't like the look in your eye."

"I shan't say. Then you can honestly claim that you haven't any idea, if anyone should ask you."

Tony groaned. "I can't decide whether I am glad of that, or sorry. I expect I shall be sorry before long."

"Nonsense. Now, tell me how to reach the place."

Reluctantly he did so, in the end sketching a map for her to use. With that in hand, she dismissed him and went up to her bedchamber to write a reassuring note to Elinor. Then she put on her bonnet once more and went out to make an unusual call. She returned home in time for luncheon, looking well satisfied, and afterward retired to her studio for the entire afternoon.

❧

The next morning, Katharine was up very early, dressed for riding. She had warned the stable that she meant to take out her mare first thing, and the horse was saddled and waiting when she came out, one of the grooms prepared to accompany her. They rode through the empty morning streets in the direction of Hampstead Heath. Katharine quickened the pace once they were away from the house, then suddenly paused at a corner some distance along the way. The groom looked puzzled, but being well trained, he said nothing.

In a short space, another rider appeared, a husky commercial-looking gentleman mounted on a brown hack. He raised his hat to Katharine, who greeted him briefly, and they continued on together, the groom looking more and more confused.

They reached the edge of the Heath as the sun was rising a few minutes before six. Katharine urged her mare to a canter and led the way along the road, up a lane, and finally off onto a track that looked as if it had seen little traffic lately. Here she slowed and motioned for silence.

They soon came to a small copse, and Katharine dismounted, leading her horse toward a tree where several others were already tied. Indicating that the groom should hold their mounts, she urged her other companion on with a gesture and began to walk swiftly around the trees to the clearing that could be just glimpsed beyond. Voices could be heard in that direction.

They emerged to find a curious scene. In the cool dawn light Tom Marchington stood with his coat buttoned up to his chin. He was facing them, but it was clear that he noticed nothing but Lord Stonenden, who stood with his back to Katharine not far away.

Three other men clustered on the left, their eyes on the two combatants. One of them was holding a handkerchief at arm's length. Katharine surged forward, but before she could voice the cry in her throat, the handkerchief dropped and two shots rang out. Smoke from the pistols floated in the cool air, but not so as to obscure Katharine's view. She had seen Lord Stonenden fire straight upward, and she had seen Tom aim directly at the other man and, appallingly, hit him!

"No!" she shouted, completing her cry and her step at the same time. "Tom, you fool!"

All of the men whirled to stare at her, but Katharine could think only of Stonenden. He had fallen to his knees at Tom's shot, and he remained there, holding his left forearm against his chest. Katharine ran to kneel beside him. "Are you all right?

Where are you hit?" In her concern, she put both hands on his upper arm.

Stonenden looked bemused. "What are you doing here?" A trickle of blood began to drip slowly from the lower edge of his coat sleeve.

"That doesn't matter. How badly are you hurt?" She started to turn back the sleeve.

"Here, here, let me," said someone behind her. "I am a doctor. Let me look."

"It's nothing," murmured Stonenden. "A scratch. The bullet grazed my forearm."

"I'll be the judge of that." The doctor knelt beside him as Katharine moved out of the way. He slit the sleeve and exposed a nasty deep scratch along Stonenden's forearm. "Hah," he said. "Not too bad. But why you gentlemen must stand up and shoot one another, I shall never understand. Pure madness." He opened his bag and began to work on the wound.

Somewhat reassured, Katharine turned on Tom. He stood in the same spot, the pistol dangling from his limp hand. He looked dazed and frightened. "You idiot!" exclaimed Katharine, marching up to him and pulling the gun away. "You might have killed him. Have you lost all common sense? Have you indeed gone mad? You *shot* a man, and for what?"

Tom blinked several times and seemed to focus on her finally. "Wh-what are you doing here?" He looked around nervously. "Elinor's not here, is she?"

"Of course she is not. Do you think me as stupid as you? She knows nothing about it. I came here for her, to try to stop you. Unfortunately, I was too late. Oh,

I am so angry I don't know what to say to you. How *could* you, Tom? How could you?"

"Do you want me to fetch a constable?" The man who had accompanied Katharine had approached, and it was he who spoke. "We can have him up on charges in a trice," he added.

Katharine sighed angrily. "I wish we might. But Elinor would never forgive me. You go scot-free, Tom. But you don't deserve it!"

"He fired in the air," murmured Tom, still seemingly amazed by this fact. "He didn't even try to hit me."

"Of course he did not! Lord Stonenden is a sensible man. You could force a quarrel on him, but you could not make him a fool like yourself."

This statement appeared to affect Tom powerfully, but whether for the good or bad, Katharine wasn't sure. He started as she spoke, looked around the clearing, then began to scowl.

The doctor had finished wrapping Stonenden's arm by this time, and the latter had risen to his feet. The whole group congregated ground Tom and Katharine, and one of the seconds said, "We are quits, then. We declare ourselves satisfied."

"Do we?" growled Tom.

"Yes, we do, Marchington. Or if you do not, I wash my hands of you. And you won't find anyone else to second you again, either."

Tom glowered at the ground.

"Come along," continued the other. "Let us go back to town and forget this ridiculous quarrel."

Tom seemed about to speak, but his second took his arm and forcibly propelled him toward where the horses were waiting. As they departed, the other second said, "I'll go fetch a carriage, Oliver. You can't ride with that arm."

"Nonsense, of course I can. I was only stunned for a moment. I am perfectly all right now."

"I would recommend a vehicle," put in the doctor. "The wound is slight, but—"

"I'll get one straightaway," replied the other, and he hurried off.

"I would also recommend that you sit down," the doctor went on.

"Oh, take yourself off," snapped his patient. "I shan't sit in this wet grass, if that is what you mean, and I am perfectly recovered. You may go in good conscience."

The man looked offended. "I shall certainly not leave until you have been conveyed safely home. I shall wait with the horses."

"Do so," retorted Stonenden.

The doctor walked away, and Lord Stonenden turned eagerly to Katharine, but his words and manner in the previous moments had brought back all her anger and outrage of the morning, and her face was stony. "I must go," she said.

He looked surprised. "At once?"

"Yes. I came only to stop this preposterous duel. I failed, and now I must go and inform Elinor that her doltish husband is unscathed."

"And what of me?" replied Stonenden.

Katharine looked up at him quickly, then dropped her eyes again. "I thank you, of course, for firing in the air. On behalf of my family."

"You can't have thought I would do anything else.

I met that young idiot only to teach him a lesson. I also failed, of course. He is remarkably hardheaded." His eyebrows came together. "In fact, why these alarms and excursions? Don't you think you might have left this affair to me?"

Realizing that she should have, but still very angry at him, Katharine tossed her head. "How was I to know that you would be magnanimous? You so rarely are. And besides, Tom might have actually killed you."

"I see. And you came to be sure that he got out of the country having done so, I suppose. Is that this gentleman's function?" He nodded at Katharine's companion, who was still standing nearby. The man tipped his hat and smiled ingratiatingly.

"No, of course not," snapped Katharine. "Mr. Rule is a private inquiry agent my father once mentioned to me. I brought him along in case I wanted to report to the authorities. Or to help me get Tom to come away, if he wouldn't."

Stonenden almost smiled. "Ah. And why did you not simply blow the whistle on us at once?"

Katharine looked icily up at him. "I am not such a cawker. I did not wish to have anyone arrested, but if that was the only way to stop you…"

He nodded. "Well, I admit I am glad it did not come to that. It would be humiliating to stand before a magistrate at my age and admit this silliness."

"You call a duel silliness?" She glared at him.

"Call it what you like. I don't seem to be able to find any phrase that pleases you."

Suddenly breathless at the pained understanding in

his eyes, Katharine turned away. "I must go back. If you will excuse me…"

"I appear to have no choice."

She glanced quickly over her shoulder, then strode away. Her feelings were in such turmoil that she could not continue to talk with him. She still felt anger, but it was now confusingly mingled with a great many other emotions, the foremost of which was admiration. He had behaved splendidly this morning; she could not but be conscious of that. And he had received nothing but a gunshot wound for his trouble. Yet he remained self-possessed and kind. His sharp words to the doctor she discounted; she hated to be fussed over herself. Indeed, as she had stood looking up at him, she had been suddenly possessed of a strong desire to walk into his arms and be held, forgetting all the confusions and misunderstandings of the last few days.

But with these feelings had come a vision of the Countess Standen as she had seen her yesterday, coming out of Stonenden's house in the early morning. And this picture destroyed the others. Perhaps Stonenden had changed; perhaps he was now a much more admirable man than he had been five years ago. But this had nothing to do with her. He might be kind to her and respect her talent, but his love went elsewhere.

With this thought, Katharine felt such a surge of misery that she almost stumbled. And in that moment, she knew that she had not been facing the truth about her emotions.

She loved Oliver Stonenden, despite the countess, despite everything. She had loved him for quite a time now. The feeling had been building without her conscious knowledge, during their pleasant hours in her studio, and now it was too powerful to be denied. Yet there was no hope in the world for it.

Reaching her horse, Katharine quickly mounted, and she was off down the lane almost before her groom could follow. In her turmoil, she was grateful for the loneliness of the Heath. She urged her mare to a wild gallop in an effort to wipe all thought from her mind.

She did not succeed. Her Cousin Mary's expression when she walked into the drawing room was enough to tell Katharine that. But Elinor Marchington was also there—she had called to be reassured yet again about Tom—so there was no chance for private conversation.

"Oh, Katharine, Tom went out before dawn this morning," said Elinor as soon as she saw her cousin. "I am so frightened. It must be—"

"Tom is all right," replied Katharine wearily. "The duel was this morning. I saw it. Tom went away unhurt."

"You saw it?" gasped the younger girl.

"Katharine!" echoed Mary Daltry.

Katharine sank into a chair and pulled off her hat. She was suddenly so exhausted she could hardly speak. "Yes. I went because there was nothing else to do. I hoped to stop it, but I didn't. Lord Stonenden is slightly wounded."

Elinor shrieked. Mary merely looked very steadily at her charge.

"It is all right," Katharine went on. "Only a scratch. Tom was very lucky that it was no more. He behaved abominably. He must be stopped, but I can't think how it may be done."

"B–but what will Lord Stonenden *do*?" asked Elinor.

"What do you mean?"

"He is such a…such a frightening man. Won't he try to get revenge on Tom? He might—"

"This 'frightening man,'" snapped Katharine, "fired in the air today, and he met your appalling husband only in the hopes of teaching him a lesson. He will *do* nothing. But *I* was tempted to deliver Tom to a magistrate, I may tell you, and see how he liked that."

Elinor quailed before the anger in her eyes. "I…I'm sorry," she murmured, clearly uncertain how she had offended.

"No, no, I am sorry, Elinor." Katharine rubbed her forehead with one hand. It seemed she couldn't bear to hear Stonenden criticized, a development which merely intensified her misery. "I am tired, I think. And discouraged. I wish I could think of some new way to help you."

But Elinor shook her head. "You have done so much. I could not ask any more of you, especially after today. No, I am beginning to think that Lady Agnes's visit was for the best after all. Tom will not listen to anyone here in London; perhaps he will listen to his father."

"Is Sir Lionel coming up to town, then?" asked Mary.

"Yes, I got a note today. He and Lady Agnes will arrive on Tuesday. It will be terrible." She shuddered. "I don't know how I will bear it. But I cannot think of anything else to try." She drooped a little, looking absurdly young. "Indeed, I am almost glad sometimes that they are coming. It seems to take a great burden off my shoulders. I need only manage through two more days, and then they will take over."

Katharine felt a certain relief herself. Though she deplored the elder Marchingtons' attitudes and methods, if they could control Tom now, she would forgive them a great deal. "I wish I might have helped you more," she told Elinor.

"Oh, no. You did too much as it was. And I do thank you."

"I don't see that I did anything," answered the other with a wry smile. "All my plans failed."

"But you kept up my spirits. And you taught me so much."

"I?"

"Yes, about how to act and what to think and… and everything!"

Katharine stared at her, astonished.

"You did, Cousin Katharine. Indeed, I don't feel nearly as low at the idea of seeing Tom's parents as I would have before."

"Well, I am glad of that. But I cannot think that I had much to do with it, Elinor. You have grown up a little, that is all." She thought of the shambles she had made of her own life and added, "I truly hope you have not taken me as your model. I make a poor one."

As Elinor protested this, Mary Daltry gazed quietly at Katharine, and when the younger girl took her leave a few minutes later, Mary came to sit closer to her cousin's chair, saying, "Tell me what is wrong, Katharine. I can see that it is something serious."

Katharine looked up, meeting her compassionate eyes. Her first thought was to evade the question

and escape to her bedchamber. She felt tears close
to surfacing. But the real sympathy she saw changed
her mind, making her realize that she needed to tell
someone about the turmoil she was experiencing.

Taking a breath, Katharine repeated what she had
discovered about herself that morning. It was very difficult to say. She faltered often, and once had to pause
to fight tears. But at last it was out. She bent her head
and drew a deep shaky breath.

"My dear..." said Mary, taking one of her hands
and squeezing it.

"Yes, it is a dreadful tangle, is it not? And I thought
myself immune to such things after Robert died."

"But, Katharine, why should it be so dreadful?
As you say, Lord Stonenden seems much improved.
He strikes me as an admirable man. And I do think
there may be some sort of misunderstanding about the
countess. He told me—"

"There is no misunderstanding. I have not told
you what happened when I tried to see him about the
duel." She proceeded to do so.

Mary Daltry frowned. "Are you certain...? Well,
but of course you are. I cannot explain it."

Katharine laughed hollowly. "I can. It is only too
obvious that Lord Stonenden is in love with the
countess. I daresay they may marry; she is a widow
now, after all. But even if they do not..." She spread
her hands. But despite her bitter certainty, she somehow hoped that Mary might contradict her, might see
some explanation that she had overlooked.

Mary, however, seemed lost in her own thoughts.
She appeared to be going over something in her mind,

pondering each step. "I don't know," she murmured to herself, "I simply do not know."

Katharine laughed shortly again and rose to her feet. "*I* know, though I truly wish I did not. I should never have entered society again. I knew it, but I let myself be persuaded. And the consequence is, I haven't helped Elinor one jot, and I have ruined myself." And with this, she ran from the room.

Twenty

MARY DALTRY WAS VERY QUIET DURING THE FOLLOW-
ing afternoon. Katharine hardly noticed; she was too
preoccupied with her own thoughts and, in any case,
she spent much of it shut in her studio. But she was
surprised when her older cousin decided to go out in
the evening.

"Well, dear," said Mary, looking a little self-
conscious, "it is Julia Anson's musical party, you know,
and I did promise her I would attend. It isn't important, of course, and if you wish me to stay with you…"

"Not at all. I am happy for you to go. I am poor
company and want only to brood alone. I suppose that
is why I was surprised."

Mary nodded and rose to go upstairs. "I shan't
be late."

When she came down a little later, pulling on her
gloves, Katharine heard her murmur to herself, "I
don't imagine he will even be there," as she passed the
drawing-room doorway. She wondered at this for a
moment, then forgot it as she was again overwhelmed
by more personal concerns.

Mary did not return particularly early, and Katharine was in bed by the time she let herself in and walked up to her bedchamber. But the older woman looked quite pleased with herself and not at all tired. She had accomplished what she set out to do, being fortunate in finding the person she sought. The resulting conversation had been eminently satisfactory—more than she had dared hope at the outset. In fact, she was nearly certain that both the problems overshadowing their family would soon be solved, and solved in ways very pleasant to contemplate. As she pulled the covers up to her chin sometime later, Mary smiled. "I *am* glad I went," she said to herself. "I was very right to do so."

She said nothing to Katharine about her outing, beyond agreeing, when asked, that it had been quite nice. But at breakfast, she initiated an uncharacteristic conversation. "You know, Katharine," she said as she poured out the tea, "I think we must go to Eliza Burnham's this evening. I saw her last night, and she was most insistent. She will be offended if we do not attend. It is her son's first appearance in society, you remember, and she is very anxious."

"I had forgotten all about it," answered Katharine. "But I cannot go."

"I know you don't wish to, Katharine. But it will look peculiar. Eliza is known to be your particular friend. It will seem as if you had quarreled if you do not go. You have attended so many unimportant occasions this season."

"I wish I had not! Oh, why did I not follow my own inclination instead of trying to interfere? I would have been so much happier."

Mary said nothing.

"I can't face them," pleaded Katharine. "There is the scandal over Tom, and over my poor picture, and now this duel. I cannot bear to be questioned in that horridly sweet way, with those sidelong glances. I can't, Mary!"

Her cousin looked distressed, but determined. "I understand how uncomfortable it is, dear, and I will help you avoid such people. But this evening is important to the Burnhams. I think you should go, if only for a little while."

Katharine rested her forehead on her hand. The truth was, she might have faced the gossip of the *ton*—she didn't care enough for society's opinion to be afraid of it—but she could not risk encountering Oliver Stonenden. She had the irrational conviction that if she saw him even once more, she would do something irredeemable. Then, abruptly, she remembered his wound. Though it had not been serious, surely he was not going out just yet, particularly not to a party such as Eliza's, which he would probably have avoided in any case. She was unlikely to see him there.

Katharine raised her head. "All right. I will go. But only for half an hour."

Mary's expression relaxed. "Certainly," she replied. And mentally she immediately began composing two notes, to be sent off directly after breakfast.

෴

Katharine dressed that evening with great reluctance. The quiet day she had spent had not made her any more eager to go to Eliza's. But she also took particular care, wanting to look her best for all the eyes that would certainly be on her. And when she looked in the mirror before leaving her bedchamber, she felt some satisfaction; no one, seeing her, would guess that she felt quite miserable. She had chosen a striking gown of coquelicot satin, which highlighted the deep brown of her hair and intensified the amber of her eyes. The dress would call attention to her, which was unfortunate, but it also made her look vibrantly lovely, which should discourage those who thought her practically in a decline over the occurrences of the past weeks. Her ornaments were of old gold, and they made the costume richer still.

When she went down to the drawing room, Mary surveyed her approvingly. "Lovely, dear," she said. "It is so good to be out of mourning at last, is it not?"

Katharine nodded absently. "Shall we go? We may as well get this over."

"Of course. The carriage is ready."

They said little on the drive, though Mary glanced at her cousin several times, and they arrived at Lady Burnham's town house in good time. Several other vehicles were discharging passengers as they climbed down, but to Katharine's relief, none were close acquaintances. They greeted Eliza warmly and walked into her drawing room, which was already filling. Andrew Burnham was holding court in one corner, surrounded by a large group of young people. Katharine waved at him. He grinned and returned her salute.

"Shall we sit down?" said Katharine then, looking for an inconspicuous place.

Mary agreed, and they found chairs near the windows. Katharine examined the crowd for people she wished at all costs to avoid, among them Lord Stonenden, Lady Jersey, and the Countess Standen. Though she did not think the gentleman would appear, the two ladies were only too likely to be present, and she could not bear the idea of talking to either of them.

More guests arrived, and the room filled so completely that it was impossible to see everyone. Lady Burnham's son Andrew came over to them and chatted until he was pulled away by one of his friends, who wished him to convince his mother to allow a little dancing. He went laughing, promising to return.

"A charming boy," said Mary when he was gone.

"He is, isn't he? Eliza should be proud."

"Indeed. There is Eliza, by the by. I believe she is coming to speak to us."

Katharine smiled. "I'll tell her she needn't include us in her rounds. She must be quite distracted trying to talk to everyone."

"Katharine! Mary!" Lady Burnham sank down in a vacant chair beside them. "I'm exhausted. Is it going well? I haven't dared look."

"Very well," Katharine assured her, her smile broadening. "Andrew is behaving charmingly."

"He is a dear boy, isn't he?" Eliza searched the crowd for her son, who was again the center of a laughing group. "He always seems so happy; he has since he was a child."

"He is very lucky."

"Yes." Eliza seemed to think of something and

straightened. "But, Katharine, I came over because I particularly want to show you something."

"Now?"

"Yes. Come with me, will you? You will excuse us, Mary?"

"Of course." Mary met Eliza Burnham's bland gaze with a look just as innocent.

"But you are so occupied," protested Katharine, as she also rose. "I could call on you tomorrow."

"No, dear, I must show you now. Come."

Katharine followed Eliza across the drawing room and down a hallway to the back parlor. There the older woman paused, then said, "Someone may come in. Let us sit down in the writing room." And she walked through a curtained archway into a very small chamber beyond. The tiny room was nearly filled by two chairs and an aged writing desk. "Yes, we will be very private here," Eliza added. She sat down and opened her reticule. "I have it here." She searched through the meager contents of the bag. "Now, where is it? I distinctly recall putting it in my reticule." She searched further. "It's gone." With an angry sigh, she rose. "I must have left it on my dressing table. Wait here a moment, Katharine, and I will fetch it."

Rather amused, Katharine said, "What is this mysterious object?"

"I must show you. You will wait?"

"Of course, Eliza."

"Good. I shan't be long." And she passed through the curtains again and was gone.

Katharine looked around the room, but there was little to amuse her. A broken pen lay on the desk, along with a few sheets of stationery, and there was a single dog-eared copy of the *Spectator* on the other chair. The branch of candles Eliza had brought in hardly illuminated the chamber, and Katharine was about to get up and move into the parlor to wait when she heard voices approaching and shrank back. She didn't want to meet anyone in this isolated room, for she might be trapped by some inquisitive person and be unable to escape.

Accordingly, when the newcomers entered the parlor, Katharine shamefacedly pushed back the edge of the curtain and peeked out at them. Perhaps it was Eliza, waylaid as she returned, or some other friend she would not mind meeting. But to Katharine's consternation, the couple in the outer room turned out to be Lord Oliver Stonenden and the Countess Standen.

She immediately let the hanging drop from her fingers and inched away from the opening. The two people she most wished to avoid, and she was trapped by them! There was no exit except through the parlor, and though she tried to steel herself to rush out with a hurried excuse, she found it quite impossible. She could do nothing but return to her chair and huddle there, hoping that they would leave or that Eliza would return to rout them.

Thus it was that she could not help but overhear the conversation between the man she loved and his mistress. The very idea made her flush scarlet—it was so low and dishonest—but her only other choice was insupportable.

Stonenden and the countess seemed to be continuing a dispute begun earlier. "You must send him about his business," the man was saying. "You must tell him precisely what you think of him, in unmistakable terms, and rid us of this embarrassment. I cannot tolerate this sort of thing any longer."

"Did he really shoot you?" replied Elise Standen softly. She sounded not altogether displeased by the idea. "Over me?"

"I have told you that he did. And he has made a spectacle of you and of himself. It must be stopped."

"Yes." The countess sighed audibly. "But you know, Oliver, it is so gratifying to be admired by a man fifteen years younger than oneself. It gives me such a lift."

"Doubtless." Stonenden's voice was dry. "But we have been over this before. If you prefer his attentions to those of older, more experienced men, there is nothing more to be said."

There was a rustle of silk. "You know I do not," murmured Elise caressingly.

"Well, then, send the boy on his way."

"And if I do?" This was spoken so softly that Katharine could barely hear it. She wished she had not.

"Then the field will be clear," answered Stonenden.

"Yes." The countess was clearly dissatisfied with this reply.

"I am weary of this discussion, Elise," added the man. "Very weary. In fact, I don't believe I wish to have it again. You must do as you please, but I cannot be expected to tolerate young Marchington any further. And, by one means or another, I shan't."

"Yes, I know, I know. All right. I will speak to him at the first opportunity."

"Splendid."

There was another rustle. "It will be wonderful to be together without *any* annoyances, won't it, Oliver?"

"I have never managed to live without annoyances," he said.

"Oh, why are you always so—?" But before the countess could complete her complaint, new voices were heard approaching the parlor. Katharine recognized Eliza's, and sighed with relief.

But Eliza was evidently not alone, for as she entered the outer room, she was saying, "I believe I saw them come in here. Yes, here they are, Tom. And if you will excuse me, I must check on the ices. I hope they are not spoiled in this heat."

There was a silence. Katharine sat frozen with astonishment. Eliza knew she was in here! Why had she abandoned her in this horribly embarrassing position?

Beyond the curtain, Tom Marchington said, "So!"

"Very dramatic," replied Lord Stonenden approvingly. "You know, Marchington, you really belong on the stage."

"You…you blackguard," retorted Tom. "You have lured the countess in here alone, but I shall—"

"Hardly lured. Eh, Elise? But the countess has something to say to you, Marchington. Go ahead, Elise."

There was a silence. Katharine could imagine the expressions on the faces of the three in the other room. The countess was obviously still reluctant to speak. Finally she said, "Tom, I believe we have made a mistake. I think the…the feeling we imagined we had for one another—"

"Imagined?" roared Tom so loudly that Katharine worried he might be heard in the drawing room.

"The countess of course speaks for herself," offered Stonenden helpfully. Katharine bit her lip to keep from giggling. This situation, though intolerable, had its elements of farce. How *could* Stonenden talk in that mocking way, under the circumstances?

"You keep out of this," growled Tom.

"The truth is," put in the countess, "that I wish you would leave me alone, Tom. I was mistaken."

"You deny all the things you said to me?"

"Well, really, Tom, I never promised anything. We had a charming flirtation; we both enjoyed it, but it was no more than that. And these things must come to an end."

Though this was remarkably like something Katharine remembered Tom saying, he responded with an inarticulate growl of rage. "*He* is making you say this," he said. "He has some sort of hold over you, and he is forcing you to give me up. But I won't let it happen."

"Tom, really." The countess sounded both annoyed and a bit amused. "It is nothing like that. I did not want to hurt you, but the truth is that I have simply wearied of your company. I'm sorry, but it happens."

"Does it? And I suppose Stonenden had nothing to do with this change?"

"You flatter me, Marchington," said the other man. "Do you want to add to the gossip with which you have surrounded the Countess Standen? Do try to behave like a gentleman."

"Of course he had nothing to do with it," added Elise, sounding much struck by Stonenden's remark. "Now, Tom—"

"I don't believe you," shouted Marchington. There was a scuffling sound; then he added, "You do love me. I know it!"

"Tom, let me go. You are tearing my gown. Let me go!"

"Here, now," said Stonenden. "None of that."

There was another scuffle. Katharine, unable to resist, pushed back the edge of the curtain very slightly. She could see them all. The countess was disheveled and looked outraged; Tom, very red, was panting and clenching and unclenching his fists before her; and Lord Stonenden stood a little back, surveying the others with what appeared to be sardonic amusement.

"You bumpkin!" cried the countess then. "You clumsy countrified lout! How dare you assault me? Get out of my sight. You were never more than mildly amusing, and now you are not even that. Get out!"

"But…" Tom looked stunned.

"Do you think I ever cared for you for a moment?" the woman continued, her temper out of control. "What vanity! I was amused to have a young man among my admirers, and I was doubly entertained by the antics of your *so outraged* family. But that is all. Now, go away and leave me alone."

Tom stared at her. Stonenden watched him curiously. "You…you slut," sputtered the former.

"Get out," repeated Elise.

"Oh, I mean to. A bumpkin, am I? A lout? Well, I should far rather be either of those than what you are. How could I have thought I loved you? You are cruel and contemptible."

"Your opinion is of no interest to me," replied the countess icily.

"That's lucky," said Tom with a short laugh, "because if anyone should ask me, I shall give it them. What a fool I have been." And with one final glare at both the others, he turned and stalked out.

There was a pause. Then Elise took a breath and turned meltingly to Lord Stonenden. "There, I have done as you asked."

"You certainly have," he said dryly, "with a vengeance."

"He made me angry."

"I could see that."

"I can't bear to be mauled about."

"I believe I can promise never to do so."

"Oliver, you are so cold. I have done what you wanted."

Before Stonenden could reply, another couple came into the parlor, followed by several more young people looking for a set of loo counters. Katharine thought Lord Stonenden looked disproportionately annoyed by these intrusions, but she herself was very relieved. She could not have endured watching a tender scene between those two.

After a while, when the others did not leave at once, the countess urged Stonenden away. He went with patent reluctance. And Katharine, choosing a moment when everyone's back was turned, was able to slip out of the writing room and back to the party. She did not encounter Stonenden there, for which she was grateful, and she paused only to gather Mary before leaving the house for home.

She would have gone with a very different attitude

could she have witnessed the conclusion of the scene in the parlor, which was just then being played out in Lady Burnham's breakfast room. Countess Standen had coaxed Stonenden there and thrown herself into his arms. But he, far from welcoming her advances, pushed her away again.

"Oliver," she exclaimed. "No one will interrupt us here."

"It isn't that, Elise."

"What, then?"

He shrugged. "I fear you have taken certain things for granted which are not, in fact, the case."

She stepped back and stared up at him, magnificent in white lace over a petticoat of dark green satin. "What do you mean?"

"My interest in this…ah, affair, was only to remove Tom Marchington from your influence."

The countess's eyes narrowed. She looked at him carefully, then hissed, "You rotten…"

"I never said anything else, if you will recall. I promised nothing."

"But you suggested a great deal," she retorted. "You know you did."

"I used your own methods against you, yes. I don't apologize for that. If you had kept to your own sphere, to men who know and understand the rules of your games, I would not have interfered. But young Marchington did not."

"Don't prate of games to me! It had nothing to do with Tom, that's obvious. It's the girl, isn't it? I suspected it when you had that ridiculous portrait done. This whole charade was for her."

Stonenden turned a little away. "I have nothing more to say. You have gotten no more than you deserved."

"Indeed? Well, it is not that easy to cast me off, *my lord*. You will be sorry for this piece of meddling. More than sorry!" He shrugged and started to walk out of the room. "You don't believe me?"

"I have no time for your threats, Elise. I thought to apologize, but your behavior makes that impossible. Good-bye."

"Blackguard!" she called after him, but he did not turn again. He walked deliberately down the corridor and back to the drawing room as if nothing out of the ordinary had occurred.

In the doorway, Eliza Burnham met him, asking eagerly, "Did it work? Katharine and Mary have gone. I did not get to speak to them again."

Stonenden shook his head. "We were interrupted too soon."

"Oh, no. I *tried* to keep people away."

He shrugged. "It was too public a place. I shall have to explain it all to her face-to-face. She will believe me. She must."

"Of course she will. Shall I go to her first? I could—"

"No. I have been too indirect as it is. I shall call tomorrow and make her see me."

Lady Burnham gazed up at him, a spark of admiration in her eyes. "Yes. Yes, I think that might be best."

Twenty-one

KATHARINE AND MARY'S BREAKFAST-TABLE CONVERSA-
tion was a trifle odd the next morning. They had
hardly spoken on the short drive home, and Katharine
had hurried directly up to bed upon their return. So
this was the first real exchange since the party. Mary
was bright and eager, full of questions about the
evening, while Katharine was heavy-eyed and silent.
She had spent a very restless night and felt miserable.
Indeed, she could not understand, and could barely
tolerate, Mary's cheerfulness.

"It was an enjoyable evening, was it not?" said
Mary when her cousin appeared.

Katharine nodded and slid into her chair.

"Andrew was looking so well. And of course there
were a great many *interesting* people present."

Katharine poured a cup of tea and drank it, surveying the food on the table with revulsion.

Mary began to be puzzled. "Did you not think so?"
she added. "I heard several fascinating conversations.
Did you?"

Startled, she met her cousin's eager eyes. Could

Mary have discovered her inadvertent eavesdropping? But how? No, her remark must be merely a coincidence. "It was a pleasant enough party," she answered. "A bit tedious, as *ton* parties often are, even Eliza's."

Mary frowned. "But did you not…that is…" She was prevented from completing this sentence by the entrance of one of the maids. "Pardon me, miss," said the servant, "but a man brought this note from Mrs. Marchington. He says it's very important, and he insisted on waiting for an answer."

"What can be amiss now?" said Katharine, tearing open the envelope. As she read, she sighed. "Sir Lionel and Lady Agnes have arrived. Elinor sounds near hysterics. She begs me to go to her, and I suppose I must."

"Oh, dear. Shall I go instead?"

"No, she asks for me particularly. She was most impressed with the way I spoke to Lady Agnes on her last visit. Of course, it is easy for me to be courageous. She is not my mother-in-law." She rose. "I shall go at once."

"Very well. But you've hardly eaten anything."

"I'm not hungry." Katharine went out, leaving her cousin frowning after her.

At the Marchington town house, Katharine found utter confusion. The maid who let her in was carrying a huge armful of linen, and in the drawing room a number of people seemed to be shouting at once.

These voices gradually resolved themselves into three as she approached the doorway. She recognized Lady Agnes's piercing tenor and Tom Marchington's sulky tone; the third, a bellowing bass, she took to be Sir Lionel.

She was correct. Tom's father stood on the hearth rug, his legs spread well apart, his hands clasped under his coattails. He was a tall, beefy man, with a shock of white hair and an alarmingly high-colored complexion, and just now he was shouting, "You will come home with us at once. At once, do you hear me?"

"That is what I mean to do," answered Tom. He looked strained, as well he might.

"Disgraceful!" continued Sir Lionel. "I would not have believed it of you. But it shall stop. I'll have no argument on that head. You are coming home."

"Tom has said he will, Lionel," put in Lady Agnes.

"What? What's that? He will?" Sir Lionel's expression was comical; he looked like a bulldog who has just discovered that squirrels can climb trees.

His wife nodded grimly. "I don't know why he has changed his mind, but he says he has."

At this point, Elinor noticed Katharine and came hurrying from the corner to greet her. "I am so glad you came," she gasped. "Sir Lionel and Lady Agnes arrived only an hour ago. I thought there would be a terrible row, but Tom seems ready to do as his father asks. We should have written him at first, I suppose." She looked doubtful. "Though he does shout so."

Katharine refrained from telling her the true reason for Tom's change of heart. She couldn't bear to speak of it. "Everything is all right, then?"

"Oh, no. They are all very angry still. But they haven't yet hit upon a subject to dispute. They will find one."

Katharine glanced at her cousin with amused

surprise, but Elinor seemed unconscious of any humorous element in her words.

In the next moment, Sir Lionel appeared to gain his second wind. "How do you explain yourself, eh?" he said to Tom. "You've been a proper jackanapes. We did not educate you to play the fool over the first lightskirt you encountered."

"Lionel!" exclaimed Lady Agnes, gesturing toward the girls.

Sir Lionel peered in their direction, obviously mystified by Katharine's presence, and added, "Sorry. I'm a plain man. I speak the truth without wrapping it in clean linen. Tom has been an idiot."

"Very well!" shouted Tom, goaded. "So I *have* been an idiot. I admit it! But men have made mistakes before this. Must we go on talking about it forever? I am ready to go home and turn over a new leaf. Is that not enough?"

Sir Lionel looked thwarted, his wife offended, and Elinor sympathetically doubtful. Katharine struggled not to laugh.

"I have done all I can," he went on. "Why can't you leave me alone?"

There was a pause; Sir Lionel's jaw worked. Katharine was suddenly moved to ask, "Have you apologized to Elinor?"

All four of them turned to stare at her.

"Who the blazes are you?" snapped Sir Lionel.

"I am Katharine Daltry, Elinor's cousin. And it seems to me that none of you have had a proper concern for Elinor's feelings in this matter."

The elder Marchingtons shifted their eyes to

Elinor, who shrank back with a piteous look of reproach at Katharine.

"You're right," responded Tom Marchington unexpectedly. "I've treated Elinor abominably these last weeks. In fact, she has a great deal more to complain of than you, Papa, Mama. But she is too gentle and kind to do so." He walked over and took Elinor's hand. "I am sorry, Elinor. I think I must have been mad. Can you forgive me?"

"Oh, Tom—"

"Don't answer him!" interrupted Lady Agnes. "He has no right to expect forgiveness just yet."

Her son glared at her, and Elinor, clinging to his hand, stoutly added, "Of course I forgive you."

Lady Agnes threw up her hands and turned away. "Young people today," Sir Lionel told her. "No backbone."

His wife nodded grimly. "We must pack your things immediately. We go home today."

"But we cannot be ready so soon," exclaimed Elinor.

"Nonsense. I shall speak to the servants."

Lady Agnes sailed out of the room, and Sir Lionel growled, "Tom, I want to speak to you privately."

It seemed for a moment that Tom would resist, but then he bowed his head and answered, "Come into the study, sir."

"That was not so very bad," said Katharine to her cousin when they were gone.

Elinor heaved a great sigh. "No, but it will get worse, and go on and on. How I wish that we need not go home just now. If only we might travel, or even go to Bath for a little while."

"I daresay this whole affair will be forgotten in two or three weeks' time," replied Katharine encouragingly.

"You do not know the Marchingtons. And my mother is taken up with the younger children." Elinor drooped, and then appeared to be struck by a new idea. "Katharine, would you come home with us, for a visit? I can bear anything if you are there to support me."

Appalled, Katharine shook her head. "Oh, no. I…I cannot. And besides, you and Tom will not want visitors just now. You will wish to be alone together."

"But that is just what we won't be. The dower house, where we are to live, isn't ready. There were a great many repairs to be made. We shall have to stay with Lady Agnes and Sir Lionel for weeks! Katharine, please come."

The idea of staying with the elder Marchingtons made the request even less palatable. Katharine shook her head again. "I cannot, Elinor. I am sorry. I have tried to help you, but—"

"Of course. You have done so much, I have no right to ask anything more. I'm sorry."

At her woebegone expression, Katharine nearly gave in. Could she make a short visit? But a vision of Lady Agnes rose before her eyes, and she shuddered. "I'm sorry," she repeated. There was a short silence; then Katharine added that she should return home. "Call upon me if I can help with your departure," she said, feeling as if she were condemning a friend to prison.

Elinor nodded, and she took her leave.

Mary met her cousin at the door when she reached

home, eager for news. When Katharine had told her what had occurred, she clucked her tongue. "They do not sound particularly suited to managing a lively young man."

"You are a master of understatement, Cousin," laughed Katharine. "I predict another shouting match before the day is out. But there is nothing further I can do. Elinor asked me to come home with her, but I could not."

"Oh, no. She and Tom must solve this for themselves."

"As they would, I think, if they were not forced to live in the same house as Tom's parents."

"Are they? Oh, dear."

"Only for a while, fortunately. I daresay things will be better when they have their own establishment. But I can do nothing in the meantime."

"No," repeated Mary. Then, looking a bit self-conscious, she added, "Lord Stonenden called while you were out. He was very disappointed not to find you. He said he would return late this afternoon."

Katharine had frozen at the mention of Stonenden's name. Now she looked at the floor. "What did he want?"

Mary assumed a rather unconvincing innocent expression. "I don't know, dear."

But Katharine was not looking at her cousin. "Perhaps he wishes to pay me what he owes for the portrait," she replied. With a bitter laugh, she started up the stairs. "It's time he did, too."

Mary looked after her, shook her head, and turned toward the back of the house. Midmorning was the time she always consulted with the cook about the next day's meals, and she could not see that varying her routine would help matters today.

When she had taken off her bonnet, Katharine settled in the drawing room. She was too restless to think of painting. In fact, she soon found that she was too restless to do anything at all. She tried to read, but her book seemed wholly without interest this morning, and she finally gave it up and sat staring blindly at the opposite wall.

She was still in this position when she heard the bell ring below and the front door open. At once she was on her feet. Could this be Stonenden again, already? She could not see him! Hoping to escape unobserved, Katharine crept to the drawing-room door and out onto the landing, but before she could get across it and away, she heard footsteps on the stairs and a female voice saying, "Miss Daltry. How fortunate. I hoped to find you in."

Turning, Katharine was astonished and dismayed to see the Countess Standen following one of the maids up the staircase.

"I must talk to you for a moment," the countess went on. "It is rather urgent."

Unable to reply, Katharine gestured toward the drawing room and led the visitor there. The maid bobbed a curtsy and left them alone.

"I must first apologize for the way I spoke when we last met," began the countess. She made a charming helpless gesture. "What you must think of me, coming here after that, I don't know. But you see, I was so upset. Now, things have changed, and I am sincerely sorry."

"Pray think nothing more about it," replied Katharine frigidly.

"You are kind. I really was dreadful. But all is well now."

What did she mean? Katharine wondered. What had changed? She shrugged.

"Thank you." Elise Standen settled herself gracefully on the sofa. "I wanted to talk to you today about Oliver's portrait. It is really quite good, you know." She looked up, seeming to expect an answer, but got none. "He was pleased with it. I know, because we were talking about it only the other day. In fact, he suggested that I have a companion picture done." The countess smiled charmingly. "For the future, you know, so that they will match."

Katharine opened her mouth, but no words came out. The other woman's implication was unmistakable. The only reason to request a companion portrait was if the two were to hang together. And if this was the case, Lord Stonenden must have offered for the countess. "I...I am not doing any more portraits," she finally managed to croak.

"Not...?" Her caller was all bland surprise. "But why? And surely you could make an exception in this case? You would not want an inferior painting hung with yours."

For a brief instant Katharine allowed herself to imagine painting the countess. It would be glorious to trace every little line, every cruel twist in her superficially lovely face. She could do a portrait that would reveal to the world the sort of woman Elise Standen really was. But she suppressed the impulse. It was impossible. And in any case, such a picture would never be seen. "I'm sorry," she answered, more in control of herself now.

"I, too." The countess smiled again. "But I will not give up so easily. Perhaps if I brought Oliver to add his pleading to mine?"

This made Katharine wince. "It would do no good. I...I am going out of town shortly, and I am not certain when I shall return."

Countess Standen's green eyes lit. "Indeed? Where do you go?"

"To visit friends. It doesn't matter. But I cannot paint a portrait."

"Yes, I see. Well, it is too vexing. Perhaps when you return?"

"I may be away for quite some time."

"Ah. And we should like it as soon as possible. Well, I am very disappointed, Miss Daltry."

Katharine looked at the floor.

"You won't change your mind?"

The younger girl shook her head.

"Perhaps you are still angry with me, and that is why you refuse my request."

"My feelings are irrelevant. And now, if you will excuse me, I am rather busy today."

"Making ready for your journey?"

"Yes."

"When do you go?" The countess eyed her speculatively.

"I am not... Today!"

Her visitor's eyes lit once again. "Oh, then I mustn't keep you. Good day, my dear."

Katharine muttered some reply, and as soon as the

countess had gone, ran up to her bedchamber and began to stuff clothes into a portmanteau. She could not remain in town and witness Lord Stonenden's marriage to that hateful woman. She would go with Elinor. Nothing could be worse than staying, not even the Marchingtons.

It did not take her long to pack. In less than half an hour she was looking for Mary to tell her what she meant to do. Her cousin, naturally, was astonished. "Go with Elinor? But, Katharine, just this morning, you said—"

"I know, but I have changed my mind. I think it would do me good to stay in the country for a while."

Seeing the portmanteau behind her, Mary exclaimed, "But are you going now? Today?"

"I know it is sudden. But the Marchingtons go at once, and I...I want to. You will take care of things here, will you not, Mary?"

"But I should accompany you."

"No. I could not ask you to prepare in such a flurry. And I shall be perfectly safe. You may come down later, if you wish."

"But, Katharine..."

"I have made up my mind." She picked up her bonnet from the hall table and put it on. "Good-bye, dear Mary. I shall write to you very soon. Don't worry."

"You make that rather difficult," replied her cousin with some asperity. "Did anyone call while I was below-stairs? Lord Stonenden, perhaps?"

"No, indeed. Why should he?" Katharine's tone was savage. "But if he does, you may tell him that I absolutely refuse his request."

"Refuse?" Mary blinked.

"Absolutely! Good-bye, Mary." Katharine dropped a kiss on her cousin's cheek, picked up her portmanteau, and was out the front door before the other could speak. She did not even wait for her carriage to be brought round.

"But how can she refuse him?" said Mary to herself. "She doesn't even know... Oh, I wonder, what has happened?"

Twenty-two

THE JOURNEY DOWN TO THE MARCHINGTONS' WAS unpleasant but, fortunately, short. Katharine rode in the traveling carriage with Lady Agnes and Elinor. The former had not been overpleased to learn that she would be receiving a guest at this delicate time, but Elinor had found the courage to insist, and her mother-in-law had finally given in with an angry shrug. Elinor herself was delighted to escape hours of Lady Agnes's sole company, as Tom and his father always traveled on horseback. As for Katharine, she was too miserable to pay much heed to the others. She spent most of the trip staring out the coach window and wondering if the pain she felt at this moment would ever ease.

They reached the house late in the afternoon and spent the time before dinner settling in. Katharine was given a pleasant bedroom in the same wing as Elinor's, looking out over a garden bursting with flowers. She unpacked her few things quickly, noting that she would have to send to town for more of her wardrobe, and then went to the window seat and stared blankly out, trying to decide what she should do. She could not continue living in London after what had happened these last weeks. Even if she stopped going out and returned to her former habits, she could not force herself to forget Lord Stonenden and his new wife. And, more than likely, she would sometimes encounter them, for she could not become a hermit—she had never wished that. No, it would be best for her to leave the city.

Perhaps she could travel. She had always wanted to see Italy, and Paris. Mary would accompany her; they could make a grand tour. But even as she thought this, Katharine sighed. A plan which once would have thrown her into ecstasies now seemed without attractions. In fact, nothing seemed right at this moment, and she could think of nothing she wanted to do or see in the entire world.

There was a tap on her door, and Elinor looked in. "I wanted to make sure you were comfortable," she said. "Do you like this room? Would you prefer another?"

"No, this is fine," replied Katharine.

Her cousin came farther into the room. "I also wanted to thank you again for coming, Katharine. It is so good of you. It will make a vast difference to me to have you here." She eyed Katharine's dour expression anxiously. "We need not stay in the house all the time, you know. We can go walking and riding, just the two of us. I hardly see Lady Agnes during the day; she is always busy with her housekeeping or one of her committees. She…she is very active in the neighborhood."

Katharine smiled a little. "If I know Lady Agnes, she *runs* the neighborhood."

Elinor giggled. "Well, she does. Or she would like to, at least. Her great rival, Lady Munsbury, is continually trying to outdo her."

Katharine grimaced. "Well, we need not become entangled in that, at least. But I must certainly call on your family while I am down here, Elinor."

"Oh, yes. Mama would be so happy to see you. We can go tomorrow, if you like. It is only six miles."

"You will be glad to see your mother," suggested Katharine.

"Oh, yes. Particularly if George has recovered; she is so distracted when one of the children is ill, she doesn't hear one word in three."

There was a pause. Both girls were lost in their own thoughts. Then a gong sounded below, and Elinor jumped. "That is the first bell for dinner. We must be down in half an hour. Oh, dear, Lady Agnes hates unpunctuality, and I have still to change."

"I too. I will meet you downstairs."

"Yes." At the door, Elinor turned back. "It really was *splendid* of you to come, Katharine," she said, and went out.

Katharine shook her head as she went to the wardrobe to get out her dinner dress. If Elinor knew the true reason for her coming, she would not, perhaps, think her so splendid. She might even, as Katharine herself did, label her cousin as sadly inept.

Dinner was stiff. Lady Agnes and Sir Lionel sat at opposite ends of a long polished table, saying little and eating heartily. Tom, on one side, did not speak at all, and Elinor, on the other, was very subdued. Katharine tried at first to start some uncontroversial conversation, but no one responded, and she soon subsided into silence as well. Her position was decidedly awkward. Her hostess clearly did not welcome her presence, and though Elinor certainly had some right to invite guests of her own, Lady Agnes made the imposition very evident in her manner. Katharine was relieved when the older woman rose and signaled the departure of the ladies. In the drawing room, one could at least read or try the pianoforte, away from Lady Agnes's piercing eye.

She and Elinor played a duet, and then Elinor played while Katharine sang a ballad. In this way, they managed to pass the time until the gentlemen came in. The strain between Tom Marchington and his father kept them from lingering over their wine.

Tom came directly to Elinor when he walked in. "Would you like to walk in the garden a little?" he said to her.

"Oh." Elinor looked at Katharine. "Well, I…"

"What a good idea," responded the latter. "I was just going upstairs to write a letter to Mary. Good night."

Both of the young people looked at her gratefully, and Katharine preceded them out of the room, saying good night to the older Marchingtons as she went. But when she reached her bedchamber, she did not go to the writing desk; rather, she sat again in the window and gazed out.

She saw Tom and Elinor strolling arm in arm down one of the paths. Tom was talking very earnestly. They sat down on a bench, and he leaned forward, occasionally punctuating his discourse with a gesture. Elinor answered at intervals, briefly. After about a quarter of an hour, Tom paused and took his wife's hand, looking down at her. Elinor hesitated, then flung her arms around Tom's neck.

Katharine rose and turned away, at once happy that the two had reached a new understanding and dispirited by her own solitary state. She shook herself and went resolutely across to the desk. She had promised to write to Mary, and she would do so. Self-pity did no one any good; it was far better to keep occupied.

The following day passed very slowly for Katharine. She went with Elinor to call on her family, and enjoyed the visit with her rather absentminded aunt, walked in the garden, tried to read two different novels, walked again, down to a stream behind the house, and finally returned to her bedchamber, amazed to find that it was only four o'clock. Boredom, added to unhappiness, was insupportable, and she berated herself for leaving her painting things behind in London. She could have sketched and done watercolors, at least, if she had them. She determined to ask Elinor if they had any paints in the house. But she also realized that she could not remain with the Marchingtons very long. A week was the most she could stand; she would break the news to Elinor tomorrow.

Dinner was a repetition of the previous day's meal, though Tom and Elinor did talk a bit more. Afterward, Katharine took a shawl and went outside. She was not at all tired, and she hoped to walk until she was ready for sleep. But the solitary stroll merely gave her more time to think of her own problems, and she soon went back in to challenge Sir Lionel to a game of backgammon. She had been told that he was very fond of the game, and so it appeared from his eager acceptance; to Katharine it seemed as good a way as any to get through the evening.

The next day began for Katharine with a sense of despair. It was with her when she woke, and stayed as she washed and dressed and started down to breakfast. She was, she admitted to herself, wholly miserable.

Thus engrossed in her own unhappiness, she did not hear the sounds of a carriage outside the house, and only when the front door was opened as she descended the stairs did she look up. "Mary!" she exclaimed then. "What are you doing here?"

Mary Daltry gazed up at her. "I came to see you, of course. I must talk to you. But first, I would appreciate some breakfast. I started out before dawn. Do you think Lady Agnes would be so good?"

Katharine raised her eyebrows a little at her cousin's truculent tone, but she said, "Of course. Leave your hat and come with me. I was just going in to breakfast. We will send the maid to tell Lady Agnes of your arrival."

Mary laughed shortly. "That will please her, I imagine."

Elinor was already in the breakfast room, so they had no private conversation during the meal. The girl was happy to see Mary, and chattered pleasantly; her spirits had improved a great deal since her talk with Tom in the garden. When they had finished, Mary pushed back her chair and said, "Come for a walk, Katharine. I want to talk to you."

Mystified, Katharine got her hat, and they went out together. Mary led her to a secluded bench at the back of the garden and sat down with the air of one who means to stay awhile. "Now, then," she said. "We shall get everything clear."

Sitting beside her, Katharine frowned. "Whatever do you mean, Mary?"

Her cousin looked stern. "I have kept quiet all along, because there is nothing I despise more than an interfering female, but now I must speak, because you are making a very serious mistake, Katharine."

"Mistake?" She smiled. "If you mean by visiting the Marchingtons, I already know that."

"I mean about Lord Stonenden."

Katharine looked startled, then stood abruptly. "I don't want to talk—"

"Sit down," interrupted Mary, and Katharine was so surprised that she did so. "I *shall* speak, whether you wish it or not. And you will listen. Because, for once, I know more about a subject than you do." She pressed her lips together and looked at her, as if daring her to contradict.

Katharine was so astonished that she could only return the stare, openmouthed.

"Good," continued Mary. "Now. I realize that you believe Lord Stonenden is involved with the Countess Standen. No, don't interrupt me until I have finished, Katharine. You are mistaken. He cares nothing at all for the countess. I know this. And I mean to prove it to you."

Katharine remained silent, less from astonishment now than from a dawning, uncertain hope.

"I will start from the beginning," said Mary. "You remember that when Elinor first came to us for help, Eliza Burnham suggested that we find someone more experienced to aid us. You did not care for the idea, but Eliza continued to think it wise, and she mentioned the problem to Lord Stonenden. Not directly, you understand, but through discreet hints."

"She did not!" exclaimed Katharine. "Oh, Eliza!"

Mary nodded. "However, he admits that he dismissed the subject from his mind until he saw how gallantly you were behaving over the matter. He was struck by that and by...well, by your character altogether, and he determined to help you separate Tom and the countess."

Katharine made an inarticulate noise.

Mary nodded again. "It was for this reason that he began to pay court to her. He thought that he could lure her away from Tom, making her lose interest in him. The countess is attracted by wealth and position, of course."

"How do you know all this?"

"Lord Stonenden told me. Wait, and you will see how. And so, he conducted a campaign, escorting the countess to some events and hovering about her at others. But he found the thing more difficult than he had expected. The countess was flattered by Tom's attentions, and she is a woman who likes to have a number of admirers. So the problem was not solved quickly."

"He might have mentioned all this to me," said Katharine.

"He was under the impression, for a long time, that you knew and understood what he was doing."

"Nonsense! He cannot have thought anything of the kind."

"He says he spoke to you about it."

"That is ridiculous. He..." Abruptly Katharine remembered several of Stonenden's remarks that had seemed quite unfathomable at the time. He *could* have been talking about this affair.

Mary noticed her changed expression. "He says he did think it. But at some point, he received the impression that you still had a low opinion of him, and he nearly abandoned the whole scheme."

Katharine flushed.

"However, he later took it up again, and finally managed to bring it to a successful conclusion. He had discovered your ignorance in the meantime, and he asked me and Eliza Burnham to arrange matters so that you could observe the final outcome."

"Is that the reason for Eliza's odd behavior at her party?" said Katharine. "You should be ashamed, both of you, for not telling me."

"I am sorry for that. I wished to, but Lord Stonenden felt that a demonstration would be much more effective. Unfortunately, the scene was interrupted before you could see the end. Lord Stonenden broke with the countess that evening, just after our departure. So, you see, he has played a noble part. Indeed, Katharine, I think he is admirable, a true gentleman."

"But is that all?" replied the girl. "Is there nothing about the portrait?"

"Lord Stonenden's portrait? What do you mean? That had nothing to do with the countess."

"No, the countess's portrait."

Mary frowned and shook her head.

"Did he not explain about that?"

At Mary's denial, Katharine told her about the countess's call on the day of her departure. "She sounded very sure of herself," she finished. "Are you certain of what you have been told?"

"There must be some mistake," answered Mary.

"Pardon me, but isn't it perhaps possible that *you* have made a mistake?"

"But why would Stonenden tell me such a complicated story if it were not true? It makes no sense."

"Why would the countess approach me for a portrait?"

Mary's face cleared. "For revenge, of course. It would be just like her. She knew that Stonenden had separated her from Tom. She would connect that with you, because of the picture."

Her implication made Katharine flush again, but she was also taken aback. It could be true.

"Katharine, is it more likely that Lord Stonenden lied to me, or that the countess deceived you? I consider myself a fair judge of character, and I would pledge my word that Stonenden was serious."

Katharine looked distressed.

"Haven't you perhaps judged him too harshly?" her cousin added.

"He was always so odiously unfeeling," replied the girl defensively.

"Always?"

Katharine remembered several occasions when he had been just the opposite. "Well, but he should have told me what he meant to do, Mary. He simply does as he pleases, not caring what other people may think," she cried, trying to recapture her anger.

"He thought you knew, Katharine."

The girl acknowledged this by bowing her head and gazing at her clasped hands. Mary's argument was convincing. Indeed, she was probably right, but something in Katharine remained stubbornly annoyed. She had not, after all, asked for Lord Stonenden's bounty, and she resented her present feelings of guilt for having misjudged him. She shrugged. "Very well. I shall thank him when I am next in town."

"But, Katharine—"

"What do you want of me? I admit that he was a great help. We could not have gotten Tom free without him. But does that mean that I must kneel in gratitude? I did not ask his help. Why did he intrude?"

"I think you know that quite well." Mary looked steadily at her.

"I don't. I can't be expected to know things when he refuses to tell me. He should have explained things himself."

"Oh, he means to. I nearly drove the servants distracted getting off before him. I decided to prepare the way because I thought he deserved a better reception than the one he was likely to get. I daresay he will arrive this afternoon."

"What!" Katharine stood. "But he can't come here. What shall I say to him? Oh, he is impossible! Why could he not write, or…or…?"

"He thought you would refuse to see him."

"So I should. So I will! Oh, Mary, why did you not tell him to stay away?"

"Because I thought he should come, of course. And I think you are acting very foolishly, Katharine."

"You don't know how I feel. I cannot face him. Oh, what am I going to do?"

"You owe him a chance to explain."

"I don't! I don't owe him anything." Katharine laughed a little hysterically. "He owes *me*, for his portrait. Perhaps I shall ask him for my fee."

"Katharine, be sensible!"

At this sharp remark, the girl regained control of herself. "I am sorry, Mary. I feel a bit unwell. I think I will lie down for a while."

"A splendid idea. You need time to think."

Katharine began a sharp retort, then shrugged and turned away. She hardly knew what she felt.

"I will find Lady Agnes and pay my respects," continued Mary calmly. "I don't suppose she will be pleased to see me. I think I will stay with Elinor's family. I haven't seen them in an age."

With this, she rose and walked up the path, leaving Katharine staring after her blankly.

Twenty-three

KATHARINE WAS NEVER CERTAIN LATER PRECISELY HOW she passed the morning after hearing Mary's story. She walked a good deal, through the house and in the garden and finally down to the stream behind the park. She remembered seeing Elinor; the younger girl spoke, but Katharine did not stop, leaving her cousin staring after her. A kind of urgent tension made it impossible for her to be still, and she felt it was imperative that she order her thoughts before Lord Stonenden's promised arrival. Yet the greater her efforts to do so, the more disordered they became.

What puzzled her most was that she felt little relief at Mary's revelations. For days she had been cast down by the thought that Stonenden loved the countess, but now that she saw the falseness of this idea, she remained dissatisfied, in a state of nervous irritation. Indeed, she was, if anything, more restless. Why should this be? And why did she not feel more kindly toward the man who had taken such pains to help her? She thought of Stonenden now with angry impatience.

At last, tired out, Katharine sat down on a large flat rock beside the stream. She had missed luncheon, but she was not hungry, and she was hardly aware of the beauty of her surroundings, though this sheltered spot was one of her favorite retreats on the Marchington estate. She leaned on one hand and bent over the water, flecked with gold in the afternoon sun. It gave back the reflection of the willow which overhung the stream here, shading the rock and dappling the current with a moving pattern of light, and of Katharine herself. Her pale primrose muslin gown blended into the bright scene, but her face was tense and anxious. After a while, however, the sound of the water began to calm her. She sighed deeply and sat back.

"Katharine," said a male voice behind her. "They told me at the house that you might be here."

Somehow, she wasn't startled. She stood and turned slowly to face Oliver Stonenden, who had stopped a little distance away and was watching her with a grave expression in his dark blue eyes. As usual, he looked complete to a shade, a little out of place in these rustic surroundings. He was dressed for riding, in top boots and buckskins, and his blue coat echoed the color of his eyes. As she met them, Katharine was abruptly unconscious of all externals.

"I'm sorry to appear so unexpectedly," he went on, "but I must talk to you. I ask only a few minutes of your time."

Katharine felt surprisingly composed now that he was actually before her. "I know all about it," she replied. "Mary told me."

"Oh." He looked taken aback, and distinctly annoyed.

For some reason, Katharine found his chagrin very satisfying. "So, you see, you needn't bother explaining."

He frowned. "I think I must. It was kind of Miss Daltry to anticipate me, I suppose. Or she meant it kindly, at any rate. But I wish she had not done so. It is for me to explain myself."

"Indeed? It is hard to believe that you think so."

Her tone clearly puzzled him. "Because I have not explained before? Yes, but I thought you knew of my plan, you see. I spoke to you about it. I thought it was something we shared."

"You could not have held to that opinion recently, however."

"No. I saw after a time that you had not understood. But then..." He smiled wryly. "I was afraid to speak of it. I did not think you would believe me. You can be quite formidable, you know."

She smiled very slightly.

"So I arranged a demonstration, and of course that too went awry, and you ran away before I could reveal the truth. I have presided over a comedy of errors. Could you not have waited one day? I left word that I would call again."

Katharine looked down. "Something...happened to make me wish to avoid you."

He stepped closer. "What?"

"The Countess Standen called on me. She said you wanted me to paint a portrait of her, a companion to my picture of you."

"Did she, by God!" Stonenden's eyes blazed with anger for a moment, then he laughed harshly. "Elise said she would have her revenge. I suppose that was it. Need I tell you that it was a lie? It was."

"Yes, that is what Mary thought."

"My ever-eager champion," he responded ruefully. "I wonder if she knows how little I want such aid?"

There was a pause; he looked at her. "So," said Katharine abruptly. "All is explained. I am grateful to you for your help. Shall we walk back to the house? Mary will want to greet you, and the Marchingtons—"

"No," he replied. "I haven't the slightest desire to see the Marchingtons ever again, and Miss Daltry will have to wait. We have unfinished business between us, Katharine. I do not want your gratitude. It was not for that that I took on the countess."

She met his eyes challengingly. She could not rid herself of a nagging oppression, even now that she knew the whole truth. Something was wrong, but she could not tell what. "Why, then?" she asked coolly.

He frowned. "But you know…no, let me begin further back. I did not forget you when you went to India, you know. I tried very hard to do so, because I was furious with you. Your refusal of my offer was a stunning blow. But you lingered in my mind, even through four years. Often I would suddenly think of you, in some quite irrelevant place, and feel…I never knew just what. There was anger, of course." He grinned. "I had never before been refused anything I wanted. But there was something else as well."

She raised her eyebrows, and his grin widened.

"Yes, I know. I was intolerably conceited in those days. At any rate, when you returned, I heard of it, of course, and I looked for you in vain on many occasions. I thought it was mere curiosity, with perhaps a bit of malice intermixed, but I know now I was mistaken. For when I saw you again at last, my one idea was to continue to see you, as often as possible. I made excuses to myself to justify it."

"Excuses?"

"I don't dare tell you. But it wasn't long before I discarded them. Your behavior with regard to Elinor's dilemma, and over your paintings, impressed me very much. I had been dazzled by you at your come-out, but I was much more deeply moved by the person you had become since then. I had not known that a woman could possess such gallantry and intelligence. And I realized that my impulse had been exactly right when I made you that long-ago offer, even if my motives had been all wrong. So I began to consider how I might win you, and that led to all the rest."

"The portrait as well?" asked Katharine a bit resentfully.

"Only at first. I have not become so selfless that I would commission a poor painting to ingratiate myself."

She smiled.

"Besides, I knew you would see through any such effort."

At this, she laughed aloud. "You are right there."

He smiled down at her. "Well. And so?"

"So?"

"I am waiting to hear if I succeeded."

"Succeeded in what?"

"Dammit, Katharine, succeeded in winning your regard. I have done all I could think of to prove to you that I am not the arrogant, selfish man you so rightly refused five years ago. Will you not tell me whether I have managed the thing?"

"I certainly think much better of you now. You have changed. It was good of you to help me, and you have my true gratitude and esteem."

"Esteem!" He sounded disgusted.

"Of course. Your kindness—"

"Blast kindness!" He strode over and grasped her shoulders. "Katharine, I have been telling you that I love you!"

"Have you?" answered the girl coolly, not moving in his grasp.

"You know quite well I have."

"How was I to know it, when you spoke so calmly of 'winning my regard'?" As she said this, emotion blazed up in Katharine, and she realized that her dissatisfaction with Stonenden was centered here. "You've been talking like a schoolmaster."

"A… Have I indeed?" He pulled her close; their eyes met across a very short distance. Then he bent to kiss her, at first very gently, then with a desperate urgency. His arms moved from her shoulders to encircle her waist, pulling her hard against his chest. Katharine felt all the pent-up emotion she had been fighting flame up, knowing this was what had been missing from Stonenden's measured explanation. Slowly her arms moved up across his shoulders and around his neck in a caress that was also a demand.

They stood locked together thus for a long moment; then he raised his head. "I love you, Katharine. Do you believe me now?"

Shakily she nodded, and he laughed.

"I was trying so hard to be fair and reasonable, to show you that I was no longer the insufferable fellow I used to be. I wanted this proposal to be as different as possible from that ill-omened first one. Perhaps I went too far."

Dimpling, she nodded again. "You were so pompous."

"Pompous? I was never pompous in my life."

"You were."

"You will pay for that!" He kissed her then, this time with a leisurely intimacy that implied possession, before releasing her to look deeply into her eyes. "*Will* you marry me, Katharine?"

Holding his gaze, she nodded once more.

"Have you nothing more to say about it?"

"You have changed," she answered, "and so have I. And I love you with all my heart."

He pulled her close again. Some time passed before they separated, but when they did, Katharine stepped back a little, taking a trembling breath.

"I'll have no more talk of schoolmasters," Stonenden told her.

Smiling, she shook her head. "But you must tell me one thing."

"Anything."

"What were the excuses?"

"Excuses?" He frowned.

"You said you made excuses to justify your interest in me. What were they?"

"Ah." He grinned wickedly. "The chief one was that I should punish you a little for rejecting me that first time."

Katharine's amber eyes blazed. "Punish me? Despicable!"

"Wasn't it?" he agreed amiably. "And quite self-deceiving, too. It was I who was to be punished by long, weary service."

She wrinkled her nose. "Which you deserved, if that is what you thought, wretch."

"Possibly."

"And I shan't let you forget it, either, not for years and years."

"The thought of your reminding me of anything, however unpleasant, for years and years, is so sweet that I don't even protest." Their eyes met again. "I do love you, Katharine."

She melted into his arms once more.

If you enjoyed *The Marchington Scandal*,
be sure to check out more Regency
romance titles from Jane Ashford

Read on for excerpts from

The Bargain

and

Man of Honour

Now available from Sourcebooks Casablanca!

From
The Bargain

LORD ALAN GRESHAM WAS ICILY, INTOLERABLY, dangerously bored. As he looked out over the animated, exceedingly fashionable crowd that filled the large reception room, his blue eyes glittered from under hooded lids. His mouth was a thin line. Revelers who glanced his way, curious about his very plain evening dress and solitary state, looked quickly away when he met their eyes. The women tended to draw their gauzy wraps closer despite the enervating warmth of the room, and the men stiffened. Whispers began to circulate, inquiring as to who he was and what the deuce he was doing in Carlton House at the prince regent's fete.

A damned good question, Alan thought, well aware that he was the object of their attention. He was here against his will, and his better judgment. He was wasting his time, which he hated, and he was being kept from truly important work by a royal whim. He couldn't imagine a situation more likely to rouse his temper and exhaust his small stock of patience.

Alan watched a padded and beribboned fop sidle up to the Duke of Langford and murmur a query.

The duke did not look pleased, but he answered. The reaction was only too predictable—surprise, feigned incomprehension, and then delight in having a tidbit to circulate among the gossips. Alan ignored the spreading whispers and continued to watch the duke, a tall, spare, handsome man of sixty or so. This was all his fault. Alan wouldn't be trapped here now, on this ridiculous quest, if it weren't for the duke. He clamped his jaw hard, then deliberately relaxed it. He wasn't being quite fair, he admitted to himself. The duke, his father, was no more able to refuse a direct command from the sovereign than he himself was.

"Well, I hope my eyes are not like limpid forest pools," declared a very clear, musical female voice behind him. "Aren't forest pools full of small slimy creatures and dead leaves?"

Somewhat startled, Alan turned to find the source of this forthrightness. He discovered a girl of perhaps twenty with lustrous, silky brown hair and a turned-up nose. She didn't have the look of the *haut ton*, with which Alan was only too tiresomely familiar. Her gown was too simple, her hair not fashionably cropped. She looked, in fact, like someone who should not, under any circumstances, have been brought to Carlton House and the possible notice of the prince regent.

Or of the dissolute-looking fellow who was bending over her now, Alan noted. He had the bloodshot eyes and pouchy skin of a man who had spent years drinking too much and sleeping too little. The set of his thin lips and the lines in his face spoke of cruelty. Alan started to go to the rescue. Then he remembered where he was. Innocent young ladies were not left alone in Carlton House, at the mercy of the prince's exceedingly untrustworthy set of friends and hangers-on. Their families saw to that. Most likely this girl was a high flyer whose youthful looks were very good for business. No doubt she knew what she was doing. He started to turn away.

"No, I do not wish to stroll with you in the garden," the girl said. "I have told you so a dozen times. I don't wish to be rude, but please go away."

The man grasped her arm, his fingers visibly digging into her flesh. He tried to pull her along with him through the crowd.

"I'll scream," said the girl, rather calmly. "I can scream very loudly. My singing teacher said I have an extraordinary set of lungs. Though an unreliable grasp of pitch," she added with regretful honesty.

Her companion ignored this threat until the girl actually opened her mouth and drew in a deep preparatory breath. Then, with a look around at the crowd and a muttered oath, he dropped her arm. "Witch," he said.

"'Double, double toil and trouble,'" she replied pertly.

The man frowned.

"'Fire burn and cauldron bubble,'" she added.

His frown became a scowl.

"Something of toad, eye of newt... oh, I forget the rest." She sounded merely irritated at her lapse of memory.

The man backed away a few steps.

"There's blood in it somewhere," she told herself.

She made an exasperated sound. "I used to know the whole thing by heart."

Her would-be ravisher took to his heels. The girl shook out her skirts and tossed her head in satisfaction.

His interest definitely caught, Alan examined this unusual creature more closely. She was small—the top of her head did not quite reach his shoulder—but the curves of her form were not at all childlike. The bodice of her pale green gown was admirably filled and it draped a lovely line of waist and hip. Her skin glowed like ripe peaches against her glossy brown hair. He couldn't see whether her eyes had any resemblance to forest pools, but her lips were mesmerizing—very full and beautifully shaped. The word "luscious" occurred to him, and he immediately rejected it as nonsense. What the devil was he doing, he wondered? He wasn't a man to be beguiled by physical charms, or to waste his time on such maunderings. Still, he was having trouble tearing his eyes away from her when it was brought home to him that she had noticed him.

"No, I do not wish to go with you into another room," she declared, meeting his gaze squarely. "Or into the garden, or out to your carriage. I do not require an escort home. Nor do I need someone to tell me how to go on or to 'protect' me." She stared steadily up at him, not looking at all embarrassed.

Her eyes were rather like forest pools, Alan thought; dead leaves aside. They were a sparkling mixture of brown and green that put one in mind of the deep woods. "What are you doing here?" he couldn't resist asking her.

"That is none of your affair. What are *you* doing here?"

Briefly, Alan wondered what she would think if he told her. He would enjoy hearing her response, he realized. But of course he couldn't reveal his supposed "mission."

A collective gasp passed over the crowd, moving along the room like wind across a field of grain. Alan turned quickly. This was what he had been waiting for through the interminable hours and days. There! He started toward the sweeping staircase that adorned the far end of the long room, pushing past knots of guests transfixed by the figure that stood in the shadows atop it.

On the large landing at the head of the stairs the candles had gone out—or been blown out, Alan amended. In the resulting pool of darkness, floating above the sea of light in the room, was a figure out of some sensational tale. It was a woman, her skin bone-white, her hair a deep chestnut. She wore an antique gown of yellow brocade, the neckline square cut, the bodice tight above a long full skirt. Alan knew, because he had been told, that this was invariably her dress when she appeared, and that it was the costume she had worn onstage to play Lady Macbeth.

Sound reverberated through the room—the clanking of chains—as Alan pushed past the guests, who remained riveted by the vision before them. The figure seemed to hover a foot or so above the floor. The space between the hem of its gown and the stair landing was a dark vacancy. Its eyes were open, glassy and fixed, effectively dead-looking. Its hands and arms were stained with gore.

A bloodcurdling scream echoed down the stairs.

Then a wavering, curiously guttural voice pronounced the word "justice" very slowly, three times. The figure's mouth had not moved during any of this, Alan noted.

He had nearly reached the foot of the stairs when a female guest just in front of him threw up her arms and crumpled to the floor in a faint. Alan had to swerve and slow to keep from stepping on her, and as he did so, something struck him from behind, upsetting his balance and nearly knocking him down. "What the devil?" he said, catching himself and moving on even as he cast a glance over his shoulder. To his astonishment, he found that the girl he had encountered a moment ago was right on his heels. He didn't have time to wonder what she thought she was doing. "Stay out of my way," he commanded and lunged for the stairs.

There was another terrible shriek, but even as Alan pounded up the long curving stairway, the apparition at the top vanished into darkness. Cursing, he kept going. He didn't believe for one moment that the ghost of a recently dead actress was haunting Carlton House, whatever the prince might say. It was some sort of hoax. And he had to uncover it, and the reasons behind it, before he would be allowed to leave and take up his own pursuits once more.

He reached the broad landing—now empty. The corridor leading off it was also completely dark, all the candle sconces extinguished. He paused a moment to listen for footsteps, and once again was jostled from behind. He turned to find the same girl had followed him up the staircase. "What the hell do you think you're doing?" he demanded.

"I must speak to her," insisted the girl breathlessly.

"I must find her. Which way?" She gazed left, then right, along the lightless hallway.

Alan was never sure afterward whether there had actually been a sound. But the girl exclaimed, pointed, and darted off to the left. After an instant's hesitation, he went after her.

The light from downstairs barely penetrated into this upper corridor, and the little there was cast disorienting shadows along the floor and walls. Alan could just see the girl blundering along ahead of him toward a half-open door, which seemed to still be swinging.

The girl reached the door, pulled it open, and went through. Alan, directly behind her by this time, followed at top speed. Then, in one confusing instant, he careened into her with stunning force, the door slammed shut, and there was the unmistakable click of a key turning in a lock outside. A spurt of eerie laughter was capped by total, black silence.

A moment ticked by. Though he was jammed into a tiny space, Alan managed to reach behind his back and grip the doorknob. As he had expected, it did not turn.

He heard a muffled sound, between a sob and a sigh. "She didn't wait for me," murmured the girl, so softly he barely heard.

"You mean the so-called ghost?" he replied sharply. "Why should it?"

"You frightened her off," she accused. "She would have stayed for *me*."

"If you hadn't gotten in my way, I would have caught it," he retorted. "What is your connection with this affair?"

There was a silence.

"Could you move, please?" the girl asked. "You're crushing me."

"I am directly against the door," he answered. "There is no room to move. I insist upon knowing—"

"We're in some sort of cupboard, then. I'm mashed into a corner. Can't you open the door?"

"It's locked," Alan replied with what he thought was admirable restraint.

"You mean, the ghost locked us in?" she said incredulously.

"Someone pretending to be a ghost appears to have done so," he amended. "To prevent discovery of the hoax."

There was another silence. Alan cursed the darkness, wanting very much to see his companion's face.

"You don't think it's really Bess Harding's ghost?" she asked finally.

"There are no ghosts," Alan pronounced with utter certainty. "That is a ridiculous superstition, rejected by all sensible people."

"Sensible," she echoed very quietly. "I suppose you're right." She sighed.

For some reason, that tiny movement made him acutely aware of the fact that their bodies were pressed together along their entire lengths. He could feel the soft curve of her breasts at his ribs, and her hip cradled by his thigh. He moved slightly, trying to disengage, but this only intensified the sensations. She had a heady, flowery scent, too, he realized. It was intoxicating in these confined quarters. "We should make some sound, so that the prince's servants can release us," he said tightly. Following his own advice, he kicked backward with one foot and produced a satisfying thud on the door panels.

"Who are you?" Alan said, personal curiosity as strong as his investigative instincts.

"Who are *you*?" she retorted with the same spirit she had shown downstairs.

"Alan Gresham," he answered.

"One of the prince's friends." Her tone made it clear that she didn't think much of the Carlton House set.

He found he didn't want her to draw this conclusion. "No," he said. "The prince summoned me here to…" Alan hesitated. The prince had made it clear that he didn't want his uneasiness about the ghost mentioned.

"To rid him of the ghost," the girl concluded, taking the matter out of his hands. "Just like him. Let someone else clean up the mess. Make no effort to really settle the matter."

"You are acquainted with the prince?"

"My mother was."

"Indeed." From her tone, and the prince's notorious romantic history, Alan concluded that the connection had been intimate.

"My mother, the ghost," she added bitterly.

"Bess Harding was your…?"

"Yes," was the bald reply.

Matters became clearer to Alan. "So you came here tonight—"

"I had to see her!" the girl exclaimed. "She can't be just…gone. I came as fast as I could from school, but by the time I reached London, everything was over. They'd buried her and…" Her voice caught, and there was a pause. "I heard about this…haunting. So I came." She sounded defiant now. "I know it isn't the thing, but no one asked me for an invitation, and I was sure she would appear tonight, so I—"

"Why?" interrupted Alan sharply. "Why tonight?"

"I was told it is the largest, most important party the prince has given in weeks," she answered. "Mama wouldn't miss something like that."

"But, Miss Harding—"

"Ariel," she cut in. "You may as well know my name is Ariel Harding. She named me from *The Tempest*." When he said nothing, she added, "Shakespeare, you know."

"I believe I've heard of it," he responded dryly.

"Umm. Well, I knew she wouldn't be able to resist such an occasion. So I came." There was a pause, then she moved slightly. "You don't think it's really my mother?" she asked again.

It was a moment before Alan could reply. Her small movement against him had sent a jolt through his entire body. This was entirely unacceptable, he told himself. He was a man of science. He was not subject to random physical attractions. "I do not," he said more harshly than he might have under other circumstances.

"But who can it be then?" she wondered, brushing against him once again.

"Someone who expects to gain from the situation," he answered curtly. "We really must get out of here." He began to kick the door again, much more forcefully this time.

"Gain, how?"

"Possibly a political opponent of the prince who

wishes to discredit him," said Alan through gritted teeth. "Perhaps someone looking for personal revenge." He kicked again, hard. "Halloo," he called. "Is anyone there?"

He was rewarded by the sound of cautious footsteps in the corridor outside. "Hello?" said a tentative voice.

"It's Alan Gresham," he replied loudly. "I'm locked in this cupboard. Open the door!"

The footsteps advanced a bit farther. "How do I know it's Lord Alan?" the voice inquired. "You might be a demon from the depths trying to deceive me."

"If I were, I should burst through this door and drag you down to hell," roared Alan. "Now, let us out!"

But the footsteps were already pounding away.

"Well, you might have known that would frighten him," Ariel Harding said. "When someone is coming after a ghost, you do not threaten to drag him down to—"

"Be quiet." The feel of her against him was becoming intense. He refused to give in to it. It was irrational; it was meaningless; it was the consequence of simple physical reflex and extremely awkward circumstances.

"Are you really a lord?" asked Ariel. "What sort of lord?"

"A courtesy lord," he replied in clipped accents. "I am the sixth son of the Duke of Langford, and thus am technically Lord Alan."

"Sixth?" murmured Ariel. "Good heavens. Do you have sisters as well?"

"I do not. And I don't see what that has to do with—"

"Alan?" put in a voice from outside.

"Father," he replied with great relief. "Can you get someone to unlock this door?"

"Unfortunately not," was the reply. "There seems to be a problem about the key."

"The numskulls have lost it," declared another voice. "But don't worry, I have them fetching an ax. We'll have you out of there in no time."

"Your Majesty! This is a cupboard. My back is right up against the door."

"Useless blunderers," said the prince. "Someone will be sacked over this."

"Your Majesty!" called Alan again.

"I heard you," answered his father. "Don't worry."

"This is like one of the French farces my mother used to act in," commented Ariel.

"I'm glad you are amused," replied Alan tightly.

"Why did the prince choose you?" asked Ariel.

"What?"

"Why did he choose you to unmask the ghost? Because you are the son of a duke? That doesn't seem like a very good reason."

"He didn't have a very good reason," muttered Alan, remembering the conversation he had had with the prince five days ago.

He had been summoned to London without warning, ordered to wait upon the regent at Carlton House. And wait he had, thought Alan bitterly. Prinny kept him kicking up his heels in a gaudy parlor for two hours before a liveried footman appeared and indicated that he should follow.

Finally, they had passed through a pair of carved and gilded double doors and into a large reception parlor that at first seemed to him crowded with people. In the center of the chamber was a small circle of what appeared to be government officials. Most of them carried sheaves of papers, and all of them looked impatient. At the far end was a huge desk with a few armchairs scattered around it. Two young men sat at the corners of the desk bent over pen and paper, busily recording the pronouncements of the man occupying the main chair, and the center of attention.

Alan's eyes followed all the others toward George Augustus Frederick, Prince Regent of England and Ireland due to his father the king's distressing illness, and found little trace of the handsome, laughing youth of an early portrait he had once seen. The prince was fat. His high starched neckcloth hid several extra chins. His extremely fashionable clothes couldn't disguise his girth. He didn't look very happy either, Alan thought. Of course, with workmen smashing power looms around the country and people marching in the streets of London to express their disgust of the ruler's treatment of his wife, he had little to be happy about.

Receiving a signal, Alan walked down the long room and made his bow before the controversial man who ruled his country.

"Langford's youngest, eh?" the prince said.

"Yes, Your Majesty."

The prince waved a pudgy, beringed hand. "No need to be formal. Your father's a friend of mine, you know."

"Yes, sir," replied Alan.

"That's why I sent for you. Sit down, sit down."

A servant appeared at his elbow with a tray, and Alan accepted a glass of wine that he did not want.

"Never see you about London," the prince commented, sipping his own wine with obvious relish.

"No, sir. I visit very rarely."

"Not like your brothers, eh?"

"No, sir." When his host seemed to be waiting for more, Alan added, "As a sixth son, I have felt able to go my own way."

"Sixth." The prince shook his head, then eyed his visitor with surprising shrewdness. "Up at Oxford, are you? Studying new inventions and the like?"

"I am a man of science, sir, a fellow of Balliol College."

"Right, right." The prince rubbed his hands together. "Just what I need. I take it you haven't heard about my little...problem?"

Alan had heard of a variety of problems, from the vilifications of the Whigs to scandals involving various women to rumors of unattractive physical ailments.

"The ghost," prompted the prince.

Alan simply stared at him.

"Glad to see the story hasn't spread outside London," was the response to his bewildered look. "It's embarrassing. A dashed nuisance, too."

"Did you say ghost, sir?" Alan asked.

"Bess Harding," came the morose reply. "The actress?" Seeing Alan's blank look, he added, "She was one of the great ladies of the stage. Gorgeous creature. Why, ten years ago, we..." He cleared his throat. "Never mind that. The thing is, Bess, er, died three weeks ago, and now she's haunting Carlton House!"

"Haunting," Alan repeated carefully.

"It's outrageous," complained the prince. "We were good friends. No reason for this at all." He looked at Alan as if for confirmation, and Alan found himself too bemused even to nod. "Makes it look as if I had something to do with her death, don't you see?" the prince elaborated.

When Alan remained uncomprehending, the regent added, "She killed herself." His voice and look grew briefly solemn. "Terrible thing. Took a razor to her wrists. I've never been more shocked. But it had nothing to do with me."

"You are asking me to—"

"Man of science," interrupted the monarch. "Just the ticket. I won't have some interfering priest in here with bells and books and mumbo jumbo. This ain't a theater, by God, it's my home. That's why you're the perfect man for the job."

"Sir, I don't think—"

"You'll know how to go on at Carlton House, fit right in," the prince continued, ignoring Alan's growing desperation. "I won't have a pack of commoners wandering about the place, sticking their noses into things they won't understand."

"But, sir, I—"

"She keeps appearing at evening parties," the prince told him in a deeply aggrieved tone. "Don't see how she could do this to me."

"Sir, surely you don't believe that this is actually, er, the dead woman."

"Bess," supplied the prince. "Don't know what to believe. Looks devilishly like her."

"But, sir, ghosts do not exist."

"Splendid. You come along and tell her so."

"I—"

"I've ordered rooms prepared for you here. Best to be on the scene, eh? You can attend meals and all my entertainments."

"Sir, I have important work in Oxford which I cannot—"

"More important than a request from your sovereign?" was the suddenly haughty reply.

Alan thought with despair of the various experiments he had in train, and of the meticulous plans he had made for the next few weeks. "Of course not, Your Majesty," he answered in a heavy voice.

Now days later all he had to show for his efforts was the embarrassment of getting locked in a cupboard. Something struck Alan sharply in the ribs. "Are you subject to fits?" demanded Ariel Harding out of the darkness. "What is the matter with you?"

"Nothing," retorted Alan, acutely conscious of his surroundings once more.

"Oh? Do you often drift off in the middle of a conversation? I suppose I shouldn't be surprised. Everyone in this house seems to be"—she appeared to search for a suitable word—"preoccupied with themselves."

"I am not part of the Carlton House set," repeated Alan, revolted. He despised those who hung about the fringes of the court waiting to offer the jaded monarch some new dissipation.

"Well…?" said Ariel impatiently.

"What?"

"You were going to tell me why the prince chose you to hunt down my mother?"

"It is not your—"

"Or whoever it is!" interrupted the girl. "You don't

seem to me like a very good choice. You can't seem to keep a train of thought in your head for more than a minute."

It took Alan a moment to gather the shreds of his temper. "I am a man of science," he answered through clenched teeth. "I am affiliated with the university at Oxford. I am conducting a series of important experiments into the nature and properties of light."

"Light?" She sounded astonished. "You mean sunlight or lamplight?"

"All types of light."

"But what is there to—"

"You wouldn't understand. The prince chose me because of my scientific interests and education. He thought that my training in the principles of investigation would allow me to uncover the hoax quickly and efficiently." That was putting the best possible face on it, he thought bitterly. No need to mention that their ruler thought he was enduring a supernatural visitation, which had nothing whatever to do with science.

"Well, it all sounds very odd to me," declared Ariel. "I thought lords spent their time hunting and going to balls and that sort of thing. Why would the son of a duke, who can do as he pleases, choose to stay in *school* forever?"

She pronounced the word "school" with deep repugnance. "My work has absolutely no relation to the pap they offer in girls' schools," he replied curtly. "And since you are constitutionally incapable of understanding anything about it, perhaps we should concentrate our energies on getting out of this damnable cupboard!"

"No wonder it is so crowded in here," Ariel said.

"Your giant intellect must take up more than half the space all by itself."

There was a sharp sound at his back, as some sort of tool was inserted between the door and jamb. A splintering noise from near the keyhole heralded a crack of light that wavered, and then quickly expanded as the lock was broken and the door pried open, finally flying back to crash against the corridor wall.

Alan felt an odd moment of regret as he took a step back and turned toward their rescuers. Ariel Harding had roused his always active curiosity, he realized. He would be rather sorry to see the last of her.

As he'd feared, the hall was full of people. Around his father and the prince stood a crowd of servants and guests all peering avidly in his direction and trying to discover what was going on.

"All right?" murmured the duke.

Alan nodded, taking another step and thus revealing Ariel to the onlookers.

"Hallo?" said the prince. "What's this, then?" He moved closer, holding up a beribboned quizzing glass for a better look and casting an experienced eye over Ariel's rounded figure. He appeared to find much to admire, taking his time to savor the glowing skin of her neck and shoulders and the voluptuous shape of her lips. "Thought you were chasin' the ghost," he admonished Alan without shifting his gaze. "Not that anyone wouldn't rather be shut in a cupboard with this—"

"We were both chasing it," broke in Ariel. "And *I*, at least, intend to find out the truth about Bess Harding's death."

"Eh?" sputtered the prince, looking uneasily aware of the crowd around him. "Truth? Everyone knows the truth. Fit of despair. Took her own life. Always a moody creature, was Bess. Terrible thing. But nothing to do with—"

"She had to have some reason," interrupted Ariel again. "Why is she coming here? I want to know—"

"Perhaps we should adjourn to some other room," said Alan in a loud voice. "I'm sure the others would like to get back to the entertainment."

"Yes, indeed," replied Alan's father. He fixed one of the senior servants with a commanding gaze. "Escort everyone downstairs."

There were some protests, but in a few minutes the hall was clear of everyone but the prince, the duke, and Alan and Ariel. "What's going on here?" blustered the prince. "Who is this girl? What's she doin' in my house? Never seen her before in my life. Don't believe I invited her, by Jove." He gave a very creditable impression of outraged virtue.

"I am—" began Ariel.

"Assisting me in the investigation," interjected Alan smoothly.

The other two men looked at him.

"I am not—" attempted Ariel.

"She possesses certain key facts that will help discredit this hoax," Alan said.

"Facts, is it?" said the prince. His sharp look faded as he examined Ariel yet again. A gleam came into his eyes and he chuckled. "I've known a few ladies who possessed some fascinatin' 'facts.' Taught me a good deal, they did." He started to turn away. "Do as you like, my boy, but don't be diverted from your task, eh? Come along, Langford, I want a drink."

The duke followed him down the corridor, in which the sconces had been relit. But he cast several curious looks over his shoulder as he went.

"Why did you say that?" exploded Ariel when they had gone.

"What?" answered Alan.

"That I am assisting you."

"You might have knowledge that could be useful," he replied. "If you do not blurt it out before a crowd, that is."

She drew in an angry breath. "I am not in the habit of—"

"As you nearly did just now," he continued. "You were about to tell them all that you are Bess Harding's daughter, weren't you?"

Ariel stood very straight. "I am not ashamed of being her daughter," she declared. "She was a great actress."

"No doubt. But that is no reason to broadcast information when you do not know who is listening."

"Who…?"

"Our so-called ghost may have been standing right here, enjoying her triumph. She had ample time to change her dress and return."

"She…" Ariel put a hand to her lovely lips. "If it's not Bess…" She faltered. "It has to be a woman, doesn't it?"

"It certainly was a woman who appeared here tonight."

"Yes," she whispered. "But who would…?"

He straightened his coat and pushed the now-ruined cupboard door closed. "Let us go somewhere private, and you can tell me everything you know about this matter."

She stiffened. "Why should I?"

Alan looked surprised. "So that I can resolve the situation and be done with it."

"The ghost, you mean?"

"Exactly."

"What about my mother?" she demanded.

Trying to temper his impatience with sympathy, Alan looked down at her. "I am very sorry about your mother. The prince was right, it was a terrible thing."

"He wasn't right, because he knows nothing about it and hasn't bothered to find out."

"Perhaps so, but—"

"I must speak to the ghost," she went on, "and ask her what she knows. I *will* discover why my mother is dead!" She glared up at him, defiance and something more poignant in her hazel eyes.

"Don't get hysterical," he said uneasily.

"I am not hysterical. I'm never hysterical. I am simply utterly determined."

"You are being unreasonable," accused Alan. "I know that as a woman, you are prone to illogic, but you must see that—"

"I won't tell you anything, or help you in any way with the ghost, unless you agree to do the same for me as I search for the truth," she said.

"Don't be ridiculous. You are a woman. You have no notion how to conduct an investigation, even if you were capable of sustained—"

"I know who my mother's friends were," she offered. "I have her things. And her servants will talk to me and no one else. They are very loyal." Her voice broke a little on the last word.

"Some of that information might be useful," he conceded.

"Well, then..."

"And it might not," he added. "This haunting may have nothing to do with your mother, if it is simply someone trying to discredit the prince."

"But you should eliminate the possibility that it is related to her death," Ariel said.

He was surprised. "That would be a logical course of action," he admitted.

"No one else is better placed to help you do that," she pointed out.

"That may be so, but—"

"So, we are agreed?" She held out her hand as if to shake his and seal the bargain.

Alan gazed at her small white hand. His eyes ran up the slim arm attached to it and met the deep hazel eyes fixed on his. This was most likely a complete waste of time, he thought. She was a woman, and thus a creature of instinct and whim rather than rational thought. She could not have anything valuable to offer that he would not discover himself. However, there was something about her... He suppressed this irrelevancy. A scientist considered all alternatives, he told himself, no matter how remote they might be. "Very well," he said. He took her hand firmly and shook it.

From
Man of Honour

"WHAT DO YOU MEAN YOU HAVE NOTHING AVAILABLE?"
demanded Mr. Eliot Crenshaw. The cold anger in his
eyes made the small innkeeper quail.

"I swear it's true, sir. My missus has took the gig,
being as my youngest daughter is about to be brought
to bed in Hemsley, the next village but one, you know.
She won't be home for a sennight. There's the old cob
left in the stables, but he won't draw a carriage, and
with this snow now..." He looked out the window of
the taproom at the driving blizzard. "Well I can't see
as how any animal could." He paused apologetically,
conscious of the gentleman's impatience.

"Damn the snow," said Mr. Crenshaw, but he
too looked out the window. It was obvious that the
weather was worsening rapidly, and having already
endured one accident on the road, he had no wish to
risk another. But his situation was awkward. "Your
wife is away, you say? Who else is here?"

Mr. Jenkins showed signs of wringing his hands.
"There's just me tonight, sir, begging your pardon.
Betty, the girl as comes from the village to help out,

went home early on account of the storm. And my stable boy broke his fool leg last week, climbing trees he was, the witless chawbacon, at his age! I don't see how I'll serve a proper supper. And the lady!" This last remark ended with something like a groan, and the man shook his head. "This ain't a great establishment, you see, sir, off the main road like we are and keeping no post horses. We ain't used to housing quality, and that's the truth. I don't know what I'm to do."

Mr. Crenshaw eyed the distraught host with some contempt. His mood had been decidedly soured by recent events. In the course of a relatively short daylight drive, his fine traveling carriage had been severely damaged by a reckless youngster in a ridiculous high-perch phaeton. His horses had been brought up lame and their high-spirited tempers roused, and though he knew he was fortunate to have escaped without serious injury, the problems which now faced him as a result of the accident did not make him thankful.

He had been escorting a young visitor of his mother's to the home of her aunts. Only his parent's most earnest entreaties had persuaded him to do so, and he was now cursing himself roundly for giving in, for Miss Lindley's maid had been badly hurt in the accident, forcing them to leave her at a cottage on the scene and walk alone to this inn. Here he found there were no females to chaperone the girl; the blizzard was steadily increasing in intensity, and there was no conveyance of any kind available, even had it been possible to go on. Eliot Crenshaw was not accustomed to finding himself at a stand, but now he passed a hand wearily across his forehead, sat down at a taproom table, and stared fiercely at the swirling snow outside. He clenched a fist on the table top. "Bring me a pint," he said resignedly.

In the little inn's one private parlor, the Right Honorable Miss Laura Lindley, oldest daughter of the late Earl of Stoke-Mannering, sat miserably holding her hands out to the crackling fire. She was chilled to the bone, her bonnet was wrecked, her cloak torn and muddy, and her green cambric traveling dress was as disheveled as her black curls. There was a nasty scratch on her left cheek and a bruise above her eye. But these minor discomforts worried her less than the rising storm and the smashed chaise they had left leaning drunkenly by the roadside. What was she to do? Her aunts had expected her a full three hours ago, and these two elderly ladies, by whom she had been brought up, were notoriously high sticklers. The smallest deviation from the rules of propriety was enough to overset them completely. What then could they feel when they knew that their cherished niece was stranded alone at a country inn with a man she scarcely knew?

Laura caught her breath on a sob. She had only just persuaded her aunts to allow her to spend a season in London. Though her twentieth birthday was past, she had never been to the metropolis, and it had required all of her argumentative skills and the help of some of her aunts' old friends, Mrs. Crenshaw among them, to get the necessary permission. She was to have gone to town next month, but now… Laura sighed tremulously. Now, it appeared that she would never have a London season. She had waited two years after her friends' debuts and argued her case with the utmost care, only to see it all come to naught because of this stupid accident. She grimaced. That was always the way of it—the things one wanted most were snatched away just when they seemed certain at last. She took several deep breaths, telling herself sternly to stop this maundering. Perhaps Mr. Crenshaw would find some way out of this dilemma. He seemed a most capable man.

But in the taproom, at that moment finishing his pint of ale, Mr. Crenshaw did not feel particularly capable. He had badly wrenched his shoulder falling from the carriage; his exquisitely cut coat, from the hands of Weston himself, was torn in several places and indisputably ruined, as was much of the rest of his extremely fashionable attire. In fact any member of the *ton* would have been appalled to see this absolute nonesuch in his present state. This was not the top-of-the-trees Corinthian they knew, and though he would not have admitted it, the elegant Mr. Crenshaw was just now at his wit's end.

With a sigh he rose and walked stiffly to a small mirror which hung over the bar. He made some effort to straighten his twisted cravat and brush back his hair. The face in the mirror was rather too austere to be called handsome. Mr. Crenshaw's high cheekbones and aquiline nose gave his dark face a hawk-like look, and this was intensified by black hair and piercing gray eyes. The overall effect was of strength but little warmth; very few men would wish to cross this tall, slender gentleman, and fewer still would succeed in beating him. Pulling at his now disreputable coat and brushing the drying mud from his once immaculate pantaloons and tall Hessian boots, Mr. Crenshaw turned from the mirror with a grimace and walked across the corridor to the private parlor.

Miss Lindley rose at his entrance. "Did you find…?" she began, but the realities of the situation made it seem foolish to ask if he had gotten another carriage, and she fell silent.

Mr. Crenshaw bowed his head courteously. "Please sit down, Miss Lindley. I fear I have bad news." And he explained what the innkeeper had told him.

Laura put a hand to the side of her neck. "Oh dear, how unfortunate that his wife should be away just at this time." She tried to speak lightly, but a sinking feeling grew in her stomach. Her aunts would never forgive her, even though this predicament was certainly not of her own making.

"An understatement," replied Mr. Crenshaw drily, "because I fear we must spend the night at this inn. It will be impossible to go on in the snow, whatever vehicle we may be able to discover." A particularly loud gust of wind howled outside as if to emphasize his point. "I would willingly ride the cob back to the village and try to persuade some woman to return and stay with you," he went on. "But I do not think any would consent to come, and frankly I am not certain I could find the village in this infernal storm."

Laura nodded disconsolately. "Of course you must not go out in such weather." She clenched her hands together and fought back tears once more.

Mr. Crenshaw looked at her. "I say again how sorry I am, Miss Lindley."

"Oh, it is not your fault. I know that. You saved us all from being killed! If only Ruth had not been hurt or if I had stayed with her at the cottage. But when that young man was taken in there as well and the woman was so eager that I should *not* stay…and I was certain we would find another carriage. I did not realize that the snow…" Her disjointed speech trailed off as she watched the storm uneasily.

"Nor did I," replied Mr. Crenshaw. "Weather like this should not come at this time of year. However, it remains that it has. We must make the best of it."

"Yes. I suppose there is no way to send a message to my aunts? No, of course there is not."

He shook his head. "I fear not. But surely they will realize that you have been delayed by the weather. I wager they will be glad you are not traveling today."

Laura smiled weakly. "I see you are not acquainted with my aunts," she said. She looked down at her clasped hands and swallowed nervously. She had suddenly become conscious that she was completely alone with a man and a stranger, a thing her aunts had never permitted in the whole course of her life.

Mr. Crenshaw frowned. "I am not. They are very strict with you, I take it."

She nodded. "They are…older, you see, and…" she faltered.

"I am beginning to," he responded grimly. "What an infernal coil! Why did I allow Mother to bully me into escorting you?"

Laura's eyes widened. "I am sorry," she said miserably. She had a somewhat clearer idea of Mrs. Crenshaw's motives than her son had. That lady had told her that the carriage ride would be a perfect opportunity for Laura to try out her social skills. No one knew better than Mrs. Crenshaw the restrictions her aunts had put on Laura, and no one felt for her more keenly. She had added jokingly that Laura must do her best to captivate her son, for she had been trying to get him safely married these past five years. The girl stole a glance at the tall figure standing beside the sofa. There could be little question of that, she thought to herself. Mr. Crenshaw appeared to take no interest in her whatsoever; indeed she found him very stiff and cold.

But the thoughts running through her companion's mind would have surprised her. He was observing that the Lindley girl was very well to pass, even in her current state of disarray. In other circumstances, at Almack's for example, he might have asked her to dance without any fear that she would disgrace him. A tall, willowy girl, Laura Lindley was a striking brunette, with a thick mass of black curls and eyes so dark as to be almost black as well. Her skin was ivory pale, particularly now after this strenuous adventure. The customary deep rose of her cheeks and lips, an enchanting color Mr. Crenshaw had noted earlier, had drained away and she looked very tired and disheartened.

Resolutely Mr. Crenshaw redirected his thoughts. This was an utterly improper time to be thinking of the girl's looks. He and the lady were in a damnable situation. The lines around his mouth deepened as he reconsidered the problem.

Watching him, Laura shivered a little. He looked so grim and angry.

"Are you cold?" he asked quickly. "Draw nearer to the fire. I have not even asked if you would care for something. Some tea, perhaps?"

Laura allowed that some tea would be most welcome, and Mr. Crenshaw went out to find the landlord.

Two hours later they sat down to dinner in somewhat better frame. Though they had not changed their attire—Laura's luggage remained with the wrecked chaise and Mr. Crenshaw had none—Laura had tidied her hair and dress and washed, as had her companion. The scratch on her face was shown to be minor when the dirt and dried blood were sponged away, and though the bruise had turned a sullen purple, it too was clearly not serious. Both felt much better as they started on the oddly assorted dishes the innkeeper had assembled. There was bread and butter and cheese, a roast chicken, some boiled potatoes, and a large pot of jam. Mr. Crenshaw eyed the repast ruefully and made Laura laugh as he, with a cocked eyebrow, helped her to chicken.

As they ate, he began to talk lightly of London. He had heard from his mother that Laura would be making her come-out, and he told her of the places she would see and the things she might do.

"There is Almack's, of course," he said. "I have no doubt that you will spend many evenings dancing there. And there will be routs, Venetian breakfasts, musical evenings, and the like. You can have no idea how busy your life will become."

At this catalog of delights, Laura could not keep a tremor from her voice when she agreed, and her expression was so woebegone that her companion said, "What is wrong? Have I said something?"

She shook her head. "No, no, it is just that… well I shall not go to London now, I daresay, and I was feeling sorry for myself." She looked wistfully down at her plate.

He was frowning. "What do you mean you will not go?"

"Oh my aunts will never let me leave after this, this…that is…" She stammered to a halt, not wishing to burden him with the certain consequences of their misadventure. There was nothing he could do, after all, and the incident was no more his fault than hers.

"Nonsense," he replied. "Why should they not? You have simply an unfortunate accident on the road."

"Yes I know, but you do not reason as my aunts do, of course. They worry so, and they do not understand modern manners. At least that is what they say. When the curate wished to visit my sister… to pay attentions, you know, they forbade him to enter the house ever again." She smiled slightly at the memory. "It was very awkward, because they are the heads of the relief committee, and the curate was in charge of that. The vicar was nearly driven distracted." Raising her eyes; Laura saw that Mr. Crenshaw had returned her smile, and hers broadened, showing two dimples.

"Was your sister heartbroken?"

"Clarissa?" Laura gave an involuntary gurgle of laughter. "Oh she did not care. She wishes to marry a duke."

He was taken aback. "A duke? Which duke?"

Laura looked mischievous. "It doesn't matter; she is determined to make a grand marriage." Her smile faded. "That will be impossible now, of course. I mean, she will never be married after this. My aunts will keep us so close, I suppose we shall not be allowed even to go to the country assemblies." Her momentary high spirits dissolved in melancholy reflection.

Mr. Crenshaw frowned once more. "You must be mistaken. They cannot be so gothic."

Laura remained unconvinced, but she did not argue further, not wishing to tease him with her problems. Silently the two finished their repast.

After a time Laura rose. "I shall go to bed, I think. I am tired out."

Mr. Crenshaw also stood. "Of course. The landlord has left your candle." He fetched it and lit it at the fire. "There is no one to take you up. Yours is the room at the head of the stairs."

"Thank you." She took the candle and started out of the room. As she was about to enter the hall, he spoke again.

"I shall spend the night in the innkeeper's chamber. It is the best I can do."

Laura's mouth jerked. "Haven't you a sword?"

"I beg your pardon?"

"Like Tristan."

Mr. Crenshaw looked blank. The girl must be on the edge of exhaustion, he thought to himself. He fervently hoped he would not be called upon to deal with an attack of the vapors.

Laura shrugged. "Never mind. I didn't mean anything. My aunts call levity my besetting sin."

The man looked at her.

"Good night," she said.

"Good night," said Eliot, much relieved.

Lying in bed some minutes later, enveloped in one of the landlady's voluminous nightgowns, Laura listened to the howling wind outside and the scratching of the snow on the windowpanes. She could not help shedding a few tears now that she was alone again. It all seemed so unfair, and she felt so helpless. Various schemes for resuming their journey occurred to her and were rejected. They were trapped for as long as the blizzard raged. If only Mr. Crenshaw were not so angry with her. That, on top of everything else, depressed her immeasurably. She was still thinking of him when the fatigue of the day caught up with her, and she slept.

Once Again a Bride
by Jane Ashford

---◆---

She couldn't be more alone

Widowhood has freed Charlotte Wylde from a demoralizing and miserable marriage. But when her husband's intriguing nephew and heir arrives to take over the estate, Charlotte discovers she's unsafe in her own home…

He could be her only hope…or her next victim

Alec Wylde was shocked by his uncle's untimely death, and even more shocked to encounter his uncle's beautiful young widow. Now clouds of suspicion are gathering, and charges of murder hover over Charlotte's head.

Alec and Charlotte's initial distrust of each other intensifies as they uncover family secrets, and hovering underneath is a mutual attraction that could lead them to disaster…

---◆---

"A near-perfect example of everything that makes this genre an escapist joy to read." —*Publishers Weekly*

"One of the premier Regency writers return to the published world. Ms. Ashford has written a superbly crafted story…" —*Fresh Fiction*

For more Jane Ashford, visit:

www.sourcebooks.com

The Brides Insists

by Jane Ashford

She thinks she's bought a compliant husband...

Although Clare Greenough has inherited an unexpected fortune, her money is in the hands of a trustee until she marries—everyone knows a woman is incapable of managing funds. What she needs is an easygoing husband, right away...

They're both in for a shock

She makes a deal with impetuous young James Boleigh, seventh Baron Trehearth: they will marry, Clare will get control of her money, and Jamie will get the funds he desperately needs to restore his lands. To stave off ruin, Jamie agrees, believing Clare will soon become a proper, submissive wife. But to expect a serene, passionless marriage was only their first mistake...

"Perfectly delightful Regency romance... Remarkably executed." —*Publishers Weekly* Starred Review

"Ashford's richly nuanced, realistically complex characters and impeccably crafted historical setting are bound to resonate with fans of Mary Balogh." —*Booklist*

For more Jane Ashford, visit:

www.sourcebooks.com

The Three Graces
by Jane Ashford

❧

When it comes to the game of love

Finding themselves suddenly impoverished and alone in the world, the three Hartington sisters must rely on their wits, charm, and unique talents to support themselves. Forced to go their separate ways, each of these enchanting sisters is brought to a dead end by the perplexing ways of men and the inequity of fate.

Three heads are better than one

Then each receives a letter that changes everything…and if the sisters are going to overcome the obstacles to love, they're going to require some astonishingly creative solutions…

❧

Praise for Jane Ashford:

"Jane Ashford's characters are true to their times, yet they radiate the freshness of today." —*Historical Novel Review*

"Ashford captures the reader's interest with her keen knowledge of the era and her deft writing." —*RT Book Reviews*

For more Jane Ashford, visit:

www.sourcebooks.com

The Marriage Wager
by Jane Ashford

An RT Reviewers' Choice Nominee for
Best Regency Historical Romance

— ❧ —

The stakes are high, the game is set...

Lady Emma Tarrant possesses little but the gambling skills
her dead husband taught her, but she's no match for a real
gamester.

Colin Wareham, Baron St. Mawr, gambles to distract himself
from devastating memories. The gaming has long since lost
its appeal, until he meets sparkling Lady Emma and finds that
she's an even better distraction.

— ❧ —

"Exceptional characters and beautifully crafted...a
delightful read for Judith McNaught and
Mary Balogh fans." —*Publishers Weekly*

"Entertaining, colorful characters, romantic... An
engaging read." —*Caffeinated Book Reviewer*

For more Jane Ashford, visit:

www.sourcebooks.com

About the Author

Jane Ashford discovered Georgette Heyer in junior high school and was captivated by the glittering world and witty language of Regency England. That delight was part of what led her to study English literature and travel widely in Britain and Europe. She has written historical and contemporary romances, and her books have been published in Sweden, Italy, England, Denmark, France, Russia, Latvia, the Czech Republic, and Spain, as well as the U.S. Jane has been nominated for a Career Achievement Award by *RT Book Reviews*. Born in Ohio, she now lives in Los Angeles.